"Whate don't make a habit of sleeping
with complete strangers."

"We're hardly strangers, Stephanie. We've known
each other since you arrived at Women's Hospital
over three years ago."

Stephanie closed her eyes. "That's just it. We've never
spent an hour together that wasn't strictly business. I
don't know how we managed to..." She cast him a
helpless glance and found he was enjoying her
embarrassment. "It was very irresponsible," she said
firmly. "And I hope you know that ordinarily I'm not
that kind of person."

"There's nothing ordinary about you, Stephanie.
Besides, the decision was hardly yours alone. There
were two of us that night, remember?"

God, she did remember. All too well. What a mess!
She took a deep breath. "Actually, Tal, there is something—"

The elevator pinged. She looked at the man beside
her. She knew next to nothing about him, she realized with a tremor of dismay.

And she was about to tell him she was carrying
his child.

Dear Reader,

When I wrote *The Silence of Midnight*, the plight of Michael, a fourteen-year-old displaced child, became an important part of the story. Then, in my next book, *Touch the Dawn*, I featured another unlucky child, a teenage girl this time. By unhappy fate, sometimes kids just seem to fall through the cracks, and there seems to be a growing number of these troubled children in our society.

Having His Baby was supposed to be about a woman who has an unexpected pregnancy that jeopardizes her position as mentor and role model to disadvantaged, pregnant teenagers. And it *is* her story, but again I became fascinated by secondary characters, a bunch of "babies having babies."

My own three daughters were fortunate enough not to have to face the problems of the young girls in this book. But still, it was a story I felt compelled to write.

Perhaps I should make a disclaimer here: My own daughter, Alison, has little in common with the Alison in this story. They are alike in name only. But I hope you will enjoy reading about the fictitious Alison as much as I enjoyed writing about her.

I think my heroine's personal journey is something modern women everywhere can relate to. And in the end, of course, she finds love. Something I hope we are all lucky enough to discover and appreciate.

Karen Young

Books by Karen Young

HARLEQUIN SUPERROMANCE

Don't miss any of our special offers. Write to us at the following address for information on our newest releases.

Harlequin Reader Service
U.S.: 3010 Walden Ave., P.O. Box 1325, Buffalo, NY 14269
Canadian: P.O. Box 609, Fort Erie, Ont. L2A 5X3

Karen Young

HAVING HIS BABY

Harlequin Books

TORONTO • NEW YORK • LONDON
AMSTERDAM • PARIS • SYDNEY • HAMBURG
STOCKHOLM • ATHENS • TOKYO • MILAN
MADRID • WARSAW • BUDAPEST • AUCKLAND

ISBN 0-373-70681-2

HAVING HIS BABY

To Alison and Doug.
You weren't really a spoiled teenager, Ali.
Never mind what Doug says.

CHAPTER ONE

Congratulations!
Pregnancy is a joyous event.
Expect tumultuous changes in both
your life and your body. Ideally,
your baby is planned for and loved
already. The next nine months can be
a time of intense spiritual as well as
physical bonding between you, your baby
and the father of your child.

—*Ask Dr. Meredith*

DR. STEPHANIE SHELDON stared in dismay at the small strip of paper turning bright pink before her eyes. *Positive!* My God, it was positive. She was pregnant. As impossible and crazy as that sounded, modern technology did not lie. No, not impossible. She had spent an evening with a man who was a stranger in nearly every sense of the word and then had gone to bed with him. *That* was the crazy part.

With shaking hands, she threw the pregnancy-test kit into the trash basket and turned the water on at the sink. A jumble of conflicting thoughts whirled in her mind as she scrubbed her fingers and palms, continuing up her arms as though preparing for major surgery. Halfway through the ritual, she stopped suddenly, her shoulders drooping. The tiny speck of life deep inside her womb wasn't a germ. It wasn't something unclean that she could wash away and dis- infect herself.

It was a baby!

A dizzying wave washed over her, forcing her to sit down abruptly. What about her career? Her reputa- tion? She'd worked so hard, overcome so much to reach the position she now held—staff physician at Women's Hospital in the field of obstetrics and gy- necology. With her fingers pressing her temples, she gave in to a moment of sheer panic. Dear God in heaven, what was she going to do?

With a groan, she remembered the class she taught. Three times a week, she preached birth control to a group of pregnant teenagers. She stressed abstinence and the importance of taking personal responsibility. When her own stomach began to swell, how was she going to explain that apparently she didn't practice what she preached? She wrapped both arms around herself and rocked back and forth. Because there was no question that there would be a baby. Abortion was not an option. She had lost one child in miscarriage before her divorce. Inconvenient as a pregnancy might be, she was going to have this baby.

And underlying her anxiety was a problem bigger than her students' and everyone else's reaction to her pregnancy. What was she going to do about Talbot Robichaux?

Closing her eyes, she experienced a feeling of un- reality. She still couldn't believe what had happened that night in Boston. It had been the last day of a medical conference. Her flight home to New Orleans was the next morning. Passing the hotel bar, she had heard music, a lone musician singing the blues. An empty evening stretched in front of her, so she had stopped in to listen. Talbot Robichaux had been inside.

Dr. Robichaux had been a featured speaker at the conference. He was also chief of surgery at Women's Hospital in New Orleans, where Stephanie practiced. She saw him occasionally and admired him for his brilliance, but they had never come close to anything approaching intimacy.

Until they spent the night together in Boston.

It was the wine. It had to be the wine. Staring morosely at her bare feet, Stephanie shook her head slowly. It hadn't been the wine, not really. It had been the date. July 31 marked five years exactly since Stephanie's divorce, and incredibly it had been precisely three years since Dr. Robichaux's wife had been gunned down in a drive-by shooting near the hospital's free clinic on Esplanade Avenue. She and Tal had discovered the mutual significance of the date as they'd shared drinks and dinner and then sex that night in Boston.

Loneliness made people do foolish things.

And now Talbot Robichaux was going to be the father of her child.

SHE STILL hadn't regained her equilibrium when she arrived at the hospital an hour later. Hoping to avoid anyone who knew her, she chose the public elevator over the private service elevator and stared at nothing while waiting for it. Aside from anxiety, she felt fine. If morning sickness was going to be a problem, it hadn't happened yet. She should be thankful for small mercies. As the door slid open, she waited while a lab technician rolled out a cart laden with blood samples.

She stepped inside, sensed someone behind her, but kept her eyes on the panel of buttons. She pressed the one for the fourth floor, stepped back and collided with a wall of male muscle and bone.

Hands went to her waist, steadying her. "Whoa!"

She knew that voice. She made herself turn and look at him. "I'm sorry, Tal," she said shakily. "I didn't see you."

"You didn't see anybody," he said, letting go while his gaze roamed over her face.

"I guess I wasn't paying attention."

"Or paying too much attention."

She thought how different his expression would be if he knew exactly where her thoughts had been at that moment. The door closed with a firm sound, and Stephanie suddenly felt crowded. She turned back to the control panel. With her finger poised over the buttons, she asked, "Where are you going?"

"Wherever you're headed."

She looked at him speechlessly.

"You've been avoiding me, Stephanie."

"Tal—"

"It's been two weeks since we spent the night together in Boston. I thought we were flying home together, but you weren't on the plane."

"I had some shopping to do."

"Right." He sounded unconvinced. "And since then, I've hardly caught a glimpse of you. Mostly I see just your coattails as you disappear on the run."

"That's ridiculous. I—"

"Is this some kind of game you're playing?"

"No! I—"

"We're two adults, Stephanie. We were lonely and stuck in a strange city. We enjoyed a meal together and then we—"

"Don't..." She put up a hand. "Don't say any more. I know exactly what happened and I still can't believe I did that."

"*We* did that."

"You know what I mean."

He studied her in silence for a long moment. "Was it so bad?"

"That's not what I meant, Tal. Whatever you may think, I don't make a habit of sleeping around, especially with a complete stranger."

He crossed his arms over his chest. "We're hardly strangers, Stephanie. We've known each other since you arrived at Women's over three years ago."

She closed her eyes. "That's just what I'm saying. We've never dated, we've never spent an hour together that wasn't strictly business. I don't know how we..." She cleared her throat. "How we managed to..."

She cast him a helpless look and found he seemed to be enjoying her embarrassment. His amusement was just the thing she needed to get control of herself. "It was very irresponsible behavior," she said firmly, "and I hope you know that ordinarily I'm not that kind of person."

Tal chuckled softly. "There's nothing ordinary about you, Stephanie," he said in a tone that threatened to fluster her all over again. "Besides, the decision was hardly yours alone. There were two of us that night, remember?"

God, she did remember. All too well. Oh, what a mess! She took a deep breath. "Actually, Tal, there is something—"

The elevator pinged.

When the door slid open, Stephanie walked out, and Tal, true to his word, followed her. People bound for morning appointments jostled them in the hall. Her own schedule was a killer today. In just six minutes, she had to meet with the pregnant teens.

"You were saying?"

She gave Tal a distracted look. "Oh, yes." He waited, studying her with the same intensity she'd noticed in the elevator. What was he thinking? "I was wondering...I need to...that is..."

His smile faded into a look of concern. "What's wrong, Stephanie?"

She drew in another deep breath. "I wonder if you could meet me for a drink this evening. Early or late, whatever's convenient for you." She could see that she'd surprised him. "Of course, if you've already made plans for this evening, then maybe—"

"I don't have any plans that can't be broken." He smiled wryly. "Forgive me, but after Boston I had the impression that you weren't much of a drinker."

She wasn't. She had broken one of her cardinal rules by having more than two glasses of wine that night, but hadn't drunk enough to undo years of sexual abstinence. No, there must have been something else at work that night. She studied Tal. With his mouth hiked up in that sexy smile, he proclaimed the genes of his French ancestors handsomely. His hair and eyes were almost black, his skin smooth and dark. He was lean and muscular, as though he spent a lot of time outdoors. When? she wondered. He worked long hours in the hospital and devoted hours each week to the free clinic. She knew next to nothing about the man, outside of his professional life, she realized with a tremor of dismay. And she was about to tell him she was carrying his child.

"Hello," he said, waving a finger in front of her nose, still smiling.

She blinked back to the moment. "I'm sorry. I was just—"

"Inviting me out for the evening. How about dinner? I know a place—"

"No! I mean, we don't need to have dinner together. If you don't want a drink, maybe we could—"

"After trying to get your attention for two weeks, I'm up for anything you suggest. So to speak." His smile flashed. "What time shall I pick you up?"

"You don't have to pick me up at all," she said, ignoring the innuendo. "No, I mean it, Tal. I'll take a taxi. I guess dinner will be okay. We'll meet wherever you say, provided it isn't one of your family's restaurants."

Seeing his expression, she sighed inwardly, guessing that he was more intrigued than ever that she apparently wanted to keep their meeting private. He was certain to be recognized at any of the Robichaux restaurants. But whatever Tal thought, he must have decided his questions could wait until that night. He nodded. "Okay, the Garden Room at Commander's. Eight o'clock. How's that?"

She relaxed. The worst was over, at least for the moment. "Eight at Commander's," she said huskily. "That's fine."

"I'll make the reservations."

"Yes, okay. Thanks. I'll see you there." Before he could say anything else, she hurried away.

THE PROGRAM to teach parenting to pregnant teen-age girls was a stepchild at New Orleans Women's Hospital. Finding space had been a problem. Stepha-nie had finally wheedled permission to use a small stockroom, but every time she entered it, she felt frustrated. From the outset, Benedict Galloway, the hospital administrator, had not been enthusiastic about a program geared to patients who were mostly poor, underage and uninsured. Stephanie walked a tightrope to appease him, trying to keep the classes alive. She might have taken Galloway's attitude as a personal affront, but the man was equally hostile to Talbot Robichaux who was single-handedly responsi-ble for the hospital's inner-city free clinic.

On her way there now, Stephanie worried about the need for more room to practice bathing and feeding infants, as well as space to learn Lamaze techniques to ease the teens' fears of labor and delivery. But her first priority was to teach them how to be good parents, and for that they didn't need much space.

As usual, there was little order in the group when Stephanie finally made it to the meeting room. None of the seven regulars was sitting down, but a tall, jeans-clad girl with long hair the color of cornsilk was on the floor, her body arranged in a classic lotus po-sition. Stephanie's gaze went automatically to the girl's middle, but if she was pregnant, she wasn't showing yet.

"Hello," Stephanie said with a smile. "I'm Dr. Sheldon."

"Hi. I'm Keely," the girl said without bothering to stand up. "I never tell people my last name because I don't happen to think last names are relevant."

Relevant. Stephanie certainly didn't hear that word from her charges very often. Most of the girls in the class had very little opportunity to expand their vocabularies. Sadly, some couldn't even read. Since the girl didn't want to reveal her last name, Stephanie guessed wearily that she was a runaway.

"Hey, I know that look," said Jolene Johnson, the acknowledged leader of the group. "Don't get your pants in a wad, Dr. Steph. Keely's just visiting."

"That's right," Keely said. "I'm not pregnant myself, personally, you know, but I know someone who is and I'm checking this out on her behalf."

"How far along is your friend?" Stephanie asked. "Has she seen a doctor yet?"

"She's just barely pregnant," the girl said, dismissing Stephanie's concern. "Don't worry. It's no big deal."

"Pregnancy *is* a big deal," Stephanie said firmly, "and especially early on. I'll get you a form and you can take it to her. Even if she doesn't join the parenting class, she should see a doctor right away. Do you know about the free clinic on Esplanade?"

"Nah, I only got into town a couple of nights ago."

Stephanie frowned. "Where are you staying?"

Keely stood up. "Jolene, I thought you said I wouldn't be hassled here."

"Keely ain't homeless, Dr. Steph," Jolene said, coming to stand beside the visitor. "She's staying with me."

Stephanie knew when to back off. It was unlikely that Keely was staying with Jolene. The oldest of four daughters, Jolene lived with her mother and sisters in a small frame house in a neighborhood where Keely's blond hair and light-colored eyes would stand out. Still, the group of teenagers was wonderfully resourceful, and since they'd obviously accepted Keely into their tight circle, they had probably managed to find a safe place for her to live.

If any place could be deemed safe in their world.

Stephanie finally got everyone settled into something that resembled a group discussion. One of the first things she had learned when the group was newly formed was that discipline was an unknown concept to most of the girls. The first couple of sessions had produced nothing more than the opportunity to air their views to someone who was light-years apart from them in a social sense. It had taken months before they had trusted her enough to allow her rare glimpses of their true feelings.

The group was racially mixed. There were three African-Americans, Jolene, Chantal and Melissa: two Caucasian girls, Chrissy and Leanne; and two Hispanics, Teresa and Angela. When Stephanie had begun the class, there were an even dozen girls, but almost half had dropped out. Those who had chosen to remain were for the most part conscientious, determined and responsible.

Today, Chantal Watson, the quiet one, wanted to begin the discussion.

"What's on your mind, Chantal?"

"You talk all the time about being responsible. Well, what about guys being responsible? Why does it always have to be the woman?"

The oldest of four children, Chantal came from a single-parent family where her childhood had been all too brief. She was determined to have a life where she was in control. With beautiful smooth skin and striking dark eyes, she had the looks of a model. Instead, at fourteen, she was six months pregnant.

"Ideally, all people should act responsibly, Chantal," Stephanie said gently. "Unfortunately, not everyone does. How people behave is based on a lot of things."

"Yeah, like if a guy sees everybody else actin' stupid, he can act stupid, too," said Jolene.

Quick and cynical, Jolene was almost too wise in the ways of the world. Stephanie looked around at the group. Without exception their sex partners had proved to have other priorities when faced with the daunting responsibility of fatherhood.

"Peer pressure has something to do with it," Stephanie agreed. "Any other ideas?"

"It's not only the guys actin' stupid," Melissa said, stroking her large belly. She was sixteen and close to term. "If you ask me, we're lookin' pretty dumb ourselves sittin' around here big as hippos."

"The night I got pregnant, I wasn't thinkin' about responsibility or anything else past that exact minute," Leanne said, studying her swollen ankles. "I've had almost nine months to learn that stuff. Forget about what Michael's responsibility is in all this, I'm gettin' my life together. You can't make a guy act like a grown-up unless he is one. That's what responsibility is all about."

"We all gotta make our own way, quit worryin' about the guys," Jolene stated, cutting to the chase, as usual. She looked at Stephanie. "Dr. Steph here wouldn't look to a man if she got herself into a fix like we did, would you, Dr. Steph?" Without waiting for an answer, she went on. " 'Course she would never be stupid enough to have sex without protection. So that's what we gotta take away from this class, I'm tellin' y'all. No more actin' without thinkin'. No more gettin' carried away by a guy's sweet talk."

"Yes!" As one, the group responded.

Stephanie had never felt like such a fraud.

"DADDY, you're not going out again tonight!"

Tal shrugged into his jacket and turned from the mirrored closet doors. "Hey, baby." He caught his thirteen-year-old daughter by the shoulders and kissed her cheek. "Mmm, you smell good. What is that, essence of chocolate chip?"

She ignored that, the way she always ignored his efforts to keep her a baby forever. "You *are* going out!"

He chucked her beneath her small chin. "I confess, I'm going out."

"You're *always* going out, Daddy. I get really lonely all by myself."

He slipped a clean handkerchief into his back pocket and caught up his keys. "You're not alone, baby. Mimi is here."

Alison made a face. "You know that's not the same. Mimi's a housekeeper. Nobody else has to stay with a housekeeper like I do."

Checking his appearance one last time, he met her eyes in the mirror. "You mean nobody else's parents ever go out? You're the only one?"

"They go out," she admitted grudgingly, "but they go with each other, you know, like husband and wife."

With an arm around her shoulders, he took her with him as they left his bedroom. "And what do they do with their offspring, leave them home alone?" There was a smile in his voice as he looked down at the top of her dark head. She was nothing like Diana, who'd been blond and blue-eyed. Her looks and coloring were straight from the Robichaux—black hair, dark, dark eyes, olive skin. What other tendencies had she inherited? he wondered.

"You have a date, don't you?" Alison asked suddenly. "This isn't business, is it?"

He hesitated. "In a way, it is. I'm having dinner with Dr. Stephanie Sheldon, a colleague of mine from the hospital."

"What do you mean, 'in a way'?"

He stopped and tweaked her nose. "So many questions, Miss Nosy-kins."

"I don't like her."

"You don't know her, Alison."

"I know she works with you, so she must be in love with you."

He stared, then laughed shortly. "Dr. Sheldon would be the first to tell you how off base that is, Alison. Now, I've got about fifteen minutes to get to Commander's, otherwise I'm going to be late."

"All those silly women at the hospital fall in love with you," Alison insisted stubbornly.

He fixed her with a stern gaze. "That's enough, young lady."

"I thought you didn't believe in mixing business with pleasure."

"Alison Robichaux..."

She turned away abruptly. "Oh, okay, go ahead. Leave me and spend the night with her. I don't care anymore."

He stopped her with a hand on her shoulder. "I'm having dinner with Dr. Sheldon and then I'll be com-

ing straight home. If it's not past your bedtime—and
that's ten-thirty sharp, since it's a school night—then
we'll talk. Work on your disposition as well as your
homework while I'm gone."

HE WAS STILL unsettled when he pulled up at the restaurant ten minutes late. He couldn't believe Alison's
behavior lately. She used to be such a sweet little girl.
Now, nothing pleased her, especially nothing he suggested. It didn't take a qualified physician to guess that
puberty was the problem. But was any parent prepared? He'd always considered adolescence a simple
medical fact until his own daughter had entered it. He
was quickly learning there was nothing simple about
it.

He got out of his car and handed over his keys to a
valet for parking. He wouldn't blame Stephanie if she
was irritated. He was seldom late for an appointment, and this one was as important as anything on his
calendar. He hadn't been able to stop thinking about
Stephanie Sheldon since the night they'd spent together.

"Good evening, Dr. Robichaux. A pleasure having
you." The smiling maître d' was well known to Tal.
"Your guest—"

"I'm here." Both men looked up. Stephanie came
forward, extending her hand as though they were
meeting for business reasons. *She* might want to pretend they had no connection other than a professional one, but for Tal those hours in Boston had
changed that. He wanted to know more about Dr.
Stephanie Sheldon. A lot more.

"I'm sorry I'm late," he said after they were seated and the waiter had taken their order. "A little problem at home."

She looked concerned. "Was it something serious? If you needed to cancel, you should have. I realize I sprang this on you at the last minute. In fact, I should have given you my car-phone number. I didn't think about it until—"

"Stephanie."

She looked at him. In the candlelight, she was beautiful. The thought came to him out of nowhere. What made her skin seem so soft and dewy? He remembered the feel of it. And her eyes. He had noticed that night that they weren't quite gray or green, but something in between, the color of a stormy sea.

"I didn't want to cancel," he said, then smiled ruefully. "It was my daughter, Alison. She's thirteen, you know. Doesn't that say it all?"

Stephanie looked sympathetic.

"I say she's thirteen, but in reality sometimes she seems three again, sometimes twenty-three. Tonight was one of those times."

Stephanie smiled. "Three or twenty-three?"

"Both."

"Adolescence is very difficult." She waited a moment, then grinned. "On parents, that is."

"You should do that a *lot* more."

"What?"

"Smile that way. It's dynamite."

"Be serious." She rolled her eyes.

His own humor faded. "Back to Alison. Since you deal with troubled teens regularly this probably won't come as a surprise to you, but I often feel completely out of my depth in dealing with her. I think this is a time when a young girl needs a mother.''

"I'm sure you do a wonderful job."

"Not really. I do a wonderful job handling a six-hour surgery or delivering a paper at a conference. I routinely make life-and-death decisions about other people, but when it comes to dealing with my own adolescent daughter, I feel . . . inadequate."

"Parenting is a complicated business," Stephanie said with sympathy. "Just try teaching it to pregnant teenagers."

He shook his head. "No, thanks. Alison may be trying my patience right now, but at least our problems are relatively uncomplicated."

Stephanie nodded.

"Maybe it's good for me to be reminded of that, to put things in proper perspective. I could be dealing with an unwanted pregnancy."

Oh, Lord, it was now or never. Stephanie placed her hands flat on the table beside her plate and looked at him. "Tal, there's something we need to talk about."

His fork stopped halfway to his mouth. "What is it?"

She dropped her eyes, studied the untouched turtle soup in front of her. How on earth was she going to tell him? "You were right today when you accused me of avoiding you," she said, glancing up. He had a tiny scar beside his eyebrow. She wondered how it got there. An accident? A childhood mishap? She should know little tidbits like that about the father of her child, but she probably never would. She couldn't imagine an intimate relationship with Talbot Robichaux. After what she had to say tonight, she might never even have another conversation with him. At least, not another civil conversation.

"Stephanie, what is it? What's wrong?"

She swallowed and touched her forehead with her fingers. "This is so hard, Tal."

"You're beginning to worry me, Steph. Does it have anything to do with your job? Is it Galloway? Has he been hassling you again?"

Initially, the hospital administrator had nixed Stephanie's idea for the teen program from the start. Then Tal had stepped in, and Galloway had reluctantly backed off, but he was waiting for the first opportunity to ax the program.

She shook her head. "No, it's nothing to do with that. It's...personal. I...I think you should finish your wine."

"My wine?" Tal frowned but picked it up, his eyes on her face.

"That night we spent in Boston..." She forced herself to hold his gaze. "It must have been the wine. I don't usually drink like that." Unconsciously, her eyes went to the mineral water she was drinking tonight. "And the occasion. You know, my divorce, thinking about the miscarriage."

"It was an odd coincidence," Tal said. "The death of my wife and the death of your marriage, both on the same day. If I believed in fate—"

"I don't know whether you'll call it fate or not— maybe a stroke of really bad luck—but we're not going to be able to just forget that night ever happened."

"Forgetting it ever happened was your idea, not mine," Tal said quietly.

"Yes, well . . ." Stephanie cleared her throat. "You may feel differently when you hear what's happened."

"Stephanie, tell me what's on your mind. What are you getting at?"

She sat up a little straighter. "How old was that condom you used that night, Tal?"

He went very still. "Why do you ask?"

"I'm pregnant."

Shock rippled across his features. As Stephanie watched, she wished with every atom of her being that she could turn back the clock. How could this be happening?

"Are you sure?" His tone was decidedly cooler.

"Yes. I took a pregnancy test this morning. It's still very early, of course, only two weeks, but I felt I should tell you right away. I don't know what your feelings are about abortion, but for me it's just not an option. I lost a baby once through no fault of my own. Although this pregnancy is v-very inconvenient . . . I don't want to do anything to . . . to terminate it. I realize that—"

He put up a hand. "Stop. Give me a minute, will you?"

"I'm sorry." She closed her eyes, wishing she could leave the table. Or the restaurant. Or better yet, leave town. That way she wouldn't have to deal with the whispers, the scandal, the sheer calamity that would soon befall her.

"The condom was new. I bought it in the men's room at the restaurant where we had dinner."

The slim rein with which she'd managed to hold her temper snapped. "Then it was defective! Because I'm pregnant."

"So you say."

She looked at him. "What is that supposed to mean?"

"It means, Stephanie, that we spent a single night together using an accepted method of birth control. Now you say you're pregnant, and I'm assuming that you want me to accept that I'm the father. That's a lot to expect of a man."

She tossed her napkin onto the table and fumbled for her purse and silk shawl.

He frowned. "What are you doing?"

"What does it look like I'm doing? I'm leaving." She snatched up her purse, but the catch gave and several items tumbled out. She began stuffing them back inside, a pen, a small compact, a money clip holding a few bills. "Apparently, this was a bad idea in the first place. I never intended you to take any responsibility for this baby, *Dr. Robichaux*. I simply felt morally obligated to let you know that you'd fathered my child. But since you don't accept that, then there's absolutely no reason for me to linger."

"Damn it, Stephanie! Will you settle down?"

She snapped the catch on her purse and stood up. "See you around, *Dr. Robichaux*."

Tal got to his feet. "Stephanie—"

Without a backward look, Stephanie threaded her way through tables of diners. At the entrance, she missed the startled look given her by the maître d'. Blinded by tears, she could hardly see where she was going. She felt an absolute fool. How had she so misjudged Talbot Robichaux? Could he really have thought that she planned to extort child support from him for the next eighteen years? Maybe he was afraid she was going to make their indiscretion public? What a jerk!

Once outside, she stood in the muggy August evening for a few seconds. The valet approached, but she turned abruptly and began walking in the direction of her house. She lived nearby and hadn't driven, which, as it turned out, was a good thing. She was in no state to drive.

She gave a yelp as a hand clamped onto her arm. "You can't walk home in your condition," Tal said, his tone a near growl.

"I'm pregnant," she snapped, "not sick."

"I meant this." Without breaking stride, he brushed her cheek where tears were falling like rain. "I'm sorry, Stephanie. I guess I overreacted. Call it shock or temporary insanity or something. It's not every day I learn I've fathered a child after being with a woman just once."

"Oh? How often does it usually take?" she asked sarcastically.

He laughed. "You want the truth?" His tone was lighter, almost mellow. "This is a first."

"Well, don't expect sympathy from me."

"No, I won't," he said ruefully. "I wish we could recall the past fifteen minutes, Stephanie. I was taken by surprise and reacted without thinking. This is the last thing I expected when you set up this date." He shook his head. "I'm still reeling. You need to give me some time."

"You can have all the time in the world," she said stiffly. "I explained why I felt I must tell you, and that's the end of it."

He stopped her with a hand on her arm. Forcing her chin up with his fingers, he said, "Listen to me,

Stephanie. We need to go someplace quiet to discuss this. Not a bar, not a restaurant. How about your place? You live alone, right?"

"No, my foster mother lives with me."

He frowned. "Foster mother?"

"Yes, Camille Landry."

"I didn't know. You don't have any family?"

She moved, freeing herself. "Does that matter? I have a house and it's nearby. We can talk in my study. Camille will give us all the privacy we need."

CHAPTER TWO

*Besides the physical changes taking
place in your body, pregnancy can
sometimes make you feel as if you
are on an emotional roller coaster.
Try to think positive thoughts. You
can be particularly needy these first
few weeks. Don't hesitate to show
your mate how you feel.*

—*Ask Dr. Meredith*

August 14, 1995/2 weeks

THE WALK to Stephanie's house took only ten minutes. They said little, nothing that mattered. It was
impossible to tell what Tal was thinking. She wasn't
sure what she'd expected from him, but she had been
hurt—surprisingly so—by his first reaction.

As she climbed the steps to her porch, she looked
through the lead glass of the front door to the foyer
inside. Camille had obviously not returned from her
evening out. Good. Tal would have the privacy he
wanted.

"You have a charming house," he said, holding the
door for her after she'd unlocked it.

"Thanks. It's small, but I like it."

Inside, she tossed her scarf over a small chair and surveyed the foyer and the rooms leading off it as if for the first time. Her house was like many in the Garden District built at the turn of the century, small but perfect for a single person or a couple. It was her first house and she had taken a lot of pleasure decorating it, in finding just the right place for the possessions she'd acquired through the years and in shopping for new ones.

A foster child at sixteen, Stephanie had been encouraged by Camille Landry to reach for the stars. Her first goal was to become a doctor. She'd achieved that. Her house might not be quite as grand as others in the area, but she had known upon her arrival in New Orleans all those years ago, traumatized and unloved, that one day she wanted to live in this neighborhood. And here she was.

"Where is your foster mother?" Tal asked, looking around curiously. "What did you say her name was? Corinne?"

"Camille. She's playing bridge with her friends. Don't worry, even if Camille were here and happened to overhear us, she would never repeat anything that might embarrass you."

He turned to her abruptly. Catching her by her arms, he spoke gruffly. "Stephanie, it was my fault that this thing started out badly. I'm not worried about your... about Camille overhearing us or betraying a confidence. You can stop being testy and defensive. I was an ass. I apologize. Now, can we talk?"

"It's not a 'thing,'" she said, looking away. He still held her arms.

"What?"

"You said, this 'thing' started out badly. My baby is not a 'thing.'"

"Aw, jeez, Stephanie." He let her go. "You know I didn't mean it like that."

She shook her head. "No, I don't know. I really don't know you at all. That's what makes this so...so incredible. So bizarre. So unbelievable."

"At least you didn't say horrible."

Her hand went unconsciously to her flat stomach. "No baby could ever be horrible," she said softly. "Not even an unplanned one."

He touched her cheek gently. "Is that some of the stuff you tell your teens?"

Unthinking, she nuzzled her face in his hand. "That and a lot of other cheerleader stuff. Anything to keep them upbeat and positive so that their babies will feel loved and wanted."

"Our baby is that already, Stephanie, loved and wanted. Haven't you already said abortion is not an option? That you plan to have this baby and keep it, raise it yourself, no matter what reaction you had from me about it?"

She gave him a determined look. "Yes."

"Well, then, can we talk about it now?"

She gave a shaky laugh and nodded, then turned and walked down the hall toward her study. "I suppose we should get it over with."

He stopped her when she headed to the chair behind her desk. "Let's sit here," he said, motioning to the small love seat beneath twin windows. "It's friendlier."

"Would you like a cup of coffee or something?" she asked, still standing.

"No, thanks." Suddenly, he looked chagrined. "Hell, Stephanie, I haven't even asked how you're feeling. Are you having any problems?"

"I'm fine." She shrugged and gave him a half smile. "It's too early for morning sickness."

They each gazed into the other's face. He actually seemed concerned, Stephanie thought, and felt a moment's regret that their relationship would be complicated by a stroke of fate instead of…instead of what? she wondered. Would he have wanted to see her again after that night in Boston?

"Hey."

She realized he was waiting for her to sit down.

"Are we going to talk standing up?"

Gingerly, she perched on the edge of the love seat. Tal sat down, looking a little too masculine against the elegant tapestry upholstery as he crossed his legs, propping one ankle on a knee. With one arm stretched out over the back, he seemed prepared to wait however long it took for her to speak. She grew more anxious. She wished he didn't look so stern, but she supposed he had a right to react with whatever emotion he felt. He certainly hadn't bargained on learning he was a father-to-be when he'd agreed to meet her for dinner.

"I don't know what you expect me to say, Tal," she began hesitantly. "I—"

"That's better," he said, nodding. "I wondered if you were going to call me Dr. Robichaux forever."

"We can worry about how I address you when we figure out what to do," she snapped.

"Stephanie." His tone was resigned. "Haven't you figured it out yet? There is only one thing we *can* do. We have to get married."

"Would you please be serious?" she cried. "This is no joking matter. There's a child to think about here."

"And two careers," he said. "Haven't you considered what will happen when the world finds out?"

"Of course. I've thought of little else since I saw that stupid strip of paper turn pink this morning."

"You're supposed to be a role model. Those streetwise girls aren't going to believe a word you say from the moment they guess that you're pregnant. They'll accuse you of preaching one thing and then doing the opposite."

She rose in agitation. "You don't have to spell it out, Tal. I know how they'll feel. I don't need you to pass judgment, too."

"My God, woman, I'm not passing judgment. What kind of bastard do you think I am? I'm the only one who knows for sure that you didn't behave irresponsibly. What I'm doing such a rotten job of is trying to make you see how difficult our positions will become once your condition is known."

"*Our* positions?" She was geared up to give him a piece of her mind, but now she hesitated. "I've told you, you needn't be concerned. I'm not going to demand any support from you, and I'm certainly not going to tell anyone whose baby this is."

"You're having my baby, damn it!" He was on his feet now, too. "You keep talking as though you're the only one involved here, Stephanie. You're not in this alone. It takes two. And I have a reputation to uphold, just as you do. Since Diana's death, I've spoken out about family values, about failing to take responsibility for one's own actions, about fatherless kids. Do you honestly think I can just walk away from you as though nothing of any consequence has happened?''

"I suppose not.''

"You suppose not.'' He studied her silently. "Then you must see that marriage is the logical solution.''

"My God, Tal,'' she whispered. "I never meant—''

"I never thought you did, Stephanie. But things are out of our control now. If you can name an alternative, now's the time.''

She shrugged but said nothing.

"So.'' Tal stood up. "I think if we get married, we should do it without delay, what do you think?''

She didn't know what she thought. She only knew what she felt. She had been almost comfortable at the thought of being a single mother. Now she felt overwhelmed. Scared. Stunned. She shook her head as though to clear her thoughts. "I can manage this alone, Tal.''

"I'm sure you can, but is that the best way to go? Is that best for the baby?''

"But marriage,'' she moaned. "It'll be a sham. And as soon as we get the divorce, everybody will know it.''

"Whoa, now. Just a minute. How do you know we'll get a divorce?''

"For heaven's sake, Tal, let's be honest, if nothing else. We don't love each other. We would be marrying for the wrong reasons. We—''

"A baby is as right a reason as I can think of,'' Tal said.

"Yes, but babies are usually conceived in love. Have you forgotten what you said that night before we went up to your room? Something died inside you when your wife was killed. You said you didn't have anything to give in a relationship. So how can you hope to make our marriage permanent feeling as you do?"

He looked away, frowning. "Love is a pretty risky emotion, Stephanie, but we've got a lot of other things going for us—careers, education, friendship..." He smiled at her, his frown gone. "Good sex. Many marriages start with a lot less."

She felt a pang that he didn't try to convince her that he felt something besides sexual attraction for her. Then in the next breath, she realized how silly that was. She wanted honesty from him, didn't she?

Which was precisely what he wouldn't be getting from her. If he knew just how ugly her childhood had been, would he want to share the rest of his life with her? Would he want her as the mother of his child? They might be in the same profession, but they were from two different worlds. Tal wasn't a snob, but would he be arguing so persuasively to share his life, his home, his daughter with her if she were suddenly to reveal all her secrets?

"What about your daughter?" she asked, her voice rising.

"Since I think we should marry immediately, we have to tell her right away."

"Right away?" Stephanie had hoped to give herself a little time. Pregnancy, marriage, stepmotherhood, any single one meant major life-style changes. All at once, it was a daunting prospect to say the least.

"Yes, right away. I've got a full day scheduled tomorrow and it's late to try and change that. It's probably the same with you." She nodded, agreeing. "Are you free around dinnertime? Could you come over then?"

"What are you going to tell her?"

"Simply that you're the woman I'm going to marry."

"She's not going to be happy."

He frowned. "What makes you say that?"

She closed her eyes. "Oh, Tal, no thirteen-year-old girl who's had her father to herself for three years is going to welcome a pregnant stepmother."

"We don't have to tell her you're pregnant right away. What do you think I'll do, walk in and say I'm getting married and, oh, yes, we're expecting . . . all in one breath?"

"Of course not, but we will only have a few weeks for her to get accustomed to the idea before Mother Nature takes the decision out of our hands."

"Alison will have come to know you by then and she'll love you, you'll see."

Stephanie laughed softly, sadly. She didn't bother to contradict him. Who knows? Maybe by some miracle he could be right. But she wasn't counting on it.

"What about your parents?" she asked.

"They're on a cruise with my sister, Abby, who lives in Long Island," he said. "Unless you have a problem with it, I don't think we'll ask them to cancel their plans. Travis, my brother, will be there. Is that okay with you?"

"Yes, of course."

He rubbed his hands together. "Okay, let's make some plans."

She gave him a startled look. "You almost sound happy about this."

"Well, I'm not *un*happy," he replied. "Are you really that miserable about it?"

She sat back down on the love seat with a plop. "I'm not miserable, especially about the baby.

But...the other...it's just so...so..." She gave him a plaintive look. "Tal, everybody will talk. There'll be whispers, snickers. They know we've never even looked at each other, and suddenly we're getting married? Come on. You're dreaming if you think we won't be the talk of the town."

"Okay, we'll be the scandal of the week. Next week, it'll be somebody else."

Stephanie stared at him in dismay. He talked so glibly about scandal, but what did he know? If he'd ever been a target, he wouldn't brush it off so casually.

"Hey..." He sat down beside her and pulled her over so that she was nestled close to him. "That's enough of that kind of talk. We were attracted to each other in Boston, right?" She said nothing, so he pulled back a little and looked straight into her eyes. "Right, Dr. Sheldon?"

"Yes." She might as well admit it.

"We can build on that."

AFTER HE LEFT, Stephanie walked the floor and tried to come to terms with the amazing fact that she was going to marry Talbot Robichaux as soon as they could get blood tests. She couldn't argue with his reasoning. It was time for some damage control, and marriage was the most logical solution.

But was it right for herself and Tal? She asked herself again, would he be so willing to marry her if he knew her background? His family could trace their bloodlines to the first planters in Louisiana. She, on the other hand, didn't even know her father's name. Tal's family owned a chain of restaurants in the city.

Until she came to live with Camille, Stephanie had never eaten in a restaurant.

The sound of Camille's voice in the foyer drew her from her reverie. She felt a wave of exhaustion, realizing it must be past midnight.

"You're still up?" It was a rebuke, gentle but unmistakable. Camille knew Stephanie's schedule almost as well as Stephanie and thought she worked too hard with too little rest. "Don't you have a caesarean scheduled for seven?"

"I couldn't sleep."

Camille's expression was shrewd as she came toward Stephanie. Nearing seventy, Camille was petite, with dark hair and eyes, and about twenty pounds overweight—a curse from her Cajun ancestors, she claimed. Now her dark eyes were fixed intently on Stephanie.

"What's wrong, chère?"

For an instant, Stephanie felt sixteen again. She wished she could simply fall into her foster mother's arms and let Camille fix everything. "Oh, Camille, you're not going to believe what's happened to me."

"What would that be, chère? And you will let me decide whether or not to believe you."

Outside on the street, an ambulance sped by, siren pulsing. Her house was only a few blocks from Women's Hospital. Whenever she heard the piercing sound, she always wondered about the emergency. Whose life was on the line?

"Chère?"

The familiar endearment sent a sharp pain to her heart. "You recall that trip I made to Boston three weeks ago? Well, I...I met someone there. In the hotel bar. We...knew each other, but not well. We work

together. He lives here." She managed to meet Camille's eyes. "I . . . I went with him to his room."

"You are an adult, Stephanie. So far, I hear nothing to shock me into a heart attack. Is he a married
man?"

"No. No, he's not married." When she'd first come
to live with Camille, she'd been willing to do anything to keep from alienating this woman who had
taken her into her house and into her heart. She had
tried to justify every act, almost every thought,
whether it was something she'd done on purpose or
something completely beyond her control. Surely she
was beyond that kind of juvenile behavior.

"Well, then . . ."

"We were two consenting adults," Stephanie said
with a bitter twist of her mouth. She closed her eyes,
breathed in deeply. "I'm pregnant, Camille."

"Oh, my." Camille sat down. Another ambulance
streaked by outside.

"I feel so . . . such a fraud, Camille. I've been trying to figure out how such a thing could have happened. What came over me?"

"Who is he?"

"You're really not going to believe this—Talbot
Robichaux."

"Ah."

Stephanie looked at her. "What? Why 'ah' in that
way?"

"You ask how such a thing could have happened,
what came over you. Look a little deeper, chère.
Maybe you don't realize how often you mention Dr.
Robichaux. Dr. Robichaux, this, Dr. Robichaux,
that." She waved her short arms. "And always with

such a look about you. How can I be surprised that you finally recognized what you feel?"

"You're exaggerating, Camille," she said, instinctively denying it.

"You slept with a man and you felt nothing for him? It was the music and the night?"

She thought a minute. "I sincerely admire him. He's brilliant. Dedicated. He's not like so many successful surgeons. He has time for patients and programs at Women's that aren't necessarily profitable. He—" Looking up, she stopped when she saw the expression on Camille's face.

"You are one hundred percent wrong about one thing," Camille said, smiling.

"What's that?"

"What's happened isn't unbelievable at all." She went over to the love seat and sat down. "In fact, it was probably inevitable."

"That I'm pregnant after a one-night stand?" Stephanie's tone was incredulous.

"No, no, chère. That you would eventually discover your partiality for Talbot Robichaux." Camille slipped off her black pumps and began massaging her feet, something she always did after wearing what she called street shoes for more than an hour. "The surprising thing is that the two of you took so long to get together."

Stephanie dropped to the love seat beside her. "We're getting married," she said.

"Good idea."

"Right away, Camille."

The older woman nodded her understanding. "It's probably for the best."

"He has a daughter. Alison. She's thirteen."

"Now, *that* could be a problem."

For the first time, Stephanie smiled. "All this non-judgmental stuff and I mention a teenage daughter and you run out of encouraging words?"

"It's a difficult age."

"Tell me about it."

Stephanie shook her head wryly, thinking of the scared runaway she'd once been herself. If it hadn't been for Camille, God only knows where she'd be now. And Tessa. As ever, when she thought of her twin, she felt an ache so sharp, so deep, it nearly took her breath away.

She and Tessa had been fifteen and wards of the state when they'd realized they would have to leave Memphis and the foster parents they'd been placed with. No two kids had ever been more frightened or vulnerable the night they'd sneaked away. With no money, they'd been forced to hitch a ride on an eighteen-wheeler. There hadn't been a plan, so they didn't know where they would end up. It turned out to be New Orleans. Luckily.

Without money, they'd been hungry and homeless. Camille Landry, a nurse at Charity Hospital, had spotted them at a fast-food place trying to talk the assistant manager into giving them a job, any job, just to get a meal. She had taken them home with her and given them much more than food and shelter. She had given them hope and affection and guidance and discipline. She had given them stability, a permanent address. Stephanie owed her everything.

She looked worriedly into Camille's kind eyes. "Tal's background is so different from mine, Camille. I worry that our differences may be too great to overcome."

"What differences? You are a man and a woman who share the same profession, the same concerns for others, you're attracted to each other and you've created a baby together." She spread her hands and shrugged. "What differences?"

Stephanie smiled. "You always know the right thing to say."

Camille reached out and patted her hand. "Everything will work out, chère, you'll see. Talbot is a good man. I trust your instincts."

Stephanie gazed silently at their entwined hands, her expression somber. "I just wish . . ."

"You wish you did not have a past. You wish that night in Boston had no consequences. You wish you could fix this situation without involving Talbot Robichaux."

"Is all that so hard to understand?"

"No, chère. Not for someone who knows you. Dr. Robichaux isn't the only honorable one here." With a final affectionate squeeze, Camille rose, shoes in hand. "Now, go to bed. Get a good night's sleep."

"Good night, Camille."

TAL LAY with his hands beneath his head, thinking. He was still reeling from the knowledge that he was going to be a father. Again. He remembered the moment when Diana had told him that she was pregnant with Alison. She had been careless about taking her birth control pills, furious that they had screwed up. She had demanded that he perform an abortion. It was his job, she'd screamed at him. She hadn't wanted the baby and had expected him to agree to destroy it. He could do it in their apartment. No one would ever know. She had never quite forgiven him for refusing.

Two pregnant women. Two entirely different reactions.

But then, Stephanie and Diana were as different as it was possible for two women to be. Stephanie was conscientious and caring. Take those disadvantaged kids, for instance. They were a big part of her life. You couldn't fake that kind of dedication.

He stared at the ceiling, at peace with the idea of marrying her, complications and all. She was a beautiful woman, smart and sexy. That night in Boston had been unforgettable. Her passion had been deep and genuine. There had been the wine, yes, but she had been with him that night. Really with him. In spite of her pregnancy, Alison, their careers, the inevitable gossip, he felt optimistic about their chances to make it work. Hell, he felt more than optimistic.

He was smiling when he reached over and turned out the light.

CHAPTER THREE

*As your child develops, you will
discover a special rapport developing
between baby and yourself. This initial
bonding has been proven beneficial.
Some studies suggest a link between the
health of the child and the mother's
mental attitude. Don't forget to include
your mate.*

—Ask Dr. Meredith

August 21, 1995/3 weeks

"PUSH, Julie, push. Good, you're doing great."
Stephanie's voice was calm. Her mind worked quickly.
The patient was fully dilated. Contractions deep and
constant now. Baby in excellent position. Glancing up,
she saw that Robert, Julie's husband, was the color of
putty. Pete Haywood, an experienced and unflappa-
ble nurse, caught her eye and nodded. Stephanie
smiled. Pete would deal with it when Robert keeled
over.

"She's crowned." That from the resident who was
assisting.

"Uh-huh. Push, Julie. Hard. Now, pant. Don't
forget to pant. That's it...that's it. Again." She

watched intently as the baby's head emerged, dark,
bloody...miraculous. "Now, just a little more."

"I'm gonna..." Robert swayed. Almost casually,
Pete caught him, stretched him on the floor a few feet
out of the way and resumed his place at the patient's
head. Caught up in the hardest work she would ever
know, Julie had no time to miss her husband.

"Hey, here we go!" Warm, wiggly, beautifully de-
veloped, the baby slid smoothly into Stephanie's
waiting hands. No matter how many times she experienced this moment, she still felt a thrill. "It's a girl!"
The couple already had three boys.

"Oh...oh...let me see." Exhausted, but happy,
Julie smiled as she was handed the little girl. "Oh,
Robert, look. Isn't she beautiful? Robert?"

"He had to take a little break," Stephanie said,
glancing to see if the six-foot, two-hundred-and-
twenty-pound welder was on his feet yet. He wasn't.

"I guess he doesn't have to cope with anything like
this in the shipyard," Julie said, smiling tenderly at
their child.

For the next few minutes, Stephanie was busy. She
clamped off the cord, dealt with the placenta, checked
bleeding, cleaned, sutured. There had been some
tearing because of the size of the infant, almost nine
and a half pounds. Finally satisfied, she stepped back
and relinquished her place to the resident.

"You can take over, Dr. Simmons." She headed for
the door, grinning behind her mask as Pete helped the
groggy father stand up. "Congratulations, Daddy."

She entered the scrub room still smiling and stripped
the latex gloves from her hands. Scrubbed and clean,
she dried her hands and then placed both palms on her
abdomen. Her own child was barely the size of a speck

of sand. She was astonished to discover how real the baby was to her, no matter how tiny. "Hi, sweetheart," she whispered. "How's it going today?"

"You tell me."

She whirled. Tal was standing in the doorway, hands in his pockets, looking amused. "How long have you been there?" she demanded.

"Long enough to discover that your conversations are remarkably one-sided."

She flushed and bent to remove the surgical booties from her shoes. Just one glance had stamped Tal's image in her mind. Beneath his white lab coat, he was wearing gray-washed Dockers and a casual polo shirt, also white. The contrast with his dusky skin and near-black eyes was stunning. It was no wonder he was considered the heartthrob of the hospital.

My God, could she really be marrying this man in three days?

"I was talking to the baby." She turned then and caught the expression on his face. "I know. It sounds goofy, but...I just like to..." She shrugged. "To keep in touch."

"Nothing about you is goofy, Stephanie," he said, coming over and giving her a kiss on the cheek.

She was flustered all over again. He was certainly acting the part of a loving fiancé.

"Do you realize how long you've been at it today?" he asked, glancing at the clock overhead. "A delivery at 5:40 a.m. Another at 8:10. Now this. I looked at the schedule board. You were supposed to perform a caesarean at seven. You couldn't have had more than four hours' sleep."

"I didn't exactly schedule all this, Tal," she said dryly. "Babies decide when to be born, and it's not necessarily in sync with a doctor's convenience.'' She tossed soiled cap and booties into a bin. "The five o'clock delivery was normal, just early. Julie, the patient who was supposed to be the caesarean, went into labor instead. She just delivered a nine-and-a-half-pound baby girl naturally.''

"No problems?''

Her smile flashed. "None, if you don't count the father fainting at the crucial moment.''

"No kidding?''

"Went down like a redwood. Actually, he's almost as big as a redwood.''

He caught her by the arm, urging her toward the door. "Come on, I'll treat you to lunch.''

They had a brief wait for the elevator, then stepped inside. "I know what you're doing, Tal, and I'll let you get away with it this once, but you don't have to supervise my diet or anything else about this pregnancy. I'm going to take very good care of our baby.''

Leaning against the wall of the elevator, he had the same look she'd noticed on his face when he caught her talking to the baby. "I believe you,'' he said quietly. "Just humor me for a few days, will you? Until I get used to the idea.''

They arrived at the cafeteria and stood in line behind Benedict Galloway. Stephanie felt Tal tense. The whole hospital knew there was bad blood between the two men. Galloway's son had died the same night that Diana Robichaux had been shot. The tragedy had occurred at the free clinic where Ben, Jr., a promising young intern, had frequently volunteered. Galloway had fought against having Women's Hospital involved with the clinic. He and Talbot had argued bitterly. There was no warmth in the man's eyes as he nodded glacially to Tal.

He turned his attention to Stephanie. "I wonder if you could see me in my office at three, Dr. Sheldon," he said, his tone clipped and cool as always. "I've heard from one of the governor's aides that your application for a federal grant is probably going to be approved."

"That's wonderful." She turned to Tal. "This could mean we get funds to expand the program for my parenting classes."

"That's an extremely premature assumption, Dr. Sheldon," Galloway said. "There are other deserving programs presently underfunded at Women's Hospital. May I remind you that your application included them, as well as your pet project. In spite of your passion, the program for the teens is not a top priority. It's still unproven. I remain unconvinced that Women's is the appropriate facility to sponsor it."

Behind her, Tal gave a derisive snort. "The board would no doubt prefer sponsoring something more along the lines of a stop-smoking clinic," he said, his tone like silk. "Or maybe stress management."

The two men locked gazes. "There is a crying need for both, Talbot," Galloway said coldly.

"And in New Orleans, at least fifty programs in as many places offer them, Benedict."

Galloway's face was like granite. "What would you do with the grant, Talbot? Set up another clinic modeled after the one on Esplanade? Or perhaps expand that one?"

"I might just do both," Tal snapped.

"Two wasted lives wasn't enough to satisfy you?"

"Three o'clock," Stephanie put in hastily. The two men were attracting curious stares. The death of Ben, Jr., was obviously not resolved between the men. Surely their shared loss should have forged a bond between the two men. Apparently it had not.

"Yes. Three o'clock," Galloway said, sweeping up his tray. "We can discuss options then. Please don't be late, Dr. Sheldon. I'm a busy man." With a curt nod at Stephanie, he walked away.

"Let the games begin," Tal murmured, shoving his tray with enough force to spill iced tea on his hamburger.

Stephanie sighed. "I can see it now. It'll be a trade-off. In exchange for money to fund more space and materials for my teens, he'll want to book some silly seminars."

"He's a pompous ass."

"You two looked like you were going to come to blows there for a minute," she said, mopping up the tea with a handful of paper napkins. "Your hamburger's ruined, Tal."

"I'm not hungry anymore."

"Do you always get into it with him like that?"

"Always. He will never—" He moved toward a vacant table, shaking his head. "Forget it. I apologize. I should know better after all these years."

They both sat down. When she didn't begin eating, he gestured at her plate. "Eat your lunch. No sense in both of us suffering."

She decided against saying more. Besides, she had no business inviting confidences from Tal until she was ready to tell him her own secrets. And that might be never, depending on how things went once they were married. They were to take the blood tests this afternoon, the ceremony itself was to take place on Saturday. Three days from today. Tonight they would tell Alison. If anything was going to put her off her lunch, it was that.

She looked at the hamburger on her plate and couldn't wait to bite into it. Apparently, nothing interfered with a pregnant woman's appetite.

HER STOMACH was fluttering when she rang the doorbell at Tal's home that evening. It was a beautiful house, one of the Garden District's most appealing. Of Italianate design, its elegance was enhanced by lavish wrought-iron trim on the balcony and at ground level. The fence, itself, intricate in design, was written up in guidebooks.

Would she be living here? she wondered, pressing the bell again. The thought was almost staggering. She blinked in the sudden glare of light overhead, then the door was opened abruptly by a teenage girl.

Stephanie smiled. "Hello, I'm Stephanie Sheldon. You must be Alison."

"I must be."

The girl was a feminine version of Tal himself, dark eyes, dark hair, dusky complexion, even features. Her mouth was pretty, even in the pout it was in now. She was pretty, period. Poor Tal, he was going to have his hands full when boys discovered her. Or vice versa.

"Come on in."

There was little welcome in her tone, but Stephanie entered, keeping a pleasant look on her face.

"You have a lovely home," she said, thinking what an understatement that was. Heavens, it looked like something out of a movie! A gorgeous entrance hallway showcased curving stairs lit by a magnificent crystal chandelier. With a quick look around, she saw that the rooms leading off the hall were just as beautiful.

She smiled at the girl. "You must feel like a princess living here."

For an instant, she thought the girl almost warmed, but then her pout returned and she shrugged.

"Do you know the history of the house?" Stephanie asked.

"It was built by a sugar planter in the 1870s, but it had been neglected something awful when my dad bought it."

Stephanie studied the medallion from which the chandelier was suspended. "Then someone did a wonderful job with the restoration."

"That was my mother," Alison said, as cool as a princess.

"Yes, well . . . it's lovely." The thing to remember here was that she was an adult and Alison was a child, though the girl would probably cringe to be so described. At a sound, she turned and saw Tal descending the stairs.

"Stephanie. I didn't know you had arrived. Have you been here long?"

"Only half a minute," she said, smiling. "Alison let me in."

He glanced from one to the other. "Did you two introduce yourselves?"

"Of course, Daddy," Alison said, tossing her black hair over her shoulder. "I know how to greet a guest."

"We were talking about your home," Stephanie said before things got any more uncomfortable. "It's beautiful, but I suppose you hear that often."

"It's always nice to hear again," he said. Touching her elbow, he ushered her past the stairs to an open door. "Let's sit in here."

Unlike the elegance evident in the front portion of the house, this room had a lived-in look. A leather sofa was flanked by two upholstered chairs. There was an abundance of pillows, most with hunting motifs. Books by the hundreds lined the shelves along two walls. The room had a masculine ambience. This was obviously Tal's domain.

He seated her on the sofa and then stood in front of her, rubbing his palms together briskly. "Okay, there's coffee, tea, a cold drink, wine. What will you have?"

"Nothing, really."

"Oh, come on."

"Well then, mineral water. Please."

He turned to his daughter. "Alison, will you bring the two of us mineral water and get whatever you want for yourself."

She looked surprised. "You're having water, Daddy? You never drink that."

"Tonight I do." He tugged at her long hair and winked. "Tomorrow, I'll resume my bad habits."

"You don't have bad habits, Daddy." Her gaze flicked to Stephanie as she turned on her heel to obey him. "At least, you never *used* to."

His mouth opened, but Stephanie touched his arm. "Tal. Let it go for now."

Reluctantly, he watched Alison leave, then sat down beside Stephanie on the sofa. When he turned to her, he looked troubled. "We should start out as we mean to go on, Stephanie. This may be difficult for her, but I expect her to obey the simple rules of courtesy. To do otherwise will make it ten times more difficult for all of us.''

He was probably right, but Stephanie felt that they needed to get this particular moment behind them before going to work on Alison's manners. The girl was going to have a lot of adjusting to do. Hopefully, giving her a little leeway tonight might pay off in the long run.

"Here it is, mineral water all around." Alison set the tray down without much regard for the three beautiful crystal goblets filled with sparkling water. Stephanie accepted hers, murmuring thanks. After passing her father his, Alison went to the chair across from Tal and Stephanie and sat. "Okay, I know something's up, Daddy. You're never home this early on weekdays except for special occasions. What's going on?"

"I'm often home by this hour, Alison," Tal said.

"Only if you're about to give one of your lectures."

"This isn't a lecture, young lady, but how would you know? It could be something nice. In fact, it is something nice."

She looked unconvinced. "We're going skiing at Thanksgiving like you promised?"

"I didn't promise, Alison. I said we'd see. And no, it's not about a ski trip."

With a mutinous expression, she flopped back in the big chair. "Then it's like I said, lecture time."

Stephanie glanced at Tal to see if he realized how adroitly Alison had seized control of the situation. He was frowning darkly, his mouth tight with frustration.

"I've always enjoyed skiing," Stephanie said, trying to inject a lighter note. "You're fortunate to learn so young. I'll never forget my first try. I had to stay on the beginners' slopes forever, it seemed."

"It's easy," Alison said shortly.

"I guess I'm just not the athletic type," Stephanie said.

Tal looked like a man whose patience was being sorely tried. "Perhaps you could give Stephanie some tips the next time we go skiing, Alison."

Alison's face filled with dismay, but to her credit she didn't say what Stephanie knew she must be thinking. "Oh, give me a break" or "I'd rather die first."

"Whether the three of us go to Colorado or not isn't the subject tonight," Tal said in the tone he used in general staff meetings at the hospital when discussion went round in circles. "Stephanie and I wanted to talk to you together. We wanted you to be the first to know that we have decided to get married."

"What?" Alison sat up straight, looking from one to the other.

"We're going to be married, Stephanie and I."

"No!" She sprang from the chair. "You can't. I won't let you!"

On his feet, too, Tal reached for her, but Alison shrugged away, her hair flying around her face. "You don't need to marry anybody, Daddy. We're fine like we are, just you and me."

"You're right, Ali. We do just fine, you and me. But that doesn't mean I never planned to marry again."

"Why do you have to do it now?" she demanded, her eyes bright with tears. "Couldn't you wait until I leave to go to college?"

"Six years?" he said, softening his tone with affection. "That's a long engagement, don't you think?"

She sniffed, then wiped her eyes with her fingers. "Maybe you'll come to your senses by then."

Tal's smile vanished. "Alison..."

"I don't care! What do you expect me to do, Daddy? Jump up and say I'm thrilled you want to marry some strange woman I've never even met until tonight and then go to my room like a good girl and leave you two down here to...to...gloat? No! I don't think so."

"That's enough, young lady!" With his hands on her arms, he gave her a firm shake. She was startled. Stephanie guessed he had seldom been pushed to use any kind of force in a confrontation with Alison. With deep foreboding, she wished that she hadn't been the cause of it.

"This isn't only about you and me, Alison," Tal said. "Stephanie is going to be my wife. I know it's a surprise, even a shock. Sometimes that happens with people. You'll understand someday. When you get older."

Oh, Tal, not that way.

"Well, I can hardly get older overnight, can I, Daddy? So I guess it'll just have to be that I don't understand."

Stephanie felt reluctant sympathy for the girl. She remembered the frustration of being thirteen. But at least Alison had a loving father and the security of knowing nothing could ever really threaten that.

"When is this going to happen?" Alison asked.

There was an uneasy silence. "Saturday," Tal said.

"Saturday! That's only two days from now!"

Tal drew in a long breath. "I'm aware of that, Alison. No doubt you'd like to argue about that, too. But since nothing you can say is going to change anything, I don't see the point in prolonging this discussion."

"Daddy, please..."

"The ceremony will be in the chapel at St. Luke's. I want you to buy something special to wear."

With a stricken look on her face, she stared wordlessly at her father.

"We'll shop for it together."

She gave a helpless cry and ran out of the room.

CHAPTER FOUR

*Not every pregnant woman suffers from
morning sickness. One in two never
experience a single episode. But be
prepared. Have plain saltine crackers
on your bedside table along with a cup
of tea. This is a moment when an
understanding mate can be worth his
weight in gold.*

—*Ask Dr. Meredith*

August 28, 1995/4 weeks

STEPHANIE WAITED while Tal opened the door of the
penthouse suite to let a bellman in bearing fruit and
champagne. She had been Mrs. Talbot Robichaux
since four o'clock that afternoon. There had been only
three other people at the ceremony—Camille, Alison
and Travis Robichaux, Tal's only brother. Travis,
more open and laid-back than Tal, seemed to accept
his brother's sudden urge to marry at face value. He
had hugged Stephanie and kissed her soundly, com-
menting that Tal was a lucky devil. Travis was the kind
of brother-in-law any woman would be lucky to have,
she thought. With a grin, he'd asked if there were any
more like her at home.

Stephanie had almost teared up. What would Travis say if he knew there was indeed another just like her. But not at home. With a heavy heart, she turned and gazed out the window, blind to the drama of the nighttime skyline.

Where are you, Tessa?

Her twin had been on her mind off and on all week long. It was troubling, not so much because she missed having Tessa beside her at her wedding, but because she felt . . . uneasy somehow. As if Tessa was nearby. Which was crazy. Nuts. The last time she'd seen her twin was almost seventeen years ago.

Oh, God, she had sworn to stop doing this. Tessa was gone and there was nothing she could do about it.

Tal closed the door and walked across the suite toward her. She watched him warily. For the third time that day, her stomach was in a knot. The first time had been in the chapel at St. Luke's as she waited for Tal. Maybe it was silly, considering the circumstances of their wedding, but she hadn't wanted to see him until they walked into the chapel together for the ceremony. He had been a few minutes late and she had nearly panicked, fearing he had changed his mind.

She had barely heard his explanation—something about Alison's dress and the girl's grandmother keeping her on the phone. The real shock had been how deeply relieved she was that he hadn't changed his mind. Until that moment, she hadn't admitted how much it mattered that she was actually marrying the father of her child.

Or was it that she was marrying Talbot Robichaux?

The second moment had come over dinner. They had decided not to leave New Orleans for a honeymoon trip. There hadn't been time to rearrange their schedules, so Tal had reserved the penthouse suite in the Royal Sonesta. How he'd managed on such short notice was a mystery to her. She suspected his family had connections that made such a feat fairly simple.

Dinner was an elaborate meal at Arnaud's in the French Quarter. It was just the two of them. Stephanie had asked that they avoid one of Tal's family's restaurants. He had agreed, apparently not looking forward to dealing with his relatives just yet any more than she was.

Tal had waited until they'd both ordered before leaning forward and saying, "We need to talk, don't we, Steph?"

"Isn't it a little late for that?" She made a big production of unfolding her napkin and spreading it over her lap.

"I wasn't referring to the wedding or the baby." He captured her hand and held it, forcing her to look at him. "I thought you might be worrying about tonight, whether or not we'll be sleeping together."

Oh, Lord, how did he know these things? How was it that she could talk about the most intimate subjects with her patients but blush like a schoolgirl at the thought of discussing sex with her husband? She was a physician, for heaven's sake!

"I wasn't worrying, exactly," she said, staring at the knot of his tie. "I assumed our marriage would be a normal one."

He smiled. "I can't tell you how relieved I am to hear you say that."

"I mean . . . well, it isn't as though we haven't . . . ah . . ."

"We've made love before."

"Yes."

"And it was good."

She looked directly at him. "Yes, it was."

"Do you have any reservations?"

Only about ten thousand. A one-night stand in Boston does not a marriage make. "Not really," she lied.

His smile deepened. His fingers were strong and warm as he squeezed her hand. He let go and settled back. "Well, now that that's settled, we can enjoy our dinner. I didn't take time for lunch and I'm starved. How about you?"

"Sounds good." When had she learned to lie like this?

When Tal's drink and Stephanie's water came, he settled back looking relaxed and mellow.

"Tell me about the kids you work with. I'll bet you've had some interesting moments with them."

"Interesting, disturbing, amusing, confusing... you name it," she said, looking down at her water glass.

"Why the smile?"

"I was just thinking about the newest member of the group, a girl named Keely. She claims she's not pregnant herself, but is coming because a friend of hers who is pregnant is contemplating joining up." She rolled her eyes. "Some of the stories I hear aren't very creative."

"You think she's pregnant and just won't admit it?"

"Maybe. Probably. Who knows? With these girls, it never pays to assume anything."

"Why would she do that?"

"Again, who knows?" She took a sip of water. "There's just something about Keely..." Looking up, she saw that he was smiling. "I try not to get personally involved, but once in a while there's a special one."

He nodded. "In what way is Keely special?"

"She's very bright and articulate. She's street-smart, too. I wonder about the circumstances that brought her to New Orleans. By her accent, I know she's not a native. Does she have a mother somewhere frantic with worry? Is she a victim of abuse? Was she forced to run to escape an intolerable situation?" Stephanie set her glass down. "There could be a dozen reasons why she's turned up here, and none of them good."

The waiter brought their plates, and while he was arranging the food, Tal seemed to be reaching back in his thoughts. When they were alone again, his eyes met hers. "I wonder if those teens realize how lucky they are to have an advocate who cares as much as you do?"

"A lot of people care. In fact, I think most people do, but most don't have any practical way of helping. I do."

"And you take a lot of heat for doing it."

She smiled. "Speaking of heat, what's the temperature in your area? Have you done anything lately to send Ben Galloway into orbit?"

He concentrated on a perfectly charbroiled filet. "Funny you should ask. Last thing yesterday, he dropped by with a little bombshell. We're being sued, he tells me, because somebody at the free clinic administered penicillin to a walk-in who turned out to be severely allergic. Fortunately, the man pulled through, but only after five days in intensive care." Tal sliced into his filet as if it were Galloway's heart. "An uninsured patient in intensive care translates to an ocean of red ink on the bottom line. His words, not mine."

Stephanie toyed with a pink shrimp. "I guess he's just doing his job, although he does seem singularly lacking in social conscience."

Tal stopped what he was doing and rested the heels of his hands on the table. "Let's not discuss Benedict tonight, of all nights. I mentioned the incident without thinking."

"Just making conversation?"

"You are a bride sharing a wedding dinner. Speaking as the groom, I think you're too tense. Only when you were talking about your teenage girls did you relax a little."

"I don't rush into marriage every day, Tal."

"I know." He put his knife and fork down. Leaning forward, he caught her hand again. "It'll be okay, Stephanie."

Now, back in the sumptuous suite, she felt her confidence slipping again. And that knot was back in her stomach. At dinner, she'd finally relaxed enough to eat, but now she was beginning to regret having had the rich seafood sauce. Only this morning she had commented to Camille that she hadn't suffered once from nausea. Had she spoken too soon?

To distract herself, she studied the suite, which was large enough to accommodate a sizable party. The bedroom/bath combination had a king-size bed that loomed as large as Lake Pontchartrain.

"Do you want the bathroom first?" Tal asked.

"Yes, thanks."

"Look, champagne." She stopped as he headed for the table where the bottle was iced and waiting.

"Your brother?"

"Yeah." He examined the label. "Way to go, Trav."

"Nice of him," she murmured, pressing her hands to her stomach.

"Do you think you can have a little?"

"Just a taste."

"Okay, I'll fix it while you freshen up."

As he walked, he shed his suit coat, tossing it casually on the love seat. She wondered if he was the kind of man who needed picking up after. It had been a bone of contention between her and Donald, her ex-husband. She liked things tidy and neat. It had come to a head during her residency. Between the hours and the stress and cooking and cleaning, her resentment of Donald's sloppy habits had grown stronger and stronger. Suddenly, panic assailed her.

What did she know about this man?

Her stomach rebelled. She groped blindly for the doorknob and rushed into the bathroom. She had only one thought—to make it to the john before losing her dinner.

She did, barely.

When she finished, she was on her knees in front of the commode. On the other side of the bathroom door, Tal was calling her name urgently. Miserable and embarrassed, she longed to be at home in bed, anywhere but where she was. There was simply no way to throw up delicately, but to have it happen on her wedding night was worse than awful.

"Stephanie, please... Open up, okay?"

Not until she was decent. In spite of shaking knees, she managed to stand up and get to the sink. Her hands trembled so much she had difficulty turning on the water. Ignoring Tal's urgent voice, she rinsed her mouth and face and hands.

"Please let me in, Stephanie. I'm a doctor, for God's sake."

Her cleanup finished, she stared at herself in the mirror for a moment or two. So much for that old saying that pregnant women were radiant. She looked like hell warmed over. Her skin was the color of paste, her lips were blue, her hair was stringy where she'd splashed it as she washed her face. Closing her eyes, she remembered that her makeup kit was in the luggage, still unpacked in the bedroom. Of course. Naturally.

Leaning her forehead on the closed door, she whispered, "Would you please get my overnight case, Tal?"

There was an instant of silence. "What?"

"My overnight case," she repeated weakly. "I need it."

He hesitated before saying, "Okay."

She heard him moving about, then he was back at the door. "I've got it. Now open up."

Still feeling drained and weak, she stood propped against the wall beside the door. Fumbling a bit with the lock, she finally managed to turn it, then waited with her eyes closed for Tal to do as she asked.

"What the hell's going on?"

Her eyes flew open. He looked tall and clean and vibrant with good health. She turned away, feeling even more grungy. "I threw up."

He caught her chin in his fingers to force her to look at him. "I guessed *that,* Steph. What I mean is, why didn't you let me help you?"

"I didn't want help. I wanted privacy."

"We're in this together, lady. I thought we had worked that much out."

"Marriage we worked out, not the throwing-up part." She gave a humorless laugh. "Believe me, you don't want to share that."

"We'll talk about this later. Come on." Slipping an arm around her, he led her out of the bathroom. When they reached the bed, she sat, feeling like a rag doll without enough stuffing. Tal knelt in front of her and slipped a shoe off her foot. "We're going to get you out of these, then you can undress, get into something more comfortable and—" Glancing up, he broke off when he saw her expression.

"Relax, Stephanie. Those beautiful plans we made over dinner tonight are scrapped," he said. With impersonal efficiency, he pulled the tails of her blouse loose and began unbuttoning it. She was wearing a sexy ivory satin-and-lace demi-bra that might have been cotton and sexless for all the reaction Tal showed. He popped the front clasp and she groped for a pillow, wrapping her arms around it. His smile was rueful. Turning to her skirt, he unzipped it and eased it down. Last, her panty hose came off, leaving her in nothing except her tiny bikini panties and grateful for the pillow.

"Sex will have to wait, at least for tonight," he said.

"Thank you," she whispered.

Tal turned away and opened her luggage. He pulled out the nightgown Camille had insisted she take. It was the same ivory satin as her bra and bikinis. He held it up—again without expression—to find the front. She reluctantly let go of the pillow and let him drop the gown over her head. He acted as though he dressed women this way every day. Or every night.

He pulled the covers down and stepped back. When she was settled, his mouth tilted in a smile. "No champagne for you, lady."

She rolled her eyes.

"Can I get you anything?" he asked, and she could see the concern in his eyes.

She shook her head. "I'm sorry about this, Tal. I haven't had a moment of nausea before now."

"I hope it's nothing personal."

She hurried to reassure him, but he simply shook his head, letting her know he was teasing. He touched the switch on the lamp and the room went almost dark. He rose to leave.

"Tal..." It was going to be easier in the dark.

"Hmm?"

"Earlier tonight at dinner when we talked about...having a normal marriage, you remember?"

"I remember."

"I lied. You asked if I had any reservations."

"And..."

"I do."

"What kind of reservations?"

"It's just that...we don't really know each other, Tal. That is, in a personal sense. You were right when you said I seemed uptight, uncertain. I am. I'm not sure that we should have a completely...physical relationship...at least not just now."

In the dark, all she could see was his silhouette backlighted by the glow from the room behind him. He put a hand behind his neck, tilting his head a little toward the ceiling. The gesture seemed one of frustration. Was he irritated with her? Did he think she was some airheaded female whose ideas now that she was married to him, were somehow different from the ones she'd held the night she had slept with him in Boston? If he did, who could blame him?

"You may think I'm making no sense, considering that we've already had sex that night in Boston and it seemed . . . good. We—"

"It *was* good. We *did* enjoy it. Nothing you can say will change that, Stephanie."

"That's not what I'm trying to say, Tal."

"Then what? Spit it out."

"I did. I don't know how I can say it any plainer. You know that circumstances forced us into marriage. We—"

"You're pregnant with my child," he snapped. "That's as good a reason for marrying as any I can think of."

What about love? But she couldn't say that. He hadn't pretended for a minute that he felt anything special for her. In fact, that night in Boston he'd been quite specific. *"I don't have anything to give anymore, Stephanie."* That was what he'd said before they'd gone upstairs together. Nothing had changed. Had it?

"I don't want to quarrel with you about this, Tal."

"I don't intend to quarrel about it. If you don't want this relationship to include sex, then I sure as hell don't want to force you."

"Marriage. We're starting a marriage here, Tal."

"Whatever you want to label it is fine with me, Stephanie. However you want to set the ground rules is also fine with me." He turned and was at the door in two long strides.

"Tal, wait . . ."

He stopped with one hand on the door frame, but he did not turn. Again, she was treated to the sight of his silhouette. This time, she could see his profile. Something about the set of his features told her how upset he was.

"I'm sorry I've disappointed you."

"I'm fine."

"You don't sound as if everything is fine, Tal. As for ground rules, I hadn't thought of it in those terms. I was simply trying to tell you what I'm feeling. I don't feel comfortable at the thought of sharing all the intimacies of marriage with you until we know each other a little better. I'm just asking for time, Tal. I'm being as honest as I know how. Please try to understand."

He turned to her at last, but his face was again in shadow so Stephanie couldn't guess what he was thinking. "Don't worry about it tonight, Steph. You're probably right. Maybe we do need time to get to know each other better."

He paused, and when he spoke again, she was left in no doubt that he meant every word he said. "One thing is certain—no marriage or relationship, affair—you label it—between a man and a woman can survive just on friendship, respect, the ties of a common career or whatever. We'll have to deal with sex sooner or later. And because it was so good with us, sooner seems best to me. But I'll leave it to you to say when. Good night."

"Good night."

It was a long time before she fell asleep.

"OKAY, Dr. Steph, you can tell us straight. Is Dr. T as good in the sack as he looks?" Wiggling her eyebrows Groucho-fashion, Jolene propped her chin on her hands and waited for Stephanie's reply.

"We're not discussing my personal life today, Jolene." Turning her back, Stephanie walked to the free-standing chart board where a list of foods was written in black letters. "Okay, let's talk about nutrition."

"Why not? Our personal lives are laid open around here for the whole world to gawk at. Is loo—oo—ve between doctors different?" she said, drawing out the word.

"Jolene!" Chantal's soft voice was reproachful.

Stephanie wrote the word *antioxidants*. "Who knows what this term means?"

Keely was on the floor in her usual lotus position. "It's an ingredient in some foods, like vitamins or minerals."

"Right." She was no longer surprised by Keely's wealth of knowledge. But so far, the girl had not revealed her pregnancy. If she didn't do so voluntarily, Stephanie was going to have to push the issue. "What foods?"

"Spinach, greens, broccoli. Mostly yuck stuff."

Stephanie listed the foods. "But good for baby."

"Why didn't you tell us you were stuck on Dr. Robichaux?" Jolene persisted.

Keely studied the ceiling with a look of boredom. "Give it a rest, Jo."

Melissa nodded. "Yeah, Jolene, if Dr. Steph wants to keep secrets, she has a right."

"What is this?" Jolene stood up suddenly, sensing mutiny in the ranks. "You're always goin' on about us trustin' you, Dr. Steph. Looks to me like you jumpin' into marriage without even a hint that you were even seein' Dr. Robichaux is what I call *betrayin'* the trust thing.''

With a sigh, Stephanie put the marker down and turned around. Eight upturned faces waited expectantly. She would have to try to explain her marriage. It was naive to assume she could return from an unplanned absence, announce she'd married Talbot Robichaux and expect this group not to ask questions. *Especially* this group. They were as familiar with hospital gossip as most of the staff.

But what to tell them? Tal had returned on Monday after their honeymoon weekend, but she had been out for another week. That had been Tal's idea, and it hadn't taken much to convince her. She had been dreading the gossip that would—did—spread through the hospital like ground fire. But she owed these girls something more.

"Okay, everybody gather round," she said, pulling a chair forward and taking a seat. "I've known Dr. Robichaux for several years," she began, her gaze touching each of them briefly. "When I came here three years ago, he was already chief of surgery. What dealings we had then were strictly professional. I was recently divorced and interested mostly in making a new start.''

"Did you know his wife?" Jolene asked.

"Not really, only to see."

"Dr. Robichaux is one good guy," Angela said. "He's been really nice to my little brother who's sick a lot. At the clinic, you know.''

"His wife was killed in a drive-by near the clinic," Jolene put in. "Did you know that?"

"Yes, I knew that.''

"Wow, that must have been bad on his kid, what's-her-name," Keely said. "Alison."

"Yes, losing her mother was terrible."

"That's probably why Dr. T's such a wuss about her," Jolene said.

Stephanie frowned at Jolene. "You don't know enough to make such an assumption, Jolene."

"Maybe, maybe not." The girl shrugged with nonchalance. "But you up and marry some guy, we want to know about him. This Alison girl is a spoiled-princess type. We checked."

"You checked—" Words failed Stephanie for a moment. "And just how did you go about checking?"

"Ve haf ways, my dear." It was Keely, twirling an imaginary mustache.

Jolene began ticking off on her fingers. "She goes to school at Sacred Heart. Plays tennis and goes to the theater." Now she was studying her nails intently.

"Poor motherless tyke," said Keely sarcastically.

Stephanie crossed her arms, eyeing the girls without saying a word. Long ago she'd realized how difficult it was to win a contest of words with them. They took no prisoners when they debated. But sometimes a significant look made them stop and think.

"Okay, okay, you want us to reserve judgment on the kid," Jolene said, stretching on the chair and resting her hands on the bulge of her stomach.

Stephanie nodded. "That would be nice."

Jolene glanced around the group. "Benedict-the-Bastard's son caught it at the same time," she said.

Stephanie sighed wearily. "Jolene, how many times—"

"No kidding?" Keely looked at Stephanie for confirmation.

Jolene was only too ready to oblige. "He was a schmuck, anyway."

"Jolene!"

"Okay." Even Jolene responded when Stephanie used that tone. "So, back to the interesting stuff, tell us more about you and Dr. T."

"There's really nothing much to tell, Jolene."

Angela spoke up. "My mother says a woman never knows a man until she's married to him for a while, anyway."

"She's probably right," Stephanie said with a smile. "So ask me later." She started up, but several of the girls spoke together. A few sketchy answers hadn't satisfied their curiosity.

"How long have you been dating him?" From Chantal.

"His family owns a bunch of restaurants. Do you get to eat free?" Leanne.

"Are you gonna tell us how he is in the sack?" Jolene.

"Does this mean you'll be moving out of your place and into the house with him and his daughter?" Keely.

"I spent the past few days doing exactly that," Stephanie said. There had been something about Keely's question, but the girl's expression told her nothing. "It was a difficult decision because I love my house and I worried about leaving Camille."

"Hey, a woman's got to live with her guy," said Jolene.

Tal's sentiments exactly, although not in those exact words. When all was said and done, there had been little choice. Tal's home was big enough to accommodate a family of twelve, while her own small place was crowded with just her and Camille. As they had discussed living arrangements, Camille had proved Tal's strongest ally, insisting she preferred to stay in the small house when Tal insisted his house had plenty of room for all of them. Before Stephanie realized it, she was moved in and unpacked and sharing the master bedroom with Tal.

He had refused to compromise on that one. Whether or not she was ready to make their relationship a physical one, they were going to share a bedroom, Tal had informed her. He had a king-size bed. She could stay on her side for as long as she wanted to, but share it they would.

And that was the way it had been since their first night. Together, but apart.

"It's like when you get married, you're supposed to leave your house and folks behind," Chantal said with unabashed envy.

"Provided you've got all that to begin with." Keely laughed then, as if the remark wasn't to be taken seriously. "How's the little princess treating you?" she asked Stephanie.

It seemed to Stephanie a deliberate effort by Keely to deflect Stephanie's curiosity. "Everyone has to give a little in second marriages," she replied. "Kids as well as adults."

"Not too good, huh?"

So much for painting her marriage in a rosy hue. These girls saw through her too well. "I suppose it's difficult for any adolescent to welcome a strange female into her home. But . . . we're trying."

At least, I'm trying.

Keely nodded sagely. "Some people don't know good luck even when it comes calling."

The familiar saying caught Stephanie off guard for an instant. She looked into Keely's blue eyes and wondered again what secrets the girl was keeping, but knew she would find out only when Keely was ready to tell her. Dealing with the teens had taught her that much. In fact, Stephanie understood the need to keep secrets better than any of them suspected. She still had a few of her own.

CHAPTER FIVE

*Family relationships can be
strained during pregnancy. With your
attention focused almost exclusively on
your baby, other members of your family
may feel excluded. Pregnancy is a
family affair! Share it.*

—*Ask Dr. Meredith*

September 25, 1995/8 weeks

STEPHANIE TURNED OFF the shower and stepped out, closing the glass door behind her. She pulled a towel from the bar and began drying herself. It had been a long day. Sixteen-year-old Melissa had delivered today. The baby was too small. No matter how often Stephanie had stressed that a pregnant mother was the only person who could provide nutrition for the baby she carried, Melissa had not taken good care of herself. The trouble was that Melissa was still a child herself. Hopefully, she would be a better mother now that the child was born. If he survived.

Catching sight of herself in the mirror, she paused to examine her abdomen. She turned sideways to see if she was showing yet but could tell no difference. At eight weeks, you weren't supposed to see anything, she told herself.

Wrapped in a towel, she freed her hair from the knot she'd hastily twisted to keep it dry and finger-combed through it. Maybe she wasn't showing, but she was gaining a little weight. One of the hints she gave her patients was that a good-quality hand and body lotion would reduce the damage from stretch marks. She opened the cabinet to get the lotion she'd bought a couple of days ago.

Frowning, she pushed bottles and boxes aside looking for it. Damn. Things seemed to sprout legs around here. First, her new mascara, then some bubble bath. She'd never had this problem until she started sharing a bathroom. She found cotton balls, soap, Tal's shaving foam. Still no lotion. Irritated, she reached for a bottle. Tal's cologne. A sound coming from the bedroom startled her. She jerked around and the bottle went flying. She tried to catch it, but it hit the ceramic floor and shattered.

With a yelp, she recoiled as liquid and glass showered her feet and legs. When her foot came down on a piece of glass, she felt a sharp pain and knew she'd cut herself.

The door flew open and Tal rushed in. "What's the matter?" Spotting the glass, he didn't wait for an answer. "Don't move." He crossed the bathroom and lifted her, towel and all.

"I broke your bottle of cologne," she told him.

"Forget it. You're bleeding like crazy."

"I stepped on broken glass. Oh, you're going to get blood on the carpet."

"It'll clean up," he told her. He set her down on a beautiful Victorian love seat, ignoring another protest, and lifted her foot to examine the cut. Blood was gushing from her instep. "There's glass in there."

"I know."

He stood up. "I'll get tweezers and bandages. Only take a second."

Ordinarily, she would have applied pressure, but the embedded glass prevented that. Gritting her teeth, she rested her head against the back of the love seat and didn't open her eyes until she felt Tal gently lifting her foot.

"I didn't know you wore glasses," she said, keeping her gaze on his dark head.

"For close work," he murmured, his attention on what he was doing.

"They're very smart."

He glanced up and something in his look made her heart beat a little faster. She remembered suddenly that she was wearing nothing but a towel. Fortunately, an oversize one, but there was still a lot of skin to see.

"Did you get it?" Her voice had a husky sound.

"Yeah." His was deep and low.

For another beat or two, they seemed caught in the moment. Then Tal moved and the spell was broken. He applied enough pressure to stop the bleeding. She winced, and he responded with a sympathetic sound. He cleaned the wound, then pressed a bandage to her instep and quickly wrapped her foot.

"That should do it." Still squatting in front of her, he rested her foot on his thigh.

"Thanks." Her voice had a breathless quality. "It was my own fault. I'll replace your cologne."

"Forget it. I have a spare." His fingers encircled her ankle and then he was cupping the shape of her calf in his hand. "In my travel kit."

"Well..." His touch was warm and the look in his dark eyes caught at her senses. She felt the flutter of her heart and wondered if it was shock from loss of blood.

"If you have any pain, I can probably find something to—"

"No. I'll be fine." Her foot was still resting on his thigh, but now both his hands were slowly moving. Along her calves, up her thighs. Her breath caught when he bent his head and slowly kissed the tops of her knees, first one and then the other. Now her heart was racing. His dark hair seemed black as midnight against her pale skin. She ached to touch it.

"Stephanie." His breath was warm against her damp skin. "You have a beautiful body," he murmured, and she shivered at the movement of his lips.

She clutched at the towel covering her as his mouth inched upward. She felt flushed all over, too warm. Dizzy. She wanted to abandon her flimsy wrap, lie back, close her eyes and let him take her away on a sea of sensation.

Was this a good idea? With the touch of his mouth heating the very core of her and his hands exploring softness and shape and quivering nerve ends, she could barely breathe, let alone think. What was it he had said to her that first night?

"Marriage can't survive just on friendship, respect, career... We'll have to deal with sex sooner or later. Sooner seems best to me."

"Tal..."

He pulled back to look at her, then with a groan he came up beside her on the love seat, tossing his glasses, and gathered her into his arms. Before she could protest, he was kissing her.

The towel melted away from her body as if it were wax and Tal was a fiery furnace. He *was* on fire and so was Stephanie. With his hands scorching everywhere they touched, his mouth devoured her. He found her ear, her throat, the curve of her neck and shoulder. Her uncertainty was gone, forgotten in the heat. His hand cupped her breast. Then...oh, Lord, his mouth was on her nipple. Hot. Wet. Streaking sensation.

Untangling her hands from the towel, Stephanie reached for him. She needed to touch him the way he was touching her. Fumbling with his shirttails, she tried to get at his naked skin.

Just then, someone knocked on the door.

Muttering profanities, Tal didn't move at first. With his forehead against Stephanie's, he managed a humorless laugh. "Can you believe this?" He glanced at the door. "Who is it?"

"It's me, Daddy." Alison sounded irritated, as if she wasn't used to waiting for an invitation into her father's bedroom. "Can I come in?"

"Just a minute." Tal stood up and watched Stephanie grope for the ends of the towel. "You look gorgeous," he said, keeping his tone low. In spite of being interrupted, he looked pleased with himself. Before Stephanie could work that one out, Alison banged again.

"Daddy!"

"Coming." He moved away, still looking at Stephanie. "Don't walk on that foot yet. I'll get you a wrap." He scooped up the negligee that was draped over the back of a chair and handed it to her, then went to the door and opened it.

Alison was waiting, arms crossed, exaggerated patience in every line of her body. "What kept you, Daddy? What were you doing?"

"None of your business, young lady."

She looked beyond him and saw Stephanie wearing the negligee, obviously fresh out of the shower. "Oh . . . *that*. I should have guessed."

Tal ignored her. "Stephanie had an accident, Alison. She cut her foot on broken glass in the bathroom. How about getting a dustpan and brush so we can sweep it up?"

She seemed about to refuse, but her rebellion died at the look in Tal's eye. Spinning around, she flounced down the hall.

Tal turned, shaking his head. "Sometimes I wonder if my house was invaded by a gremlin who took my sweet little girl and left a smart-mouth brat in her place." He gave Stephanie an apologetic look. "Have patience, will you, Steph? This will surely pass."

He seemed more in need of reassurance than she did. "Of course it'll pass," she said. "And just for the record, you don't have to keep apologizing for her. I've invaded her territory and she hasn't come to terms with it yet."

"Will she ever?"

She smiled. "Before she's old enough for college? Who knows?"

"Great. Thanks a million. That's just what I needed to hear."

He seemed to think then of his disheveled state and began tucking in his shirt. Suddenly, Stephanie realized how she must look. She tightened the sash of her robe and tried to restore order to her hair. Each was conscious of the other. Neither was thinking about the rebellious teenager. Alison had interrupted a moment that would have changed the course of their relationship. Another minute and they would have been in bed together.

"What are you thinking?" Tal asked, his hand resting on his belt.

"That Alison did us both a favor."

He took a step toward her. "Stephanie—"

"Here it is." Alison was back. Eyeing them suspiciously, she thrust the dustpan and brush at her father, who refused it.

"Be careful," he said. "There are glass slivers everywhere."

"You want *me* to clean it up?" From her expression, it was obvious she would rather have eaten a spider.

"I do," Tal replied firmly.

"Why?" she demanded. "I didn't break it."

"Because while you do that," Tal explained patiently, "I'm going to get Stephanie settled. She can't put her weight on that cut until the bleeding is controlled."

Two stubborn people, Stephanie thought, watching the exchange. They seemed remarkably alike, used to having their own way. With a final stormy look at Stephanie, Alison went into the bathroom to do as she was told.

"And be careful," Tal told her. "Any splinters you miss could wind up in somebody's foot."

There was a mumble from the bathroom. They couldn't make out the words but could guess at the sentiment. It wouldn't be Alison's foot, so who cared? They laughed softly. It was a warm moment, one of those little times that tended to seduce Stephanie into believing—almost—that her marriage was going to survive in spite of the many cards stacked against it.

"How'd this happen, anyway?" Alison demanded from the bathroom, raising her voice over the rattle of the dustpan on the ceramic floor.

Tal bent and lifted Stephanie so that when she answered, her voice sounded breathless. "I...ah...I dropped a bottle of your dad's cologne while looking through the cabinet for some body lotion."

"Oh." For once, no smart comeback and no mumbling.

Still holding her, Tal looked into Stephanie's eyes. "Did you ever find it?" He was so close she could see the tiny gold flecks in his eyes.

"No." For a long moment, they both seemed caught in a mix of sensations—his strength, her own vulnerability, the feel of her body against his, his heartbeat, her heartbeat, the inexorable flowering of their relationship in spite of everything.

"I'm done." Again, Alison shattered the intimacy of the moment. Did the girl do it purposely? There had been times in the weeks since Stephanie had moved into Tal's house when his daughter's hostility was so strong that Stephanie was convinced Alison would never come around. It was not to be ignored. If Alison kept this up, the house would resemble an armed camp. What about her own future then? What about her baby's future?

Tal moved, easing her down on the bed. "Would you stack a couple of pillows against the headboard, Alison?" he asked in a gruff tone. "And grab one to elevate Stephanie's foot, okay?"

"What am I, a maid?" the girl muttered. But she did it, and in placing the pillows, came close enough for Stephanie to catch a faint familiar scent. The same scent as the missing body lotion.

Oh, no. Was Alison responsible for Stephanie's things disappearing?

"Will you be okay for a while?" Tal asked quietly.

"Yeah, I need to talk to my dad," Alison put in.

"I'll be fine." Stephanie looked at Tal. They needed to talk, too, but it could wait. "Go ahead, Tal."

As she watched father and daughter leave, her eyes were troubled.

"HOW'S THE FOOT?"

Stephanie looked up from the papers spread around her on the bed. Tal walked toward her, unbuttoning his shirt. Her pulse quickened as she watched the now-familiar ritual. First his shirt, then his shoes and socks, then his pants. In his briefs, he stepped into the walk-in closet and came out seconds later in a pair of sweatpants that rode low on his hips. She didn't think he owned a pair of pajamas. He wore the sweats out of consideration for her, she suspected, and only when he was lounging before bedtime. When it came time to get into bed, he stripped to briefs only.

"It's okay. By Monday morning, I'll be able to walk on it."

"How are you doing otherwise? I didn't have a chance to ask earlier."

"You mean the pregnancy?" With a shrug, she capped her pen and put it on her bedside table. "Except for wanting to sleep a bit more than usual, I don't feel much different than I did before." She stacked the file folders neatly and leaned over, pulled the drawer on the bedside table open and placed them inside.

"Good." He came to her side of the bed and sat down. She slept in a big T-shirt, but with his eyes on her she felt as if he could see right through it. She thought of the passion they'd shared earlier and knew by the look in his eyes that he was remembering it, too. It was going to be difficult to pretend she didn't want more of the same.

"How did it go with Alison?" she asked, trying to head him off.

"How does it always go with Alison these days?" he said, rubbing a hand over his mouth. "One minute she's reasonable, and the next she's like a two-year-old having a tantrum. It's enough to drive me crazy."

"If it's any comfort, she's probably as bewildered over her behavior as you are." She laughed ruefully. "Actually, I can't blame her. I feel turned upside down myself."

"You shouldn't." His thigh was firm against hers.

Separated from him by only a thin sheet, she could feel his heat. Yes, she definitely recognized that look in his eye. If it wouldn't have been too obvious, she'd have pulled the covers up.

"What did you tell her?" she asked.

"Not much. It's none of her business what goes on between you and me. We're married. She's going to have to accept it." A moment passed as they each mulled over the possibilities of that. Then Tal gave a crooked smile. "For my part, I wish she'd been about ten minutes later."

"I wanted to talk to you about that, Tal."

There was a small silence. "So, talk."

She pulled her knees up and wrapped her arms around them. "I'm not sorry we were interrupted. And before you jump in and say how good we are in

bed, I'll grant you that, Tal. We seem very compati-
ble that way, but it's not enough." He would have
spoken, but she stopped him with a look.

"I keep remembering what you said that night in
Boston before we slept together. You warned me that
you didn't have anything to give, and I think you
meant in an emotional sense." By his frown, she
guessed he didn't like being reminded.

"I said that without thinking," he replied. "We
share a lot, Steph—mutual respect, friendship, our
careers. We're even alike in our political philoso-
phies."

"I share the same things with about twenty other
people I know," she countered. "And I don't want to
be married to a single one of them."

He looked at her. "Do you want to be married to
me?"

She sighed. "That's not the point. I—"

"The hell it's not!"

She rubbed her forehead. "I'm trying to explain,
Tal."

"Forget it! I don't need you to draw me a picture."
He rose, pulling at the string of his sweatpants.

"What are you doing?"

"I'm getting ready to go to bed." He pushed the
pants down. One foot caught and he swore, off-bal-
ance. He sat down again, bouncing the bed, and with
a jerk finally had the pants off.

He bent and picked them up, then tossed them angrily at the clothes hamper. They landed short.

"I hate it when you do that," she said, yanking the
covers up past her waist. "You can see the lid is closed
on the clothes hamper. What if I just tossed my things
at it instead of putting them inside? The bedroom

would be chaos. Or is that it? You expect me to come along behind you and tidy up?"

He stalked to the hamper, jerked the top off and angrily shoved them inside. "There. Does that make you happy?"

"Not necessarily, but it keeps the bedroom neat."

"Fine. Wonderful." He yanked the covers down on his side and got into bed. "You can turn out that light anytime you get ready."

Without a word, she snapped it off.

Silence fell. Heavy, dark silence. Beside her, she could sense the emotion emanating from Tal. It wasn't desire consuming him now. It was fury. That was one way to quash the need for sex between them. Become a nag. Stephanie felt the sting of tears behind her eyes.

So much for talking out their problems.

STEPHANIE MET with the teen group the next day in a small office on the second floor of the hospital. Once every three weeks, she personally checked their blood pressure and weight. Most of their prenatal care was administered from the clinic, but she liked to keep an eye on them. Left on their own, they sometimes neglected their routine checkups.

Today she planned to examine Keely, whether the girl liked it or not. So far she had resisted all Stephanie's efforts. Stephanie had broken the rules by allowing Keely to sit in on the group meetings without submitting to a physical examination. She was afraid that if she pushed too hard, Keely would simply disappear. This way, the girl was at least learning some basic principles of health care.

Stephanie stripped away the blood-pressure cuff and made a notation on a chart. "Excellent, Chantal. One-twenty over seventy-eight." While she wrote, Chantal stepped onto the scale.

"Look at this, Dr. Steph! One thirty-three. I've only gained two pounds since I got weighed last week."

"Great. Keep that up, and after the baby is born you'll be back to size eight in no time." After making a note, Stephanie closed the chart. "Who's next?" She purposely avoided looking at Keely.

"Me, I guess," said Jolene, stepping up and holding out her arm. "But you're gonna be ticked off. I pigged out last night."

"Where's Angela?" Keely asked from the back of the room.

"I scheduled an ultrasound for Angela. She should be back any minute." Stephanie fitted the blood-pressure cuff around Jolene's arm, then pumped it up. As she listened, she frowned. "It's a little high, Jolene. Let me take a look at your ankles." She waited while Jolene climbed onto the examining table. As she suspected, the girl's ankles were swollen. "Hmm, looks like you *did* pig out last night. There's a lot of salt in fast food."

Instead of lecturing Jolene, she directed her remarks to the group. "Remember, we talked about the danger of retaining too much fluid? The kidneys have to work hard during pregnancy. Some very dangerous things can happen if they don't function properly. Give them a break. Go easy on the salt, and if you want to slim down quickly after giving birth, remember to choose lots of fruits and vegetables."

"Why's Angela having an ultrasound?" Keely asked.

"She'll tell you herself when it's done." With her stethoscope draped around her neck, Stephanie collected the charts, all except one. She opened it, then looked at Keely. "Am I ever getting a chance to write in your chart, Keely?"

"I told you, I'm not pregnant. I'm only attending these classes for a friend of mine."

Jolene rolled her dark eyes. "You still hangin' with that story, Keely? We know you ain't got no frien' in a delicate condition that you advisin'. Look at us." Her gesture included everyone in the group. "We got no secrets aroun' here."

Keely put her hands on her hips. "I thought you people didn't ask personal questions."

"We don't lie to each other, either," Chantal said in gentle reproach.

For a moment, Keely looked stricken. Then she turned and headed for the door.

"Keely!" Stephanie started after her, but before she reached it, the door flew open and Angela rushed inside. She was panting, her hands cupping the bulge of her belly. One look and everyone could tell she was bursting with news.

"What! Tell us, girl." Jolene closed the door and stood in front of it. If Keely was going to leave, she would have to wait until after Angela had her say.

"I'm having twins!" Angela cried.

There was a chorus of reactions.

"Really?" Jolene asked. "No foolin'?"

"Man, I guess you can forget breast feeding, huh?" Jolene sat down. Clearly the prospect of two babies at once was daunting even to her.

Stephanie was not surprised by the results of the ultrasound. She had suspected as much. "It's possible to breast-feed twins," she told Angela. "It just takes a little more dedication."

Angela's dark eyes filled with tears. "I'll never get Ramon to marry me now."

Jolene was up again. "Who says? If he doesn't like it that you're havin' twins, then the hell with him. He's not good enough for you anyhow." She stood beside Angela, looking fierce and protective. "Lots of single mothers raise two kids. What's the difference if they're both born the same time?"

Chrissy was shaking her head. "Wow, that's two times the diapers, two times the formula, two beds, two car seats, two—"

Jolene whirled. "Knock it off, Chrissy!"

"Besides, she doesn't have a car," Teresa said.

"Two times the *work*," Chrissy finished, heedless, for once, of Jolene.

Keely spoke up suddenly. "I think you're lucky."

"I don't feel lucky," Angela said tearfully.

"You should," Stephanie put in. "Think of it this way—two times the love and two times the joy."

To distract Angela, Stephanie pulled the girl's chart and recorded her blood pressure and weight. A lively discussion followed about twins, identical and fraternal. It was a subject Stephanie knew well. She noticed that Keely seemed interested, as if her impulse to leave was forgotten. Watching her, Stephanie hoped she would have a chance to try to persuade her not to leave. Something about Keely set her apart from the other teens in the group. Stephanie wasn't sure what it was. Sometimes she had a look . . .

"My mother was a twin," Keely said suddenly.

There was immediate interest from the group. They all looked at her, Stephanie included. "Your mother?" she repeated.

"Yeah, my mother," Keely said, her blue eyes flashing. "I may be homeless, but I'm not motherless."

"No, of course not," Stephanie murmured, knowing she had offended her. After months of running this group, Stephanie knew not to react strongly to anything the girls said. Why she forgot the rules with Keely, she didn't understand. She was so afraid that Keely would run, that she would never see her again. She couldn't explain the strange kinship she felt with this girl. "I'm sorry if I sounded rude, Keely."

Keely shrugged. "Not that she was anybody to brag about, my mom," she said, her young face hard. Studying that look, Stephanie's heart began to pound. Tilting her head like that, Keely seemed so familiar. She looked—It couldn't be! What she was thinking was crazy! She finally managed to ask, "Where is your mother now?"

"Beats me." Keely crossed her arms and looked away. "She put me in foster care two years ago and split. That's the last I ever saw of her."

"Foster care. Where was that?" Stephanie's lips moved, but almost no sound came out. She was still, waiting for Keely to say it.

"Memphis."

"Memphis." Stephanie sank into a chair. Inside, she felt a pain so keen she brought her hand up to her chest even though she knew nothing was going to help. She managed to look into Keely's eyes. Familiar eyes. How could she not have guessed? "Your mother's name . . . is it Tessa?"

Keely turned away, pretended to study the poster on the wall depicting the growth phases of an embryo through eight weeks. Stephanie moved closer. She forced herself not to touch the unruly hair, fine as cornsilk. So like Tessa's at that age.

So like my own.

"Keely, please. I need an answer."

One shoulder went up, then down. "What's the big deal, anyway? Does it matter who my mother is?"

"More than you can ever know," Stephanie replied, her voice shaking. "Is it Tessa?"

Keely turned then. "Yeah, it's Tessa."

Tessa. Stephanie's twin.

"Dear God," Stephanie whispered as a great wave of joy swept through her. She longed to open her arms and draw her sister's child close. All at once, everything about Keely seemed familiar—the shape of her face, her cocky smile, her voice, the unrestrained movements of her hands when she talked, those long legs, even yoga!—all of it, familiar, beloved. All of it, Tessa made over.

Her impulse to embrace her niece died in the coldness of Keely's gaze. Those eyes, so like her own, had seen too much. So Stephanie settled for a smile, tentative and loving. But inside, her heart rejoiced. Nothing could change that.

CHAPTER SIX

You will want to avoid taking
upon yourself any added
responsibilities which might
increase your stress level.
Pregnancy itself is stressful enough.
Perhaps this is a time to ask your
mate to share responsibilities.

—*Ask Dr. Meredith*

September 26, 1995/8 weeks

STEPHANIE AND KEELY sat on a bench overlooking the
murky water of the Mississippi and watched a long,
fully loaded oil tanker inch past. It had been some
time since Stephanie had climbed the levee to the
Moonwalk. It was a tourist activity, but she had agreed
to go without a word when Keely declared that if her
aunt wanted to talk, then that's where she wanted to
do it.

Behind them, the French Quarter teemed. Mixed
with the cries of gulls were bursts of jazz and laughter, car horns, traffic. Familiar New Orleans sounds—
bawdy, bold, fun. But Stephanie heard little, so intent was she on what Keely had to say.

The girl had both shocked and amused her. The
story of Keely's life wasn't pretty. With her hand

pressed to the ache in her chest, Stephanie wondered what in the world Tessa had been thinking when she abandoned her daughter to foster-care. Hadn't she learned anything from their own horrible experiences as wards of that system? Another city, yes, another state, but for a displaced child, what difference did it make?

"Tell me how you got to New Orleans."

The breeze off the river had picked up. Holding back flyaway strands of her long hair, Keely shrugged. "Like everybody else. I hitched."

Familiar horrors flashed across Stephanie's mind. Dear God, it was true: history did repeat itself. But nothing showed in her tone when she asked, "Did you have any problems?"

"Not really. I guess I was lucky. I wouldn't do it again, because...well, this guy at the last rest stop in Mississippi got really pushy, but I got away and a couple of retired people in a van offered me a ride." She drew one leg up onto the bench and wrapped her arms around it. "They were nice. Like grandparents, or something."

Or something. Like Tessa and Stephanie, what would this child know about grandparents?

Assuming an air of indifference, Keely rested her chin on her knee. If it hadn't been for her niece's eyes, wary and watchful, Stephanie might have believed that there was nothing at stake for the girl. That she had come to New Orleans like many runaways, simply because the weather was mild and at that moment there was no other place she wanted to be.

Both knew that wasn't true. Keely had deliberately chosen New Orleans because her mother's twin lived there. She had come to search for Stephanie.

"Why did you wait so long to tell me?" Stephanie asked.

"I like to do things my way, in my own time. I waited until I knew you a little better. What if you were one of those tight-ass types, the kind to phone the welfare caseworkers 'for my own good'? Hey, I wasn't about to let myself in for that hassle again."

"What makes you so certain I won't do that?"

"Well, I know you're gonna try and tell me what I should do next, where I should go, what to wear, what to eat, where to sleep, but I figure we can work it out. I wouldn't put that kind of power in some stranger's hands."

"After we work it out, can I assume you'll accept what I suggest so long as I don't call the authorities?"

"It depends."

"On what, Keely?"

With her cheek resting on her knee, Keely looked over at Stephanie. "On whether or not I can still be my own person. I have to be free, Dr. Steph. I've been on my own too long to listen to a bunch of stupid bureaucrats trying to tell me to just say no—or just say yes, depending on the question—about my life. They don't know squat about my life. About what I've been through."

Stephanie touched her forehead. How had a sixteen-year-old acquired such a veneer? Her thoughts in chaos, she wondered what in the world she was going to say to Tal when she brought another teenage girl into his home to live. Looking at Keely's face, she realized she didn't intend to consider any other alternative. She and Tessa had been torn apart when they were sixteen. She had lost a part of her heart then. It was a tearing wound that had never healed. Nothing could fill the special niche that was Tessa.

So, of course Keely would live with her and Tal. And Alison.

Dear God. Alison. That would make two volatile, opinionated adolescents in Tal's formerly peaceful, uncomplicated household. And in a few more months, the baby.

The thought of her child calmed her. Unconsciously, she touched her abdomen as if to protect the tiny life nestled there. And as her palm rested on her abdomen, she felt a quick, intense connection with Tessa. Her sister seemed close. If she closed her eyes, she could almost hear her voice. That happened sometimes. Once they had been so attuned to each other that wherever one might be, the other always knew. Once, in spite of their dismal existence, one's happiness was the other's, one's pain was the other's. Somehow, that connection had been severed when Tessa ran away.

Where are you now, Tessa?

The long, mournful whistle of a riverboat sounded across the water. In Memphis, they used to sit on the high banks of the Mississippi and fantasize about boarding one of those boats and sailing somewhere to a better life. Anywhere. Gazing at the river bright with sun, Stephanie felt tears spring to her eyes. She knew beyond a doubt that somewhere Tessa was thinking of her. Beside her, she reached for Keely's hand and squeezed it. Her heart lifted. She had almost given up the thought of ever seeing Tessa again, but sitting beside her on a bench in the sunshine was Tessa's daughter.

Stephanie turned, putting out a hand to capture a bright blond strand of her niece's hair. "Will you tell me your whole name now?" she asked.

Keely smiled. "Keely Ann Hamilton."

Keely Ann. Both Stephanie and Tessa had the same middle name. A hokey idea that their mother had dreamed up. They'd never understood it, had laughed over it. But secretly liked it. Keely Ann.

I'll take care of her for you, Tessa.

She stood up and smiled at Keely. "Come on, I want to introduce you to someone special."

STEPHANIE WAS WAITING for Tal when he got home that night. It had just rained, a brief but heavy downpour. He came inside stamping his feet and grimacing. His hair was wet and curling and the shoulders of his jacket were damp. When she wordlessly handed him a drink, he gave her a quick look, and before accepting it, shrugged out of his jacket and ran a hand over his hair.

"Thanks. Cheers." He swallowed half of it at once, holding her gaze. "What's up?"

She glanced up the stairs to make sure Alison wasn't hovering. "Can we talk in the den?"

One dark eyebrow went up, then he gestured in that direction with exaggerated gallantry. "After you."

In the den, she took a seat on the leather sofa and watched him pour himself a second drink, much stronger. She sensed his fatigue, his impatience. His suspicion. "This has been a helluva day," he said after settling opposite her. "I get the feeling whatever you've got to tell me isn't going to improve it."

"Not really."

"Is it Alison?"

"No." At least, not yet.

"Is everything okay with you?"

She looked at him blankly before his meaning dawned. "Oh, you mean the pregnancy? I'm fine. It's nothing to do with that."

Since dropping Keely off at Camille's house an hour ago, she had rehearsed what she would say several times. Once in her car, then in the bedroom, finally in the kitchen while she'd put together a salad for dinner. Now, sitting across from him with the moment upon her, it was harder than she expected.

"It is personal, however," she said.

"Just say it, Stephanie. The suspense is getting to me."

"I'm sorry." She stared at her hands, then met his eyes. "My niece is here."

"I didn't know you had a niece."

She got up from the sofa and began to pace. "I didn't either. I mean...I just learned about her today."

He stared. "You're kidding."

"No. I wish I were." Agitated, she pushed a hand through her hair. "She's in my teen group. Can you believe that? All these weeks and not a word. I mentioned her to you. Keely, the special one, remember? She's not pregnant—so she says. She's refused to let me examine her. Today I pushed, knowing she was holding something back, but you could have knocked me over with a feather when she said...well, when she dropped the bomb."

She glanced at him uneasily, but couldn't tell what he was thinking. Once he had heard everything—and especially after last night's scene—he might wash his hands of her, baby or not. But she had to tell him.

"One of the disadvantages of marrying the way we did, Tal, is that we don't know each other very well." At his impatient sound, she hurried on. "This isn't about sex again. It's about...other things. Details about who we are."

She stopped then, stared at the painting of his grandfather that hung over the mantel. The resemblance to Tal was striking. She didn't even know her grandfather's name. Either of her grandfather's names. "I don't know anything about your background, not really. And you don't know about mine."

"I don't care about your background," he said. "I know who you are today, Stephanie. Isn't that what matters?"

"In a perfect world maybe," she said with a wry smile. Turning suddenly, she went to the fireplace, needing a little distance to finish this. "I never told you, but I have a twin sister."

He set his drink down carefully.

"Her name is Tessa," she said.

To her dismay, she felt the grief of loss welling up in her. A tightness in her throat silenced her momentarily. Tal started up, but she stayed him with a fluttery movement of her hand.

"I haven't seen her for nearly seventeen years." Tears threatened and she opened her eyes wide to stem them. "We hitchhiked to New Orleans from Memphis, if you can believe that. After a few days, we met Camille Landry. I still consider it the first stroke of good luck to come our way ever. For some reason, Camille took us in."

Using both hands, she wiped the corners of her eyes. "We hadn't put much emphasis on going to school until then, but Camille soon convinced us that it was important." Remembering, Stephanie managed a smile. "She was tough. She had to be, considering our background. I lived for praise from her and she was generous and loving, so long as we tried our best." Her smile faded. "Tessa didn't take to our new circumstances."

Stephanie gazed straight ahead thoughtfully. "She didn't seem to adjust the way I did. She hated everything about school, the other girls, the rules, the absence of freedom to make our own choices. She was constantly in trouble with the nuns. It was only a matter of time before she decided that the price of respectability was too high. One day she just left."

Upstairs, the volume on Alison's CD player was too high. The rhythmic vibrations of the bass notes rattled some loose items on the coffee table.

"I never saw her again."

"Never?"

She shook her head. "Camille tried to locate her, of course. The authorities never reported a single sighting. She just disappeared without a trace."

"How do you know this girl—Keely—is actually your sister's child?"

With a lift of her shoulders, Stephanie smiled. "I know," she said simply.

After a moment, Tal got up and walked to the door. Opening it, he stepped into the hall. "Alison! Turn the volume down to a decent level or turn it off completely."

"Aw, Daddy, do I have to? This is my new CD. It's—"

"Down or off, Alison!"

He looked harassed, but when he sat back down he patted the space beside him, inviting Stephanie to sit.

She perched on the edge of the sofa. "Where is Keely now?" he asked.

"With Camille. I thought that would be the best place for her, at least for tonight."

"Where is her mother?"

When she answered, her voice shook with pain. "No one knows, Tal."

He gave her a sympathetic look which threatened to shatter what little control she had left. "What would you like to do about this, Stephanie?"

All she was capable of was a helpless, mute gesture. With a grunt, Tal moved closer and gave her a wordless hug. For a moment, she allowed herself the comfort he offered. Then she moved to sit up a little straighter. This discussion was going to be difficult. As much as it comforted her, she couldn't manage it in Tal's embrace. But he wouldn't let her go. He shifted, tucking her snugly against him. "You'll want her to live here, of course. With us."

"I had hoped—"

He didn't wait to hear what she hoped. "Camille is what? Nearly seventy?" He shook his head. "I know how wearing it is to raise a teenage girl. Camille's too old for it, no matter how sweet-natured your niece is."

"Yes."

He gave her a final squeeze. It wasn't particularly sympathetic, certainly not sexual. It was purposeful, as though the decision was made. "We'll move her into the room next to Alison's first thing tomorrow morning."

Just like that. "My house is your house," Tal had insisted when they had discussed the problem of where to live after their marriage. Now she'd produced a runaway niece and he was opening his home to her, too. But along with profound relief, Stephanie felt something else. If this were truly her home—if her marriage were truly real—perhaps she wouldn't feel as if she were somehow exceeding the limits of their relationship.

"What's the problem?"

She shook her head. "It's just...this is so unexpected. I was floored. It was the last thing..." She sniffed and felt teary again. "This is ridiculous," she exclaimed, fumbling for a tissue from the box on the end table. "All this weeping..."

Tal offered his handkerchief. She took it and with trembling hands mopped at the tears and blew her nose.

"It's the pregnancy," she said shakily, laughing a little. "It has to be. I haven't been this emotional since—"

But she stopped there. Tal had taken the news about Keely better than she had ever expected. She had no intention of revealing any more secrets.

TAL PARKED his car and sat unmoving for a moment watching the house where Camille Landry now lived without Stephanie. Ten o'clock, but through the glass door he could see that lights were still on, both in the front room and beyond. That front door was beautiful but impractical. He must remember to ask Stephanie if there was a security system. The elderly were particularly vulnerable if they lived alone. He got out of his car before he could change his mind, and quickly walked to the door.

The bell had an old-fashioned ring, another example of Stephanie's care in restoring the house. How much did she miss it? he wondered suddenly.

Through the leaded glass, he could see someone coming. A girl, pencil-thin, long blond hair, in jeans and a cropped T-shirt. Stephanie's long-lost niece. He had needed to satisfy his own mind as to the girl's identity, and in one look it was done.

She peered at him through the glass for an instant, then turned the lock to let him in.

"Hi, I'm Talbot Robichaux."

"I know. I'm Keely."

He smiled. "I guessed that. You look a lot like my wife."

"Dr. Steph."

"The same." He glanced beyond her. "Is Camille here?"

Keely stepped back to let him in. "Actually, she's on the phone. She shouldn't be long."

"I know it's late and I didn't call first, but—"

"Where's Dr. Steph?"

"I left her napping in the den." Emotionally drained after discovering a niece she never knew existed.

Keely looked down at her hands. "I guess I really shocked her today."

He nodded. "You could say that."

She looked at him, her blue eyes wary. Then, "Can I get you something? We've got some iced tea."

"I think I'll pass," he said.

They stood for a moment, mutually assessing. This was the way his daughter might look if Stephanie was carrying a girl, Tal thought. Although the eyes were different—Stephanie's were in between gray and green—Keely's face had the same sculpted cheekbones, the same firm but feminine jawline and straight nose. Like her aunt, she would be a beautiful woman one day.

"What is it, Dr. T?"

He gave a laugh. He'd never been called Dr. T. "Did you get that from Steph?"

"It's what the kids in the group call you."

He wasn't aware that the young mothers-to-be even knew who he was. Suddenly, he wondered if they knew about Stephanie's pregnancy. Had she revealed it to them without discussing it with him first?

"What's the matter?" she said. "Do you prefer being called Dr. Robichaux?"

He looked at her blankly, then realized he was frowning. "What? No, Dr. T's fine." He motioned toward the front room, softly lit by a lamp. "Could we go in there for a minute, Keely? The truth is, I came to see you tonight, not Camille."

"To see me or to talk to me? Which?"

He stopped and met her eyes. She did not give an inch. Not many sixteen-year-olds were so self-possessed. Amused, he replied, "Talk. I came to talk to you, Keely. Are you this prickly with everybody or is it just me?"

She sat down on the sofa, crossing her legs beneath her. "Prickly means difficult, I guess. I don't mean to be. I'm just looking for honesty. If people would be honest, life would be a lot simpler, don't you think?"

"Simpler," he said, smiling. "But not necessarily less difficult."

She thought a minute, then shrugged. "I've been around a lot of adults who don't seem to understand how to be honest. It sort of makes you cautious, you know? Anyway, I took Dr. Steph by surprise today when I told her who I was. She might not have really

meant it when she told me she wanted to take me home
with her to live. I know she just got married and she
didn't have a chance to talk to you before she said all
that. I just want you to know that I've been around the
block a few times, and people sometimes say things
they don't mean. I understand that."

"She meant it, Keely."

"Okay. Whatever. But just so you know, I'm not a
tender flower here, like your daughter. I won't self-
destruct or anything if she has to renege."

"Why do you say Alison's a tender flower?"

She looked at him as if to be certain he was serious.
"Because she is. She's been sheltered all her life. Hey,
I'm not knocking it. Her good luck if you ask me."

"She was barely ten years old when she lost her
mother."

"At least she *had* one to lose when she was ten."

She waited a few seconds to see if he could top that
one, then went on. "Like I say, I won't take offense if
you're here to check me out—sort of over and above
what Dr. Steph told you about me." Her expression
changed as a thought struck her. "She did tell you
about me, didn't she?"

He nodded, liking her better with every word.
"Yeah, she told me."

"Okay." She gave him that straight-to-the-heart-of-
it look again. "So, why are you here, Doctor?"

"I'm not quite sure." It was the truth. Curiosity?
Caution? Duty? On the way over, he told himself that
as Stephanie's husband it was his responsibility to
make sure she wasn't being duped by some street-wise
runaway. If he didn't buy into Keely's story, somehow he would fix it so that Stephanie would be spared
any more pain. Increasingly, he found himself feeling

protective of his wife-in-name-only, but that wasn't
something he felt ready to explore. Not tonight.

"Are you sure it's not to tell me Stephanie made a
mistake?"

"No, that's not it, Keely." Looking into her eyes, he
recognized suddenly that in spite of her bravado, she
was anxious about her future. He found himself
wanting to reassure her. "Stephanie wants you to come
and live with us. She doesn't know I'm here. I admit
to being curious. I hope that's excusable."

"Who could blame you?"

"Just so you'll know, the invitation to live with us
comes from us both, Keely."

Again she subjected him to a long, solemn look.
"What about Alison?"

"Alison." He wondered what to say. "We're talking honesty here, right?" She nodded. "Well, Alison
will probably live up to your assessment of her, at
least, for a little while. She's not a total brat, although at times lately she would try the patience of a
saint. She'll come around."

He got up then, and pulled her with him. "We're a
family now, Keely. Stephanie, me, Alison, and now,
you."

She still looked skeptical, but she didn't argue.

If he could have eased her mind, he would have, but
he had learned a lot about family dynamics since his
marriage. The truth was, things would probably be
pretty tense around the house when Keely first moved
in.

"Meantime, first things first. We've got to get you
enrolled in school. Steph and I talked about Sacred
Heart Academy. That's where Alison goes. She'll be
able to show you around. You'll need clothes, uni-

form skirts and blouses, and so on. Again, Alison knows the drill. She's been there since kindergarten. She'll never admit this, but she's intimidated by the older kids. You're a junior. No matter what else she may feel, she'll respect you on that basis alone.''

Keely rolled her eyes. "Oh, sure.''

He chucked her under the chin. "See you at six tomorrow. Tell Camille hello.'' He talked over his shoulder as he walked to the door. "Sorry I missed her. G'night.''

" 'Night.''

He sensed her watching him as he got into his car and pulled out into the traffic. He wondered how long she would stand there. He would have given anything to know what she was thinking.

"SHE'S NOT GOING to Sacred Heart!''

"Alison, one more rude outburst and you will find yourself grounded." Tal stood in the den feeling like a referee. "It's a big school. There's room for you *and* Keely.''

For the third time in as many minutes, Alison sprang from the sofa. Waving her arms, she paced, ignoring Stephanie and Keely. "What will my friends think! They'll talk behind my back. It'll be awful.'' She stopped and gave him a pleading look. "Why does she have to go there, Daddy?''

"What a question, Ali. Why shouldn't she?''

With a disgusted sound, Alison flopped down on the sofa, folded her arms huffily and glared straight ahead. Watching her, Tal thought how like her mother she was when Diana was in a rage. He sighed wearily. He should have expected this. Since Keely had moved

in a week ago, there hadn't been an easy meal or a relaxed hour in the house.

"We've been over this ten times, Alison," he said
patiently. "Keely is living with us now and she's going to have the same opportunities as you. Have you
thought how selfish you appear over this?"

"I don't care. I hate her!"

"Alison!" Tal took a furious step forward, but
Stephanie sprang to her feet to stop him.

"Tal, maybe we should discuss this later, just the
two of us."

"How about hearing what I think?"

All eyes turned to Keely. It was the first time she had
spoken. She looked at Tal. "Since we're being honest
here, I'd like to say that I don't particularly look forward to going to the same school as your daughter, Dr.
T. In the first place, we come from separate planets.
Maybe you don't see it, but since I've been here, Alison and I have discovered it's true. Seems to me that's
what she's trying to get across to the two of you." A
quick glance included Stephanie.

"The kids at school will have a field day over this.
Everybody knows you people never heard of me until
a few weeks ago. Alison knows how it'll be. She'll be
embarrassed. It's not something to look forward to. I
can't blame her."

"You see?" Alison gave Tal a significant look.
"Even *she* knows it's a stupid idea!"

"Did you have a suggestion, Keely?" Stephanie
asked quietly.

"You probably won't like it."

"Try us," Tal said.

"I can go to the high school where my friends are."

"The pregnant ones?" Alison looked repulsed.

Keely gave her a cool stare. "Some are and some aren't."

"Okay, enough." Tal rubbed the back of his neck. He felt as much stress as when one of his patients was in a life-or-death situation. He looked at Stephanie for guidance.

Stephanie looked at Keely. "You're sure about this?"

"I'm sure."

"It's not as safe."

"It'll be interesting."

"The students come from every conceivable background."

"I always wanted to meet a Russian."

Stephanie laughed. "Well, maybe not Russia."

"I think she's nuts," Alison put in, disgusted.

"I think you're a snob," Keely retorted.

Stephanie held up a hand. "Okay. Truce." She looked at Tal. "Maybe we should consider it. Keely obviously prefers to make her own choice here. I'm willing to try it, at least temporarily." Beside her, Keely stirred, but Stephanie forestalled her. "I know how independent you are, Keely, and I'm trying to honor that."

"You promised," Keely said.

"I know." Stephanie looked at Tal. "Can we give this a try? It doesn't really matter where she attends classes, does it? The classwork will be the same."

Classwork, maybe, Tal thought. But nothing else about the two schools was remotely alike. There had been reports of violence at the public school where Keely's friends went. What concerned him more was the fact that it was located on Esplanade Avenue where Alison's mother had been killed. Alison's school

was located in the Garden District, as safe as any place
could be in New Orleans. How could he accept less for
Keely?

"Please, Tal..." Keely touched his arm. "It's what
I want. I'd feel out of place at Sacred Heart."

He looked at them, the women in his life. He knew
when he was overruled and, reluctantly, he agreed.

UPSTAIRS, Keely sat on the edge of the bed and gazed
around at the bedroom that was now hers. *Hers!* She'd
done this every night since Stephanie had brought her
up here and opened the door, telling her to make herself at home. *Make herself at home!* She still found it
almost too good to be true.

She settled in bed against the headboard, drew up
her legs and wrapped her arms around them. She
simply could not believe she'd found her mother's
sister at last, that she was in New Orleans, and that the
people who lived in this fabulous house had taken her
in. Even in her most outlandish fantasies, Keely had
never dared to dream that big.

The room was a mix of old stuff and new. Her favorite was the tall armoire on the opposite wall.
Stephanie told her that armoires used to serve as closets in the days when people didn't have closets. Now
it held a color TV with a CD player. There was even a
fireplace. And in front of it was a funny little stand
that had a round dropleaf. A fire screen, Stephanie
had called it, to shield ladies' faces in olden times from
the heat of the fireplace.

Keely had searched for Stephanie Sheldon for more
than two years. Her foster parents in Memphis had
been okay, but she didn't belong with them. She had
believed then that she belonged with her mom. Fam-

ily was family, wasn't it? But that last time, when her mother promised to come for her and didn't show up, Keely had washed her hands of Tessa Sheldon. She blinked away a sheen of tears and rested her cheek on one knee. She was going to make a place for herself here with her mother's sister. The way she figured it, being her mother's identical twin made Stephanie closer than an aunt, almost a mother to Keely. She had found her, hadn't she? Against all odds. That was an omen. A sign. Maybe some people didn't believe in signs and omens, but Keely did, and she was here because it was meant to be.

She frowned, watching a small moth fluttering around the rose-colored lampshade beside her bed. There were a few things that bothered her about her new situation. This hurry-up marriage, for one thing. Not that Dr. T and Stephanie weren't made for each other, they were. That fact was as plain as day. But the kids in the group said Stephanie and Dr. T hadn't dated at all when they suddenly turned up married to each other. And there was a sort of... tension between them that Keely had noticed. Nothing bad, but... not the kind of atmosphere you'd expect if a sexy guy like Dr. T and a smart, beautiful woman like Stephanie got married.

Her look drifted to her door. Just down the hall was the bedroom they shared. She knew how people acted when they were head over heels in love and somehow those two didn't give off the right vibes. She would have to wait a while, do a little more analysis of the situation before she could tell exactly what was going on there. Until then, well, she was one lucky runaway.

With one little catch, of course. Alison, the darling of this fabulous house, was not exactly overjoyed to open home and hearth to someone like her. With a finger, she touched the fringe of the lampshade and watched it sway. She sighed. Nothing came easy in this life. Alison was a selfish little twit—not that Keely expected anybody else to share her views on the daughter of the house. The kid was spoiled rotten, and if Keely was right in her assessment of the situation, Alison did not exactly adore her new step-mom. Keely's mouth twisted. No accounting for taste there. The little brat should have had a few years' mothering from somebody like Tessa. Then she'd know good parenting when she saw it. She'd appreciate a person with a heart as big as Dr. Stephanie Sheldon's.

She reached for the switch on the lamp, wondering how twins could be so different. Stephanie and Tessa, born the same hour, the same day, reared the same way. One made all the right choices and the other made all the wrong ones.

She didn't want to think about her real mother anymore. She lay back in the dark and closed her eyes. She didn't have a real mother anymore.

CHAPTER SEVEN

*Miscarriage! The fear of losing the
baby is a universal one. Many women
lead busy, demanding lives. Pace
yourself. You should consider reducing
the number of hours you work. If
financially feasible, you may consider
putting your career on hold. This
calls for a frank discussion with your
mate.*

—*Ask Dr. Meredith*

October 16, 1995/11 weeks

TAL WAS BONE-TIRED as he exited the hospital parking garage at a few minutes past eight. A patient had suffered cardiac arrest during a radical mastectomy at 7:00 a.m. He had brought her back, but it had been a harrowing few minutes. Afterward, he'd seen patients until four, then sat in an interminable meeting of the board, where he'd been harangued by a succession of retired colleagues over getting too involved with issues that didn't make money for the hospital. He knew he had Benedict Galloway to thank for putting him in the hot seat.

Behind him, somebody honked. He hesitated. A right turn would take him directly home, but no one

was there except the housekeeper. It was Friday and
Alison was sleeping over at a friend's. Keely was with
Stephanie at the clinic. He turned left.

He had tried to talk Stephanie out of working nights
altogether at the clinic. A steady stream of patients
showed up on weekends, when street violence dou-
bled. Friday night was the worst. He didn't draw an
easy breath when she was there. After Diana's death,
he couldn't cope with that kind of loss again. But since
their wedding, he had learned something about Dr.
Stephanie Sheldon's independence, especially where
her work was concerned.

He was at Canal and Rampart when he heard the
first wail of a fire engine. Pushing buttons, he lowered both the driver's and passenger's windows to try
to get a fix on the location. New Orleans was particularly vulnerable to fire. Day or night, the maze of
narrow streets in the Quarter were choked with tourists and traffic. Just getting to the scene was a problem. He made an illegal turn on the median and
stopped beside a police unit. "How bad is it?" he
asked the driver.

"Three-alarm." The radio squawked and the cop
raised a hand while he listened. "I'm not ticketing you
for that illegal turn because I've got to get to the scene,
but next time—"

"I'm a doctor," Tal explained. "Maybe I can help.
Where is it?"

"Esplanade and Royal, the Burgundy Inn." He began pulling away. "If you're going, you'll need an es-
cort. Follow me."

Tal knew the place, a small hotel with a Victorian
look, one of the converted mansions of New Orleans's past. It was what advertisements called

"quaint, with atmosphere." In reality, it was seedy and run-down. Old. A firetrap. And less than a block from the clinic, which would probably receive all the injured. Tal peeled out behind the cop. Stephanie was going to have her hands full.

The waiting area was in chaos when he walked in. Clinic staff and three EMTs were administering oxygen, soothing hysteria and checking for anything more serious. Most of the fire victims were suffering from smoke inhalation and trauma. A man sitting apart was holding a bloody handkerchief to his lower arm. His shirt was ripped to shreds, his chest crisscrossed with bloody welts. Tal identified the wounds as knife cuts. In an alcove separate from the waiting area, two uniformed policemen were questioning a couple. The woman seemed distraught, crying and gesturing toward the rear of the clinic. Tal sighed. Business as usual.

He spotted Keely comforting a frightened toddler and headed toward her, but there was no sign of Stephanie.

"Oh, hi, Dr. T," she said, jiggling the crying child up and down in her arms. "If you're looking for your lady, she's busy. A woman brought her little kid in with a gunshot wound. It looked pretty bad." She glanced at the jammed waiting room. "And now this. It's shaping up to be a long night."

"Has Stephanie called for help?"

"Sure, but with the traffic and all, who knows when they'll get here." The child's mother appeared, and the toddler began to wail in earnest. Keely set him down and he dashed over to her.

Tal looked toward the treatment rooms. "Where is she?"

"Number one, I think."

He started off, then stopped and drew some money out of his pocket. "You need to go home soon, Keely. Stephanie and I will be late. Here, get a taxi."

"Aw, Dr. T, I'm helping. Can't I stay?"

"Not past eleven."

She wanted to argue, but after a moment she shrugged and gave him a cheeky smile. "Okay, but now you're here, can I drive Dr. Steph's car home? No sense in you two driving home separately, is there?"

"I suppose you're right."

"Then it's okay?"

"Well . . ."

"I've had my license a whole week, Dr. T. And Dr. Steph let me drive on the way over, honest."

Knowing he had been outmaneuvered, he shook his head. "All right, I guess. But lock the doors and go straight home."

"Yes!" Her smile was jubilant.

"And call the front desk to check in the moment you get there. You got that?" He fought to sound stern. Keely's exuberance was infectious.

"Got it!"

"Good girl." He winked at her, relieved to be spared a major confrontation over curfew. Alison, even if she'd been old enough to drive, would not have given in so easily. As he headed toward the treatment rooms, he wondered if it was just the difference in their ages—thirteen and sixteen—or if his own daughter was simply hopelessly spoiled. He would have to remember to ask Stephanie. She was the expert on adolescent girls.

He found his wife in the first curtained cubicle. She and a nurse were bent over a small boy, frantically trying to stanch heavy bleeding from a wound on the child's torso. A bag of blood swung from an IV pole. One glance told Tal the child was critical.

He called Stephanie's name softly. "Do you need any help?"

"Not here," she replied, barely sparing him a glance. Her hands on the child were deft and quick, exploring, swabbing, pressing. "But check the patient in the next cubicle, would you?" Without looking up, she indicated the direction with a movement of her head.

He started to leave, then remembered Keely. "Don't worry about Keely. I gave her permission to drive your car home. She promised to be careful and indoors by eleven."

Stephanie looked up quickly, startled. "Is it that late already?" He knew the feeling. Time and everything else had slipped by while she was working to save the life of the child. She gave him a distracted smile.

"Dr. Robichaux. I thought I heard your voice. Thank goodness!"

He wrenched his attention from his wife and turned to the agitated nurse at his elbow. "Ellen. Need some help?"

"Do I ever!" she said fervently. Glancing behind her at the curtained area, she dropped her tone. "The guy in there was in the fire at the Burgundy, but he's not burned. It's drugs. Somebody brought him into the clinic and dumped him here without saying anything. I don't know how long he was unattended before we realized he was in bad shape."

Tal was behind the curtain before she finished. A young male lay on the examining table. Mid- to late twenties, Tal thought, registering a range of facts at once. Gray cast to the skin, profuse sweating, rest-lessness, incoherence. Mike Whitcomb, a crackerjack nurse, was urgently speaking, trying to get a response, but the most he got was a weak groan.

"What did he take?" Tal asked, ramming his hands into latex gloves.

"We don't have a clue," Mike said, standing back after taking a blood-pressure reading. "But it's big and bad. His pressure's skyrocketing."

Drug reactions were common at the clinic, but usually the team had some idea which drug the patient had taken. Tal chose an instrument from an array of tools precisely arranged on a tray and moved close to examine the man's pupils. Just as he bent to have a look, the man stiffened and began to convulse.

For the next few minutes, Tal and the two technicians worked desperately. Not knowing which drug they were fighting was a major drawback, but even worse was the lack of sophisticated equipment to monitor vital signs. In a hospital trauma unit, there would be machines showing heart rate, breathing, blood pressure, to name only the basics. In the clinic, Tal had only instinct and whatever medication he decided might counteract the lethal substance.

Finally, the convulsion ended and Tal relaxed slightly. Opposite him, Ellen and Mike breathed a little easier.

"Jeez, it was touch and go there for a minute," Mike said, watching Tal place the stethoscope against the man's chest. "Whatever this guy sampled nearly killed him."

"Quiet!" Tal snapped, drawing two startled looks. He swore. "His heart has stopped!" Tossing the stethoscope aside, he called out, "Get the crash cart!"

CRASH CART. The words made Stephanie's heart stumble. Cardiac arrest. As busy as she was with her small patient, a part of her followed the drama being enacted in the next cubicle. Thank God Tal had walked in tonight. Until then, she had been the only physician at the clinic, and she was already working on the little boy when the drug O.D. had been discovered, unconscious, in the waiting room. As soon as she'd seen him, she had known he was in critical shape. But so was the child. She had issued a call for the physician on call, but he was stuck in the traffic jam caused by the fire.

"Stand back!"

The order came from Tal. Stephanie's hands stilled for an instant, braced to hear the explosion of electric shock. There it was.

"Again!"

Another explosion.

Come on ... come on ...

She caught herself urging the junkie to fight. Beneath her hands, her little patient whimpered, began to stir restlessly. Thank God for the resilience of children. She listened to his heart, his pulse, studied him with an eye trained by too many similar situations in the year that she'd been volunteering at the clinic. She drew in a deep breath, satisfied that he was stabilized and could now make it to the hospital.

"Good job, Gloria." She smiled behind her mask at the aide, who gave her two thumbs-up. Small victories were what kept them going at the clinic. Pulling off her mask, she turned to leave the cubicle just as Tal gave the order for the third shock to his patient. She stopped.

Another explosion. A moment of silence. She imagined Tal bent over the man's chest, listening intently, silently pulling for him. Then a chorus of sighs.

"Hey, okaa-ay!"

"He's back!"

"Way to go, Dr. Robichaux!"

"Somebody get an ambulance! This guy needs to be moved out!"

"One's on the way!"

Stripping off her gloves, Stephanie headed for the front of the clinic. The on-call physician should be here soon, as well as Dr. Derek Morgan, for the midnight shift. The clinic was inadequately equipped to handle burns, and she was relieved to see that the seriously injured had been transferred. Still, the waiting room was full. Several victims of the fire looked at her hopefully. Suddenly, she was reminded that she hadn't eaten since lunchtime. Her back ached, too. The hours were catching up with her. Behind her, she heard Tal's voice and was tempted for an instant to tell him she was going home. But that was hardly fair. He'd had a long day, too.

With a sigh, she accepted the chart Ellen handed her and called the next patient.

"Wow, what a night." With a groan, Stephanie climbed into Tal's car and settled back against the soft leather, content to let him drive her home. Glancing at the clock, she grimaced. Her day had begun at six, and she'd been working steadily for more than eighteen hours. She was glad Tal had given Keely permission to drive her car home tonight. She didn't think she had enough energy left to find her way to the Garden District.

"Twenty-two people treated for smoke inhalation plus various minor cuts and bruises in the fire," she said with a weary chuckle. "And two major emergencies. That's a busy night, even for the clinic."

"Yeah."

While he was negotiating the rotary at Lee Circle, she stole a look at him. His features appeared stern in the glow of the dashboard light. "How is it you happened to drop by tonight?"

"I didn't have any other plans."

Uh-oh. Something on his mind. She sighed, too tired to deal with anything else tonight. She still felt a nagging backache, and a single cup of yogurt at midnight hadn't quite banished the headache. "Well, it's a good thing you did show up. The drug O.D. might have died otherwise. He owes his life to you."

"I'm sure the boy who was shot will say the same about you."

"It was touch and go there for a while for both of them."

He said nothing more, and after a moment Stephanie turned to look out the window. As they headed out of the business district, dilapidated and derelict dwellings gradually gave way to neater, well-maintained properties. They sped by Loyola and Tulane universities, now dark and quiet. On the left, Audubon Park was deserted; its huge oak trees, draped with Spanish moss, silent sentinels.

Tal slowed at last and drove between the two impressive pillars at the entrance to his neighborhood. *Her* neighborhood now, she reminded herself, surveying the luxurious residences they passed. In seconds, he reached for the remote, and the iron gates that protected the property swung slowly open. The violence of the area around the clinic seemed light-years away. What did people here know about hope-lessness and despair?

"You should have seen her face," she murmured, studying the splendid columns on the front of Tal's house.

He looked at her. "Whose face?"

"That little boy's mother. She said he'd found the pistol under her mattress and he was playing with it when it went off. But I don't think that's what hap-pened. She had a fresh bruise on her cheekbone and her lip was split."

"The mother?"

Stephanie nodded. "I think she and her boyfriend were in a fight and someone had a gun. It was fired and the child was the victim."

"Did you question her about it?"

"The police brought her in and they would have al-ready questioned her. If she fired the gun, she's pun-ished enough for nearly killing her own child. If it was her boyfriend—who happens to be the child's fa-ther—she doesn't want him jailed."

"What do you think should be done?"

She rubbed her forehead. "I'm not sure. One thing I've learned since working with the teens and the clinic, is that these situations are far too complex for snap judgments. To be honest, I'm just as glad to leave it to the cops, and to deal with the physical or emo-tional fallout when I'm called upon to do so."

"Okay. That's it, Stephanie!" he said abruptly.

Startled, she turned to look at him. "What?"

He'd driven straight into the detached garage and now stopped abruptly. With a sound that was almost a growl, he faced her. "I don't want you working at the clinic anymore."

"What are you talking about?"

"Not what you think. I know you're doing good work there. I know your heart's in it. You don't have to convince me. Hell, I've gone out on a limb at the hospital about providing services for people nobody seems to care much about. I work one afternoon a week at the clinic. I make speeches in Baton Rouge to the legislature to try and make a difference. I throw in a good word for the program whenever I get a chance in meetings here and in other cities."

Stephanie put her hand on her abdomen. It was a habit she'd acquired since becoming pregnant. Whenever she felt threatened in any way, her first thought was to protect her baby. "Then why do you want me to stay away?"

He drove a hand through his hair. "It's too much risk right now, Steph. The kind of medicine you have to practice at the clinic is stressful. Even dangerous. Too many of the patients are loose cannons. The person who shot that little boy is an accident waiting to happen to anybody in his or her world. At the clinic, you're too close to danger."

"But I wasn't until you married me, right?"

"Don't I have the right to express concern for my wife?"

"Concern, yes. But you don't have the right to dictate to me."

"I think I do. You're not thinking straight, Stephanie." He paused a moment. "It isn't just that the clinic is a stressful, high-risk environment, there's also the fact that you need to consider your condition now. You worked eighteen hours today. That's an excessive workload for anyone, but especially for a pregnant woman."

"Tonight was an exception. We don't have a three-alarm fire every Friday."

"But you have other disasters. Weekends are total chaos, so here's what I propose," he said.

"I can't wait to hear this."

"I don't want you working nights anymore. Especially weekend nights. You can keep your weekday shifts."

For an instant she was speechless. Did he really believe he could tell her when and where and how much she could work? Did he actually think she would give anybody that kind of control?

"I'm serious, Stephanie. No more night duty." His tone was as implacable as the look in his dark eyes.

She didn't waste a heartbeat. She simply reached for the handle on the car door and wrenched it open. "I think we've finished here," she snapped.

"You're almost three months pregnant, Stephanie."

"Oh, gosh. Thanks for helping me keep track." She got out and slammed the door with a crash that would have awakened neighbors if there had been anybody within two acres.

He caught up with her striding across the patio. "If you won't think of yourself, think of the baby."

"My baby's fine." She fumbled in her purse for her keys.

"Excuse me," he said. "I thought this was *our* baby. And you're wrong thinking this is settled. It isn't, not by a long shot."

In the act of shoving her key into the lock, she turned to face him. "Oh, yes, it is settled, Tal," she said quietly. "You know where I stand, I know where you stand. You just told me. In no uncertain terms. It's obvious to me that you expect me to go along with your dictates. Well, what about my wishes? What about what I think?"

He clearly did not intend to reply. In the moonlight, his features were a chiseled mask. Stephanie felt a rush of frustrated anger. "Damn it, Tal, this is my choice. And I've been making my own choices for a long time. I'm going to do as I see fit!"

Suddenly, her words sounded childish and unreasonable. The night was quiet and still, even beautiful. A full moon cast silvered shadows over the house and patio. Maybe that's why they'd been so busy, Stephanie thought. At the clinic, they had long ago discovered the waiting rooms overflowed on the nights of the month when there was a full moon.

The clinic. She felt connected and useful at the clinic. How could she let that go?

"It's late," she murmured, her shoulders slumping wearily. "It's too late to discuss this. I'm exhausted and you must be, too."

Without a word, Tal reached around her, turned the key in the lock and pushed open the door. They went inside and in the soft glow of night lamps, made their way up the stairs to their bedroom.

They undressed in strained silence. Stephanie inquired politely if Tal would like to shower first. He declined, saying he would use the guest bathroom down the hall. He needed to check on Keely anyway, he told her. Stephanie felt a stab of guilt. Since receiving the message from Keely that she'd got home safely, Stephanie's hadn't worried about her niece.

She was trembling with fatigue as she undressed and stepped into the shower. A luxurious soak would have been nice, but she was too exhausted to take the time. Besides, lying in the Jacuzzi afforded too much time for thinking, and thinking was the last thing she wanted tonight. But the thoughts kept coming. Had she overreacted to Tal's request? He was only showing concern for her. Maybe she'd been hypersensitive. Standing under the warm spray, she cried a little. Damn. Nowadays she seemed to spend a lot of time crying.

She was drying herself when she saw the blood.

Her cry was instinctive, sheer anguish wrenched out of her before she had a chance to think anything.

Dear God, not my baby. No...no...no...

Tal was beside her in an instant. "What's wrong? What is it, Stephanie?" She was naked, holding the towel against her body. Her eyes were wide with fear.

"The baby...I'm bleeding."

Shock held him still for a heartbeat. "It's okay," he said eventually, even though he knew no such thing. Gently, he pried her fingers away from the towel. "You need to lie down."

"Yes." With his help, she made her way to the bed. Tal flung the covers back and urged her to sit down. "I'll get a nightgown."

"Yes."

He fumbled in the dresser drawer, grabbing the first silky thing that he touched. Back beside her, he slipped it over her head. It was some sort of top, short and sleeveless with a row of tiny buttons. As soon as she had it on, he pushed her gently down. With her eyes closed and her hair spread over the pillow like melted honey, she looked spent. He watched slow tears slip from the corners of her eyes and was swamped by a depth of feeling that stunned him. He wanted to take her in his arms and promise her that everything would be all right. But she was a physician herself. She knew such promises would be meaningless. Only time would tell if she was losing the baby.

He was shaken to discover how much that scared him.

"I'm going to call Dr. Duplantis now," he said.

Evelyn Duplantis was her gynecologist. Stephanie nodded and turned her face away.

Tal made the call while sitting on the edge of the bed watching Stephanie's face. When he hung up, she was clinging to his hand.

"Evelyn said to stay in bed," he said, lacing his fingers through hers. "Don't get up except to go to the bathroom. If the bleeding stops, take it easy for several days. If not, and you start to hemorrhage, get to the hospital immediately."

Stephanie managed a ghost of a smile. "We both knew all that."

"Yeah, but she's the expert and I'm glad to defer to her judgment where this is concerned. I don't feel like a doctor right now."

Her gray-green eyes met his. "How do you feel?"

"As anxious as any man in my shoes would feel."

She closed her eyes. "You don't have any shoes on."

"Okay then, as any expectant father."

She nodded. "Me, too."

"You're an expectant mother."

Her eyes opened. He could tell by the way she looked at him that she couldn't speak. He squeezed her hand and her eyes flooded. "Don't worry."

He studied her, the way she lay open and vulnerable now, so different from the assertive, indignant woman who had stormed upstairs an hour ago. Something came to him then. He saw it in her eyes. "Don't blame yourself, Steph. You know that the threat of miscarriage is greatest in the first trimester."

"You're right, I do know that," she said, her soft lips trembling. "So why did I work eighteen hours today?"

"You didn't plan to. And once you were at the clinic, you could hardly walk away from people who needed you. You're a doctor."

She sniffed and rubbed her nose. "Then why am I feeling so guilty?"

"Pregnancy. Hormones. Fatigue, for God's sake."

Shaking her head, she shuddered. "I'm so scared, Tal."

"Oh, baby." He let go of her hand and went around to the other side of the bed, pulled down the covers and got into bed with her. With a tiny strangled cry, she turned to him. "Come here," he said.

He put out his arms and she came willingly, clutching at him, pressing her face into his chest, holding on tight. She was trembling all over. He tucked her head under his chin and held her close. She felt small and fragile. She began to weep softly, helpless sobs that tore through him. Stroking her hair, he murmured soothing sounds. It was all he could do.

Tal fixed his gaze on the silvery panes of the window. Usually when they got into bed and turned out the light, there was a reserve between them. But tonight, now, at this moment, that reserve was gone. They were simply two people with a shared concern. For the first time, he felt truly married.

"Tal?" Her voice was scratchy, tear-drenched.

"Uh-huh."

"I won't be going back to a full practice until the baby comes."

"We'll see."

"No, I mean it." She stirred, not moving away, but arranging herself so that their bodies were more comfortably entwined. The smell of her soap, delicate and floral, drifted up to him. "You were right about cutting back my hours. Now that I'm pregnant, I can't do everything I did before."

"No one could."

"I can't give up my work with the teen group."

"No."

"And I have to do some work at the clinic." When he stayed quiet, she sighed. "No nights. Not because of your safety concerns so much, but I really shouldn't overdo. I can give them an afternoon if I cut back on my practice. Wednesdays, maybe."

"As you said, it's your decision." He wondered if she would move away now, go back to her side of the big bed, and the night would end up like all the others with the two of them separate. But she stayed.

"I don't want to do anything to put our baby in jeopardy," she said in a husky tone. "You were right, I'm burning the candle at both ends and I'll cut back gladly. Let's just pray this is nothing serious. By morning, we should know." She turned slightly and rested a hand on his chest. He wondered if she realized that her fingers were sifting through the hair on his chest. He sure as hell was aware of it. "I'm sorry I jumped all over you, Tal."

"I asked for it," he admitted, stroking her back through the silk. She was sleek but curvaceous, just as he remembered. "I meant well, but I suppose I sounded dictatorial."

"You did, a little."

Silence fell then, broken only by the muted sounds coming through the window from the distant street. Outside, an ambulance raced past, its siren screaming. For some reason, he saw the face of the patient who'd overdosed. Felt again the wild thump of his own heart when the man's had quit. It brought back another moment, one he'd spent three years trying to forget.

"Your heart is beating so fast," she said, pressing her palm flat on his chest. "What are you thinking about, Tal?"

Diana. Ben, Jr. Death. In the dark, he closed his eyes, willing the image away, and held Stephanie a little closer. She was soft and warm. She smelled good. She felt good. He didn't want to remember another woman. Another time. With desire throbbing in his groin, he wanted to turn Stephanie fully into his arms, pull her up and taste her, find the same joyful release that he had experienced with her in Boston.

Great timing, Robichaux. And real class on your part. Your wife is in the throes of a possible miscarriage and you're fantasizing about having sex with her.

"I was working at the clinic the night Diana died," he said in a rush, before he could change his mind. "I was reminded of that tonight."

"The child with the gunshot," Stephanie guessed.

"No, it was my patient, the overdose. When that kid's heart stopped—"

She waited for him to finish, but when he didn't, she continued, "Diana was beyond help of any kind, wasn't she? At least that's what the media reported."

"The media only had half the story. Diana was in the neighborhood to buy drugs. Ben Galloway's son was with her. Ben, Jr., was on duty, but he was a user, too. They'd already made a buy from a crack dealer doing business on the street behind the clinic."

"Oh, no."

"Ugly, isn't it?"

"It's sad. Tragic. I had no idea—"

"Nobody knew. Their deaths appeared to be the result of random violence. There was no need to reveal more. And because I was at the clinic that night, I got to the scene before Ben, Jr., died. His wound was serious, but he could have survived it." His tone changed. "Except that he had O.D.'d. While I was trying to keep him from bleeding to death right there on the sidewalk his heart stopped."

"Like the boy tonight," Stephanie said, suddenly understanding. "What about Diana? Was it drugs, too?"

"No, she was killed by a bullet, but she would be alive today if she hadn't needed cocaine," he said bitterly.

She looked up at him, her hand still on his chest. "I'm sorry."

He gave a halfhearted shrug. "It seems a long time ago now."

Stephanie was silent, thinking. "Does Benedict Galloway know this?"

"No."

"Really? Benedict thinks his son was killed because he was on duty at the clinic that night?"

"Yes. I didn't see the point in telling him otherwise. For my own reasons. Everything would have been out then—not only his son's addiction, but my wife's, as well. Why would I tell the world that the mother of my child was a junkie? I want Alison to believe the best of her mother. All she has are memories."

"Yes, I understand that. But Galloway's hostility to you still puzzles me."

"He believes I could have done more to save his son, and, of course, he has never approved of Women's Hospital catering to the class of people that frequents the clinic," Tal said. "You know that."

"True," she said, idly moving her hand on his chest. "I'm convinced my own difficulties with him about the teen group stem from his personal prejudices."

Tal laughed shortly. "The truth is, Benedict Galloway is a bigot. In a sick, sad sort of way, his rage over the death of his son is mixed up with his contempt for the people served by the clinic. He sees my support of the clinic as a stumbling block to getting rid of it...."

"I hate the way he tries to discredit you at the hospital," Stephanie said, her tone taking on heat. "Every chance he gets. It's so unjustified. If he only knew."

"It seldom works. I think most people dismiss it as professional rivalry," Tal said, enjoying her defense of him. My God, the differences between her and Diana! He gave her a small squeeze. "But anytime you want to scratch his eyes out on my behalf, I'll stand back and watch."

She laughed, a soft, low laugh that was sexy as hell, and snuggled a little closer. "You're too nice sometimes for your own good."

"Hardly."

"I mean it. First you marry a woman who turns out to be less than a bargain. Then you get mixed up with another woman who somehow defies the odds and gets pregnant, and you marry her to save her reputation."

"It's my reputation, too."

"And on top of that, you don't even get to sleep with her." She reached up and kissed his jaw. "You're incredible. A present-day knight in shining armor."

"I'm sleeping with you now."

"You know what I mean."

He turned, cupping her chin in his hand, and kissed her. She tasted delicious. He took the kiss deeper, unable to resist grabbing a moment or two of selfish pleasure. When he stopped, he had the satisfaction of knowing that she was aroused, too. He rolled to his side, pulling her close until they fit together like spoons. With his palm, he caressed her tummy, silently urging the baby to stay put. The night had been a turning point. He knew now, without a doubt, that he wanted this baby. Added to that, he wanted Stephanie.

"Now you know my secrets," he murmured, his mouth close to her ear. He felt her breath catch. And then he slept.

CHAPTER EIGHT

*Do not be surprised to discover that
you are capable of intense sexual
desire during your pregnancy. Let your
mate know how you feel. Don't be shy.
This can be a time of meaningful growth
in your relationship. Who else is more
intimately connected to the miracle
taking place in your body?*

—Ask Dr. Meredith

October 30, 1995/13 weeks

IT WAS TWO WEEKS before Stephanie was able to put
aside her fear of miscarriage. She stayed in bed two
full days—as Evelyn advised—then resumed a dra-
matically scaled-back schedule. Mornings were still
highlighted by routine bouts of nausea. By now, she
wondered if it would ever pass. The instant she awoke,
she dashed to the bathroom, threw up, staggered into
the shower and stood under the spray on trembling
legs until her stomach quieted and the grunginess was
washed away. By the time she came out of the bathroom, she felt great.

It was crazy.

It was inexplicable.

It was pregnancy.

Tal had learned to leave her alone. At first, he had wanted to do something to help.

"What can you do?" Stephanie had muttered. After suffering the inevitable, she was standing at the vanity sink brushing her teeth. "Even if you could do it for me, I don't think you'd like throwing up so regularly."

"But when will it pass?" he asked, watching her comb her fingers through her hair. "Three months, according to the experts, right? Surely you won't do this the whole nine months?"

"I'm a week past three months, as of today," said Stephanie, still a little pale. "So much for that statistic."

He frowned, thinking back. "I don't think Diana upchucked even once."

"Lucky Diana."

"I feel so useless . . ."

"Forget it. You've done your part."

He chuckled suddenly, and Stephanie met his eyes. She laughed with him. It *was* funny. Sort of.

He leaned casually against the door frame. "All the feminist rhetoric seems to be true when it comes to pregnancy. No man in his right mind would volunteer for nine months of this. There must be a hormone or something that gives a woman the fortitude to tough it out."

Stephanie suddenly felt better, completely recovered. With a thoughtful expression, she put her hands on her tummy, unconsciously caressing the small life she carried. "It's a funny thing, Tal. I remember how horrified I was the day I discovered I was pregnant, but that seems like a strange dream to me now. I can't imagine rejecting the thought of this baby. I feel overwhelming love for him. I'm protective and anxious and optimistic, all at the same time. I spend an amazing amount of time daydreaming about him. I think about how he'll look, what he'll be like, what kind of mother I'll be. And I'm not a daydreamer," she said ruefully. "Just ask Camille."

Tal studied her, smiling softly. "What makes you think it's a boy?"

"I don't really know. It just seems right." She smiled back at him. In sweatpants and nothing else, he looked sexy as sin. She became aware of her own skimpy attire. After drying off, she'd slipped into a silky kimono that barely reached the top of her thighs. She fumbled for the sash and tightened it. "Do you think it's a boy or a girl?"

"I don't know." He pushed away from the door and came closer. She knew her hair was a mess, curling wildly around her face. Tal tucked some wayward strands behind her ears, then stood looking into her eyes. "Boy or girl, I don't care. I just want a healthy baby."

"Me, too."

The next thing she knew, he had pulled her into an embrace. He did that sometimes now, as though he enjoyed simply holding her. She relaxed against his naked chest. Since the night she had almost miscarried, she felt safe and comfortable when Tal held her. She could almost believe the difficulties complicating their relationship might be worked out.

But could they? When he knew her, *really* knew her, would he still want her in his life? But, dear lord, with his breath warm and tingly at her ear and his hands lazily exploring her backside, she could almost be persuaded to believe he would.

"Tal..."

"Mmm, you feel good." His hands slipped under her kimono and found bare skin. He squeezed her waist, then cupped her buttocks. Oh, he was so smooth. She remembered now...that night in Boston. He hadn't rushed her. Like the song, he'd been a lover with a slow hand. He had taken his time building a fire in her, hot and consuming for all his patience. He had kissed her as no other man had ever done. Just remembering made her breathless. When she felt the bulge of his arousal, she made a small moan and turned to meet his mouth.

He tasted minty from toothpaste, cool yet warm. His tongue entreated and she opened to him, surrendering to the sheer pleasure of kissing. He was hard and strong pressing into her softness. She scooted a little closer, lifting her arms around his neck, wanting to feel him all over. Her nipples tingled. Pregnancy, she had discovered, made her breasts more sensitive. She wanted him to touch her there.

As if he could read her mind, he closed his hand over her breast, found her nipple and brought it to a peak. She closed her eyes, so intent on the pleasure of the moment that she didn't even hear the commotion outside their bedroom door until it suddenly burst open.

Alison ran straight over to the vanity. "Daddy, Keely's in the shower and I need to get in there. This is the second time this week. I don't have any privacy anymore!"

"Alison!" Tal's tone stopped the girl in her tracks. "I didn't hear you knock."

She gave the two adults a quick, startled look. An instant later, she made a face and shrugged. "Oops, sorry."

Behind Tal, Stephanie straightened her kimono, fumbling with the sash to close it. She was too flustered to look up.

"This is disgusting, Daddy," Alison said, rolling her eyes. "It's so early. How can you?"

For a heartbeat, Stephanie thought Tal might throttle her. "Alison," he said softly, "I'm giving you exactly three seconds to clear out of here. Like you, Stephanie and I value our privacy. Do I make myself clear?"

Anybody else would have scuttled away, but not Alison. "But what about Keely? I need to take my shower first. I've timed it. It takes me—"

"Alison!" It wasn't a bellow, but it was close.

Keely suddenly appeared behind her. "It takes you an hour, princess. If I want to be on time for school, I have to grab the bathroom before you barricade yourself inside."

"What am I supposed to do, leave it open so we can share? And don't call me princess!"

"Then start acting like a real person and I'll treat you like a real person."

"I am a real person!" Alison screeched. She turned to Tal. "Daddy, see how awful she is? I hate it here since she came. Why does she have to live with us?"

"Enough!" Tal put a hand on each girl's shoulder and marched them across the bedroom to the door. "This room is private and off limits to both of you from this moment. If you want to come in, knock politely and wait." He emphasized the last word with a deliberate stare at each. "If you don't get an answer, you don't come in. Do you both understand?"

Alison shrugged.

"Alison . . ." Tal looked at her, waiting.

"I understand, I understand."

He looked at the other girl. "Keely?"

"Got it," she said. "I shouldn't have barged in, but I heard her in there whining—"

"I was not whining!"

"Okay, let me rephrase that," Keely said with sarcasm. "Tattling. Do you like that one better?"

Alison whirled to face Tal. "See, Daddy? She talks to me like that all the time!"

"No, I don't. Only when you deserve it, princess."

"Don't call me princess!" Alison shrieked.

"I said, enough!" Tal roared. "The two of you had better put a lid on it or I'm grounding you until you're old enough to vote!" He made a disgusted sound, looking toward the ceiling. "Keely's right about one thing. All I've heard for the past week is whining, or bickering, or nitpicking, or backbiting . . . I could go on until you both miss your rides to school. I've had it. Stephanie is sick of it, even Mimi has complained about it. When will it end?"

Nobody responded.

"Look, we're a family here," Tal said, gentling his tone. He looked from one to the other. "Have you forgotten that? Like all families, we're different from each other. Just because you're not blood sisters doesn't mean you can't live together in peace and harmony. We've all got to make an effort. But I'm telling you—keep it up as you're doing and this household will be like a war zone most of the time."

Alison was staring sullenly at her feet. "It's not my fault."

Keely's eyes flashed at her. "It's mine for intruding on your perfect little kingdom, right?"

Tal put his hands on his hips. "Did either one of you hear a word I just said?"

Alison rolled her eyes. "We both heard it, Daddy."

"It's okay, Dr. T," Keely said, drawing a resigned breath. "It's not about the bathroom. Shoot, I can understand where Alison's coming from. I'd probably bitch, too, if a total stranger dropped out of the sky and changed life from the way I wanted it."

Alison gave an outraged huff. "You hear that, Daddy? Even when she's apologizing, she makes me sound awful!"

It was Keely who rolled her eyes heavenward this time. But before she could zing Alison again, Stephanie came out of the bedroom. Considering what Alison had interrupted, it was difficult to look normal. She stopped close to Tal. She was no expert on parenting, but she knew enough to present a united front before these two hotheads. Besides, she was responsible for one of the hotheads.

"I wish I could have recorded this," she said, assuming a stern tone. "If I had, you would have been embarrassed listening to yourselves."

Both girls had some difficulty looking her in the eye. "Tal is right. If we want to make it as a family, we all have to put forth extra effort. That means setting aside some of our own desires sometimes. It means considering other people."

Tal draped an arm around Stephanie's shoulders.

Alison stole a look at Keely.

Keely stared at Alison.

Amused, Stephanie's tone softened. "This is a very big house, ladies. Both of you have your own rooms. We also have extra bathrooms, so there shouldn't be any conflict over facilities. If you find it impossible to share the one closest to your two rooms, then maybe somebody should consider using one downstairs."

She could see at a glance that Alison wasn't about to go for that idea unless, of course, Keely was the one who went downstairs.

"Well, what do you think?"

Keely and Alison refused to look at each other.

Finally, Keely spoke. "I'll take the back bathroom downstairs. I like that big old-fashioned bathtub, anyway."

"Good." Alison smirked. When everyone glared at her, her expression changed to uncertainty.

"All right." Tal rubbed his hands together, giving Stephanie an approving smile. "This is more like it. Let's see if we can get along for a few days without a squabble, okay? Give us all a rest. Tell you what. I'll leave instructions with Mimi that you can order pizza tonight. Stephanie and I have plans for dinner out." He appeared not to notice the quizzical look he got from Stephanie. "How does that sound?"

Keely shot a hard look at Alison. "It sounds fine," she agreed before Alison could voice her objection. The younger girl chewed on her lip, obviously torn. If she didn't go along, it would look as if Keely's unflattering accusations were right.

"Alison?" Tal was looking at her.

"It's fine, Daddy. Just don't be too late, okay?"

"Hey, forget that. You two take your time. Have fun." Keely reached out and playfully punched Alison's upper arm. "Me and the princess here can get along for one night."

Shaking his head, Tal disarmed a fuming Alison with a hug before she could light into Keely again. "I think you should drop the royalty thing, Keely."

"Thank you, Daddy," Alison said primly.

"Aw, no problem," Keely said, her blue eyes dancing wickedly.

Stephanie hastily turned to go back into the bedroom before the fragile truce broke down again. Throwing her hands up, she wondered if this marriage could be saved. With two warring teenage girls in the house, it seemed doubtful. She could only imagine how it would be when they discovered her pregnancy.

THE TEEN GROUP MET that afternoon. Stephanie had the room set up for a hands-on demonstration on how to bathe a baby. It would be a lively session because she had prevailed upon Leanne, whose baby boy was now eight weeks old, to provide the baby.

"A real live baby?" Jolene asked, her big brown eyes round. "You gonna let us practice on somebody's real baby?"

"Not just somebody's baby. Leanne's. His name's Tyler."

"I know his name," Jolene said, easing into a chair and managing with much grunting and groaning to get her feet onto the chair in front of her. Her ankles were swollen again. Stephanie made a mental note to check the girl's blood pressure.

"Here she is!"

Leanne came in grinning with the baby suspended on her chest in a cloth harness. What little order there was in the class ended as everyone clustered around to get a look at him. Stephanie smiled as the girls oohed and aahed. There was no point in trying to begin the demonstration before they had examined the baby and heard from Leanne every detail of her labor and delivery.

"Look!" While patting the baby's bottom with one hand, Leanne stuck out the other. A ring sparkled on her middle finger.

Angela squealed.

"Is that what I think it is?" Jolene asked, eyeing the gold band with some suspicion.

"Michael and I got married," Leanne said, displaying the ring proudly.

"Wow!"

"Lucky, lucky, lucky."

"Why's she lucky?" Jolene challenged. "Leanne's a fine piece. That dude Michael knows a good thing when he sees it. He's the lucky one, you ask me."

"Yeah!"

"You got it!"

"All *right*!"

They high-fived it all around.

A happy ending, Stephanie thought, hoping the young couple would beat the odds. Marriages between fifteen- and seventeen-year-olds were statistically at high risk.

"Okay, class." Stephanie clapped her hands. Finally, she got them quieted down. "We're happy for you, Leanne. Best wishes to you and Michael."

"Thanks, Dr. Steph."

"And thank you for bringing Tyler." Gently, she touched the downy fuzz on the infant's head. "Let's show these ladies how to bathe a baby."

She rolled a steel cart to the front. A small plastic bathtub sat on top of it. Alongside it were all the essentials for the exercise—soap, no-tears shampoo, hooded towel, tiny bath-cloth, baby powder. Stephanie filled the tub from the sink in the bathroom. Rolling up her sleeves, she bent down to the lower shelf to get a few pamphlets she planned to hand out.

As she was straightening up, the room tilted. Dizzy and weak suddenly, she closed her eyes to fight the vertigo. With no chair within reach, she was forced to cling to the sides of the cart while a rushing roar filled her head. The girls were looking concerned. She knew Jolene was speaking, but the sound seemed far away.

And then everything went black.

STEPHANIE CLOSED the door of Evelyn Duplantis's office and started toward Tal. He was on his feet before she reached him. "I'm fine," she assured him. "I told you it was nothing."

"Why did you faint if it was nothing?"

She shrugged, allowing him to usher her out into the crisp October air. "Who knows? But Evelyn says everything's fine and I believe her. Pregnant women faint. Who knows why? Oxygen deprivation when I stood up suddenly, I assume."

"You scared the hell out of me."

She chuckled. "You and the girls. They were worse than you. Most of them have seen people shot in their neighborhoods, but let me faint and they overreact. It's weird."

"They care about you."

She smiled. "I know. And now they know I'm pregnant. Our secret is out."

"They would have guessed that in another week or two, anyway," Tal said, reaching around her to unlock the car door. It was dark and the parking highrise was nearly deserted. He moved closer and placed his palm over her abdomen from behind, rubbing slowly. "You've got a little bulge here. I noticed it this morning."

"I've gained six pounds." Stephanie leaned against him, enjoying the intimacy. Since when had she become such a sensual creature? Was it just pregnancy? Or was it Tal? Something else besides a baby was happening within her. If she could only be sure that Tal was feeling it, too.

He pulled her closer, fitting the curve of her derriere against his front. "Feel good?" he asked.

"Uh-huh." She tipped her head back, resting it against his chin. In the circle of his embrace, she felt safe and protected. While his hands caressed her tummy, he was doing lovely things with his mouth. His lips moved against her temple, grazed the corner of her eye, trailed down her cheek . . . to her ear. Closing her eyes, she rocked gently to and fro, giving herself up to the pleasure. She loved the smell of him, his warmth, his strength, the sound of his breathing . . . as rushed as her own. The unsatisfied cravings he'd unleashed that morning were back, full force. She admitted it now. If Alison hadn't burst in on them, they probably would have ended up in bed.

"Steph . . ."

"Hmm?"

"We've got to get in the car."

"Uh-huh."

Tal released his breath in a rush and reluctantly turned her to see her face. Her cheeks were soft, flushed with desire. Her eyes were a dreamy gray, the color of the lake on a cloudy day.

He gave her a lazy smile. "Where to?"

She blinked, like a cat coming awake. "Ah . . . what time is it?"

"Six forty-five."

She nodded, still looking dazed. "Well, I could go back to my office, but nobody is there except the insurance clerk. My patients were rescheduled, of course." She touched her forehead as if trying to think her way through a fog. "I could take care of paperwork, I suppose."

Exasperation and amusement were on his face as he propped an arm on the open car door. "That is not what I meant, Stephanie. Where to means shall we go home and let you put your feet up, or do we keep our dinner date?"

"Oh."

"I vote for dinner . . . provided you feel up to it."

"Are you?" she asked.

"Up for it?" His smile was wickedly male. "Oh, yes. For both. And anything else."

She sat down abruptly and reached for the seat belt. With that remark and her senses in an uproar, she didn't trust herself to say another word. When he closed the door for her and started around the car, she caught a look at his face. He was still smiling.

"WHAT'S SO FUNNY?"

Tal leaned back at an angle in his chair, twirling his wineglass. "You. That." He looked at her plate, empty except for a sprig of parsley and a piece of squeezed lemon.

"I was hungry." Her tone was defensive.

"I'll say."

Instead of responding to his teasing, she was suddenly uncertain. "I must seem insatiable," she said, looking with chagrin at her plate. "This is something the girls talk about all the time, their phenomenal appetites. I never truly understood until now. Food never tasted this good."

"My brother will love hearing that." He glanced beyond her shoulder. "Here he comes now."

Stephanie turned to see Travis Robichaux approaching their table. The man was easily recognizable as a Robichaux, although not as tall or as dark or as handsome as Tal.

"Hello, strangers." Smiling, Travis pulled out a chair and sat down. "I was wondering if Mimi's cooking was so fabulous you weren't going to eat out ever again."

"How's it going, Trav?"

"Hi, Travis," she said.

He looked at Stephanie's plate. "What's this guy doing, starving you?"

A smile flicked at the corner of Tal's mouth before he winked at Stephanie. "She eats like a lumberjack."

For a beat or two, Travis studied them both. "Uh-huh. So, how about dessert . . . on the house?"

"On the house?" Tal repeated as though such a gift was almost too much to believe.

"Yeah, I'm thinking we're celebrating here, right?"

Stephanie reached hastily for her coffee cup. Tal would have to handle this. She was startled when he reached for her hand. Her eyes flew to his.

He was smiling. He brought her fingers to his mouth and kissed them. "Yeah, we're celebrating. My lady's pregnant."

"Get out of here...." Travis leaned back, eyeing them skeptically.

Tal returned his stare blandly.

"Jeez, this is great!" Travis turned and gestured to the nearest waiter. "Forget dessert. This calls for champagne." He gave Stephanie a quick look. "Just a taste, right? I know it's bad."

She smiled. "Okay, just a taste." She stole a look at Tal and felt a rush of heat at the expression in his dark eyes. Whatever he was thinking, he wasn't trying to hide it from his brother.

"To baby," said Travis, holding up his glass for a toast.

"To health and happiness," Stephanie said.

Tal met her eyes with a look that sent her heart flying. "To us."

THEY DROVE HOME almost leisurely. With each caught up in private thoughts, neither had much to say. Stephanie commented on the excellence of the restaurant and Tal absently agreed. After living with him for three months, she realized he took very little notice of his family's wealth and position. That same lack of pretension was part of Travis's personality, too. It stemmed from a lifetime of belonging, of stable family ties and financial security. She had ceased to wonder what he would think about her own sordid upbringing. She never intended to reveal it.

Travis's uncomplicated acceptance of her pregnancy was a welcome relief. One more obstacle overcome, she thought. Now, if only Alison would take it as well, she could relax a little. After Travis left their table, they had talked briefly about when to tell Alison and Keely. They didn't think Keely would be a problem, but Tal had admitted that he couldn't be sure about Alison. And he also admitted he didn't want to deal with her reaction—whatever it was—right now. Especially not tonight.

Tonight they were going to make love. They hadn't talked about it, but she knew. The knowledge was so strong, it was almost a presence in the car with them. Everything from the kiss that morning to the celebratory toast at dinner had been foreplay leading to the moment when they would enter their bedroom and for the first time share the bed as lovers. Stephanie was oddly free of misgivings about taking the step that she'd shied away from until now. She knew that she had turned a corner somehow. Tal had accepted her pregnancy, had insisted without hesitation on marriage, had taken her responsibility to Keely as his own. She wasn't even certain anymore what she had been holding out for.

They turned in the driveway to the house and found every downstairs light on. Tal drove through quickly and parked in the garage. They hadn't made it across the patio, when Alison jerked the door open. One look and they could see that she had been crying. Stephanie's heart stumbled. Her first thought was for Keely.

Please don't let her be hurt.

"Daddy, I've been trying to call you at the restaurant! Uncle Travis said you left thirty minutes ago. Where have you been?"

"I've been in the car, Alison. It takes that long to get through traffic." He spotted Keely halfway down the hallway. "What's wrong?"

Alison wiped her cheeks with both hands and sniffed loudly. "Keely told me the biggest lie, Daddy. She said you and Stephanie were going to have a baby!"

Tal swore beneath his breath.

"It's not true, is it, Daddy? I told her if it was, you would have told me. Isn't that right, Daddy?"

For an instant, Stephanie felt the girl's betrayal. Everything comfortable and familiar in Allison's life had changed in such a short span of time. The poor kid probably didn't know what was coming next.

Tal gave a resigned sigh. "Can you wait until we get inside the house to talk about this, Alison?"

"Just answer me, Daddy!"

He shouldered past her, pulling Stephanie with him by the hand. Alison blinked, but didn't show any intention of giving up. "Come into the den," he said calmly. "Both of you."

In his hurry, he propelled Stephanie forward with a hand on her waist. As they passed Keely, she spread her hands and gave him an elaborate shrug. Unamused, he pointed to the den door. When they got there, Alison began to talk again, but he silenced her with a sharpness that, for once, did the trick.

"Sit down, both of you," he began at once, his expression grim. For the life of her, Stephanie could not look the girls in the eye. Tal could say what he would, but with Alison's hostility like a thundercloud in the room and Keely's respect for her damaged, she knew they would blame her.

She was startled to feel Tal's arm going around her waist. He pulled her close before saying quietly, "Stephanie is pregnant."

"Dad-*deee*..."

Alison's wail earned another reprimand from Tal. "Do you want to whine or do you want to hear what I have to say, Alison?"

"You never used to talk to me like that, Daddy."

"I never needed to, Alison."

"I think this is all my fault," Keely said suddenly. "I shouldn't have said anything." Her look included the two adults. "I'm sorry. I didn't know it would upset her like it did."

Tal looked at his daughter. "I'm sorry you're upset, Alison. I wish you had learned about the baby from Stephanie and me. We intended to tell you."

Alison gave him a wounded look. "When, Daddy?"

The question stung. "Soon, baby. It's the truth. I guess we just wanted to keep it to ourselves a little longer. We knew it would be a big surprise."

"It's a big surprise to everybody, I'll bet!" Alison cried. "Oh, what will my friends think? You're not supposed to be having babies! You're too old!"

Amusement won out over exasperation. "I'm not too old and neither is Stephanie."

"But it's too soon. You just got married!"

He hesitated a split second too long on that one.

"Couldn't you have used a *condom!*"

Tal's expression was almost comical. Stephanie felt sympathetic. Was it Daddy's first inkling that his little girl knew about such things? She decided he needed help. "A condom isn't always reliable, Alison," she said quietly.

Alison gave her a sulky look. "That's not what it says on TV."

"Take it from me, it's true," Stephanie said dryly. "But we can discuss birth control for the rest of the night and it won't change the fact that your dad and I are having a child.'' Her tone softened. "He or she will be your little brother or sister. Have you thought of that?"

Alison looked away. "I don't need a brother or sister," she said, but with less belligerence.

"You like babies, don't you?"

She shrugged.

Tal gazed silently at his daughter. Stephanie guessed how he must be feeling. He loved Alison so much and he had indeed turned her life upside down with this pregnancy. Given a little time, she would probably come around, but in the meantime, nothing much was going to make the idea of a baby brother or sister a happy event for his little girl.

She turned to Keely. "How did you find out?" she asked.

"I heard it at school," Keely said, still looking apologetic. "The kids said you fainted and that Dr. T rushed to your room looking like he was gonna pass out, too."

"People exaggerate," Stephanie said with a glance at Tal.

"Did they exaggerate, Dr. T?" Keely asked.

"I was concerned," Tal admitted, moving to the door and putting an end to any more questions. "Speaking of which, Stephanie has had a long day. She needs to get some rest." He waited while the two girls and Stephanie filed past him. She glanced at his face but could read nothing in his expression. With a sigh, she went upstairs.

TAL WAS WAITING when she came out of the bathroom, and he wasn't wearing his usual sweatpants. Her eyes widened.

"Don't say a word," he told her. She tried anyway, but before she found her voice he had taken her into his arms and was kissing her breath away. It was startling and masterful and arousing. It was as if he thought she needed persuasion and was ready to do what it took. Maybe he wasn't as upset over the scene in the den as she'd thought. Wondering how far he would go, she wrapped her arms around him and kissed him back.

He ended the kiss at last, only to begin urging her backward. "Let's go to bed."

He kissed her again, a hot melding of their mouths, then tumbled her onto the mattress, following her down, taking care that she didn't bear his full weight. Then he rolled her on top of him. He was hot and hard, all male angles. He took only a second to look into her eyes. "This is driving me crazy, Steph. My daughter's unhappy, my household is in chaos, I'm besieged at work and hounded by the administrator…" He looked away for a second before gazing back into her eyes. "But the hardest thing of all is wanting to make love to my wife and everything in the damn world conspiring against it."

She traced the line of his mouth with one finger. "I'm sorry."

"Don't apologize. I understand why you've been hesitant," he said, his tone dropping huskily. "And I've tried to give you time. God, it seems like years…"

"A little over three months."

Holding her eyes with his, he slipped a hand beneath her silk kimono and cupped one breast. His thumb moved slowly back and forth over her nipple. She closed her eyes, shuddering involuntarily. The pleasure was almost painful.

"Look at me."

She didn't know if she could. Deep inside her, desire was building, making her ache. Now his hands cupped both her breasts. His touch had her nipples taut and tingling. She wanted to savor it, revel in the feelings that poured through her like warm spring rain. "How much longer do we have to wait, Stephanie?" he asked hoarsely.

"Don't wait," she whispered.

His breath left him in a great gust. In seconds he had her naked, the kimono flung to the floor. For Stephanie, the time to come to terms with her marriage and her pregnancy had been necessary. But her hunger for Tal had been there all along, ever since that night in Boston.

But somehow tonight felt new. They touched and kissed and sighed and smiled. They delighted in rediscovering sweet, remembered places—her flat abdomen, now gently rounded, his rough male flanks, the womanly softness at the apex of her thighs, the strength and hardness of his passion. Tal sank his fingers into her and found her ready, then his mouth claimed hers with an urgency that brought them quickly to the edge. With a fierce shift of his body, he took his place.

Inside her.

He made a sound, unable to mask the emotion that roared through him. Stephanie answered, a sweet sigh of surrender. And then they fell into a perfect rhythm. Another sweet memory. If she had let herself recall just how sweet, she would never have been able to resist this long. Swamped in wave after wave of pleasure, Stephanie strained toward that final hurdle. Shameless in her passion, she heard the sounds coming from her and knew no man would ever touch her heart as he did.

I love you.

She wanted to say it, then tasted the saltiness of her own tears because the words must stay locked inside. What he'd said that night in Boston still haunted her. Before she opened her heart to him, she needed to know Tal's feelings were based on more than physical desire. With quickening passion, she felt the tension in Tal. As his climax neared, her desire peaked. Her thighs gripped his hips. His hand was between them, touching her. She needed . . . She wanted . . . She cried out as she was vaulted into splintering light. And in the next moment, with a shout of satisfaction, Tal followed.

CHAPTER NINE

*With your hormones in an uproar, you may overreact
from time to time. Your temper may
flare. Your insecurities may surface.
Keep these moments in proper
perspective. Nevertheless, your mate
can do wonders here. But only if you
tell him what you feel. Again, don't
be shy!*

—Ask Dr. Meredith

November 27, 1995/17 weeks

STEPHANIE LEFT the delivery room, stripping off the cap and mask as she walked. She glanced at her watch. Fifteen minutes late; no time to take off the surgical scrubs if she didn't want to be even later getting to Benedict Galloway's office. He was a stickler for punctuality, but Mother Nature outranked him, at least in Stephanie's specialty. In this case, the early onset of Martha Landingham's labor was to blame. Then the baby presented in the breech position. So, to avoid a caesarean Stephanie had had to try to turn the baby. Fortunately, she had managed the tricky maneuver and Eric Graham Landingham III, was finally born.

Galloway's secretary greeted her with a frosty smile and a deliberate look at her watch. Still on an adrenaline high from her success in the delivery room, Stephanie was impervious to the woman's disapproval. She responded with a bright smile. After a brief knock, she opened the door of Galloway's office.

To her surprise, there were only two people in the room, the administrator and Tal. Not a staff meeting then. Something else. The two men were unsmiling. She sighed inwardly, sensing her day was about to take a downward turn.

Galloway nodded briefly. "Here you are, Dr. Sheldon."

"Sorry I'm late, Benedict." She closed the door softly behind her and slipped into the chair next to Tal's. "An unexpected delivery."

"Yes, well. We've covered a few points in your absence. Talbot will no doubt fill you in later." Was that an oblique reference to their marriage? If so, it was the first from Benedict. While others had offered warm congratulations when she and Tal had announced their marriage, there had been nothing from the administrator. He glanced at her loosely tied top without any expression whatsoever. By now he must have heard about her pregnancy, but she wouldn't hold her breath waiting for his good wishes.

She looked questioningly from one man to the other.

"I can fill you in right now," Tal said in a curt tone. She looked quickly at him. She knew that look. He was furious. Breathing fire.

What on earth?

"Benedict has called us both in here to let us know that yesterday he was put in the unhappy position of having to defend the hospital."

She was bewildered. Defending the hospital was the administrator's job.

"Specifically, he was forced to defend you and me."

"You and me?" She thought back, trying to recall a patient who might have a genuine grievance but could think of none. Especially someone that both she and Tal would have treated. She looked questioningly at Galloway.

He regarded her coldly. "I'm not surprised by this disaster, Dr. Sheldon. I believe I have warned you often enough that your activism at that clinic is not only a threat to your career, but places the hospital in jeopardy, as well. Now an incident has confirmed my worst fears."

"What are you talking about, Benedict?"

"Get to the point, Ben." Tal rose abruptly and went to the window.

Galloway gestured to a yellow pad on his desk. "My visitor complained about a patient you treated at the clinic on the sixteenth of October. He claims the man received substandard care. In spite of the fact that his condition was life-threatening, he was ignored by Dr. Sheldon, who was on duty when he came in, and that when Dr. Robichaux finally got around to looking at him, his condition had deteriorated to the extent that he suffered cardiac arrest."

"In other words, we *caused* his heart to quit," Tal clarified, clearly disgusted.

Galloway pushed his notes toward Stephanie. "Here, see for yourself." She picked up the pad and began reading.

"The patient's heart stopped because he'd been binging on cocaine for days!" Tal retorted.

"This is ridiculous!" Stephanie said, glancing up from the notes. "This man was dumped at the clinic. Whoever brought him left without saying a word. He didn't get immediate attention because the waiting area was overflowing with victims from a three-alarm fire. If whoever came with him had bothered to tell us, we would have responded appropriately. I don't 'ignore' any patient, Benedict."

"That isn't the way it was reported to me," Galloway said.

Stephanie tossed the papers back on his desk. "Then your visitor has misled you. The clinic was a madhouse that night. Ask anyone. I was the only physician on duty. A child had been shot and I was trying to save his life."

"You *did* save his life," Tal put in curtly.

She barely acknowledged that. "And if it hadn't been for Tal arriving just when he did, this man would have died from the effects of a cocaine overdose."

Abruptly, Galloway sat forward. "Do you know who my visitor was?"

Tal turned from the window, frowning. Stephanie glanced down at the notes, but saw no name. "No, who?"

"Irving Connaught."

"The state representative?"

"Exactly." Galloway nodded coldly. "The person you neglected was his only son, Anthony Connaught."

"He was not neglected!" Stephanie said.

"Does he know his son is a cokehead?" Tal asked with sarcasm.

"Irving is a very visible public figure," Galloway said. "This could be a major blunder."

"What blunder?" Tal demanded with an incredulous look. "He went into cardiac arrest, and we brought him back!"

Galloway pushed on, ignoring Tal. "The repercussions could cost us dearly."

For an instant, Tal regarded him with disbelief. "For God's sake, Ben! Is that what this is all about? Damage control? Did you call us in here because we've inadvertently caused some bad publicity?"

"There would be no damage control necessary if the hospital wasn't linked to that clinic," Galloway said scathingly. "He threatened to sue!"

"And tell the world his son's secret?" Tal's expression was scornful. "I doubt it."

"At the very least, we stand to lose Connaught's support in the state capital. Thanks to you, that's probably at an end."

"Connaught is only one legislator," Tal said impatiently. "I assume you're worried about future state grants. This hospital has other friends in Baton Rouge. The governor, to name just one."

"Hear me on this, Dr. Robichaux," the older man said in a threatening tone. "I don't intend to sit by idly while you take this hospital down the tubes. One lawsuit has already been filed. We don't need another."

"What really galls you is that you've never approved of the clinic or of any program that didn't guarantee beefing up the bottom line. Isn't that right, Ben?"

"This hospital is not a charity institution," Galloway said.

Tal sighed. "Come on, Benedict. The hospital is insured for this kind of thing."

"The perceptions of the public remain whether we are insured or not," Galloway said stiffly. "That is the point I'm trying to make here."

"You're overreacting, Ben."

Galloway stared at him for a moment. When he spoke, he sounded coldly furious. "Overreacting, am I? I receive a legitimate complaint from an important public figure and I'm overreacting? Time and time again, I've warned you about that miserable clinic. But do you heed me? Does it make any impression on you? No. None. What does? Your own wife shot and killed on the premises, and my son...my son..." His voice caught.

He drew in a long breath. With what seemed an effort, he managed to bring himself under control. When he spoke again, his voice vibrated with emotion. "You enticed my son to that hellhole and then watched him die on the sidewalk."

Tal put out a hand. "Ben—"

Galloway rose, his look daring Tal to touch him. "I don't think we have anything further to say." He glanced at the notes he'd taken, then tossed them on his desk. "I'll send a memo about Connaught's visit to our attorneys. They will no doubt be getting in touch with you. Dr. Sheldon . . ." He turned to Stephanie. "Your personal relationship notwithstanding, your own liability in this matter is quite apart from Dr. Robichaux's. My advice to you is to get your own lawyer."

"Let's get out of here, Stephanie." Tal caught her by the arm. In half a dozen steps, they were at the door, but Stephanie suddenly turned back.

"Benedict, don't you think—"

His gaze went right through her. "I have another appointment. Good day."

TAL ERUPTED from Galloway's office like a man shot from a cannon. He strode past the administrator's secretary, pulling Stephanie along with him out into the hall, heading for the parking garage. At least, that's where Stephanie assumed they were going. People stared curiously as they passed. Understandable, she decided, stealing a look at the scowl on Tal's face. Long before they reached his car, Stephanie had a stitch in her side.

"Nothing like a solid show of confidence," he said bitterly, throwing open the car door.

"You know how he is, Tal," she said gently, hoping he would simmer down before he got behind the wheel.

"What did he expect us to do at the clinic that night? Make a quick check of the sick to see if there were any VIPs, then take them first?"

She chuckled, pressing her aching side. "Probably."

"Hasn't he ever heard of triage? We treat people who are sickest first."

"Provided we know they're there."

"Anthony Connaught is one lucky junkie," Tal said, his hand on the open car door. "His old man ought to spend some time considering that instead of threatening a lawsuit."

"You would think so," she said, wincing a little.

He noticed her favoring her side. "What's wrong?"

"Just a stitch. I'm not used to sprinting down the halls of the hospital."

He swore. "What am I doing?" The question was put to the vast concrete ceiling in the garage. "Are you okay? Is it the baby?"

She sat down in the car, smiling. "I'm fine. Close the door. Now that I've caught my breath, I'm hungry."

It took a second, then a laugh burst from him. "Naturally. For a minute there, I imagined there was something more important than your next meal." He was still grinning and shaking his head when he reached the driver's side. As the car idled, he looked over at her. "Where to?"

"Something light because we have the charity reception at the Fairmont tonight, remember?"

He made a face. "The truth is, I forgot." With his wrist propped on the steering wheel, he looked resigned. "I'd hoped I wouldn't have to look at Ben Galloway's face again for a few days."

"Sorry." There was common accord in the look they shared. Galloway's persistence in trying to discredit the clinic was a bond that drew them closer. For a long drawn-out minute they sat there enjoying the sight of each other.

Tal stirred first. "But that's tonight," he said briskly. "So, what's your pleasure for lunch?"

She studied the roof of the car. "Well, let's see..."

While she thought, he said, "How about our place?"

Something in his voice made her glance over at him. He didn't look as if he was thinking about lunch. "Our place?"

"Yeah, it's Mimi's day off."

He *wasn't* thinking about lunch. And neither was she when he looked at her like that. That's all it took.

A look and she was ready to fall into bed with him. A touch. A thought. A whiff of his after-shave. The sound of his voice. It had been this way for a month now, ever since they had made love.

That had been a turning point. Somehow, that night she had been able to let go of the misgivings that had kept her from making her marriage real. Tal didn't love her, she didn't deceive herself into believing that, but he did desire her. With the same hunger that she craved him. By concentrating on that, she managed to put from her mind the what ifs in their relationship. After the baby was born, maybe there would be something upon which to build a permanent relationship. Provided the two teenagers in the house would learn to get along.

The night when Alison and Keely had met them at the door with the fact of her pregnancy still haunted Stephanie's thoughts. At that moment, she'd been sure Tal would like nothing better than to be a bachelor father again. She wished she could undo the way Alison had learned about the baby. Fortunately, Alison didn't suspect yet that pregnancy was the reason for Tal's marriage, although in time she was bound to. Stephanie sighed, not looking forward to that day. Keely, of course, probably suspected. But she had said nothing.

"Big decision, huh?"

She looked over at him, then dropped her gaze to his mouth. He had a gorgeous mouth. "What time is your first afternoon appointment?"

"Two. And yours?"

She smiled at him. "Two, too.

"No kids, right?"

"They're both in school," she told him, still smiling. "At least they'd better be."

He reached over, wrapped a hand around her nape and brought her close for a kiss. It was slow and deliberate, an erotic blending of their mouths replete with the sensuality that came so effortlessly now. Stephanie closed her eyes, delighting in the taste of him, the smell of him, the wonder of knowing that he took pleasure in kissing her.

He was breathing hard when he finally let her go. With a groan, he resettled behind the wheel, fidgeting to ease an obvious ache. She glanced at his lap and laughed. His dark, hot look held desire and promise.

"Buckle up," he told her gruffly.

She did, still smiling.

SHE MADE her two o'clock appointment with a few minutes to spare. Strolling down the hall on her way to the teen group, she felt relaxed and energized at the same time. Shameless might be a better word, she thought. She blushed to think of the passionate hour just past. But it wasn't shame she felt; it was happiness. Anticipation for the next time. And the next. She hardly knew herself anymore. Sex in her first marriage had been nothing like what she shared with Tal. Was it pregnancy? But pregnancy in her first marriage hadn't released the kind of emotion she felt now. She had become a slave to the appetites of her body. Food, sleep, sex.

At the door, she paused, then went inside, hoping as she greeted the girls that the way she'd spent her lunch hour wasn't written all over her face.

Of the original twelve teenagers in her group, seven had given birth, all without serious complications.

Only Jolene, Chantal, Chrissy, Teresa and Angela remained. Statistically, there would be some problem with one in twelve pregnancies. Scanning the friendly faces greeting her, she hoped this group would beat the odds. Heaven knew, they'd gotten precious few lucky breaks in their young lives.

With a frown, she noticed that Jolene was missing. With the girl's pregnancy almost at term, Stephanie had tried to convince her how important it was not to skip a meeting.

"Has anybody seen Jolene today?" she asked.

The four girls exchanged looks. Nobody knew.

"Was she at school?"

"She has algebra with me," Chantal said in her soft voice. "She wasn't there. I saw her last night, though."

"Was she feeling okay? Did she say?"

Chantal shrugged. "Just that she's miserable and doesn't feel like doing much of anything. But lordy, she was so puffed up, Dr. Steph, her ankles, her hands, even her face! She's gained a lot of weight in a few days, you can see it. I told her how you said that's a danger sign."

"She thinks *she* feels fat and miserable," said Angela, whose enormous bulk was almost comical. "She oughtta try walking around with twins inside. Talk about fat and miserable!"

Stephanie heard them out with a sense of foreboding. Jolene was at risk for toxemia. Stephanie had cautioned her over and over, but it was like talking to a child. With a sigh, Stephanie selected a videotape for discussion and popped it into the VCR. Today was Friday. The group wouldn't meet again until after the weekend, but she'd made it clear time and again that in an emergency she could always be reached. She hoped Jolene would remember that. In the meantime, she'd alert the girl's caseworker.

THE FAIRMONT HOTEL was one of the oldest in New Orleans. Elegant in a way the newer hotels could never be, it was the perfect location for the charity reception. Stephanie ascended the lushly carpeted stairs to the mezzanine level with Tal. She responded mechanically as people turned, waved. Smiled. Spoke. As always at these events, her stomach was in a knot.

To Tal, another charity reception was boring rather than intimidating. No one here tonight had the power to make him feel other than what he was: well-born, successful, highly respected.

Stephanie began the silent litany that sometimes helped overcome her nervousness. She was a physician in a difficult specialty. She had graduated cum laude from a top university. She had survived the torture and training of med school. Now she was Dr. Stephanie Sheldon, respected, admired, even envied by some. A world that she had once been denied was suddenly open to her. The world outside the hospital. She had never admitted to anyone—not even to Camille—how bewildered and intimidated she felt in that world.

"Are you cold?" Tal asked, giving her a concerned glance as they reached the top of the stairs. "Your fingers are like ice."

She cleared her throat. "Just a little nervous."

"Why?" He looked genuinely mystified. She looked good; she could see it in his eyes. She had chosen soft, flowing silk in a coppery shade that complemented the amber highlights in her hair and made her eyes greener.

"Because it's our first public appearance as a married couple," she told him. "Besides, it's obvious that I'm pregnant."

With a slow smile, his glance fell to her middle. "Are you talking about that little paunch I was kissing at lunchtime?"

She made a helpless sound. "Tal!"

He had been casually holding her hand. Now, with a soft chuckle, he pulled it through his arm, drawing her a little closer with the gesture, covering her fingers with a hand that felt warm and reassuring. "The hell with 'em," he growled, giving her a quick kiss on her temple. "There's not a man here who doesn't envy me."

She flushed with quick, heady emotion.

They were at the top of the stairs. Tal advanced without hesitation into the glittering throng of the New Orleans elite, and she had no option but to go with him.

"Tal," a man's voice said. "It's been a while."

Tal's smile to the sleek couple was polite. "Jack. Catherine. I thought you two were still in Europe. How are you?"

Jack and Catherine. Stephanie's stomach took another plunge. There was no mistaking the resemblance between this woman and Alison. These people had to be Diana Robichaux's parents. Jack Sterling's face bore no smile as he greeted his former son-in-law. Tall with a thick head of iron gray hair and steely gray eyes, he was the hospital's chief counsel. Catherine was as trim as rigid dieting and an expensive health spa could make her. Her hair was champagne blond, and her face was classically beautiful. There was no warmth in the look she gave Tal before turning to Stephanie.

"I don't believe we've met." Maybe it was multiple plastic surgeries that made her smile seem insincere, Stephanie thought, giving her the benefit of the doubt.

"This is my wife," Tal said at once. "Stephanie, Catherine and Jack Sterling, Alison's grandparents."

"Hello." Stephanie politely shook hands with Catherine, then Jack. As Alison's grandparents, these people would be a part of Stephanie's new life. "I guessed who you were," she said to Catherine. "Alison resembles you, Mrs. Sterling."

"Actually, she's a carbon copy of her mother," the woman said without a particle of warmth.

"I'm afraid I never met Diana."

Catherine looked at her. "How odd."

"I knew her to see her," Stephanie explained, "but we were never formally introduced."

"Oh, I see. And where are you from?" Catherine asked abruptly.

"Tennessee, originally, but I've lived in New Orleans since I was fifteen." Stephanie hated these polite interrogations. She always felt like an oyster being pried open and examined for a rotten spot.

"Then it's quite incredible you didn't meet Diana."

"Hmm." Not so incredible. Runaways didn't have much occasion to hobnob with debutantes. Squeezing the clasp of her evening bag, Stephanie glanced at Tal, but he seemed intent on his conversation with Jack Sterling. "Did you enjoy Europe?" she asked, ignoring the remark about Diana. She lived with enough reminders of Diana Robichaux, as it was.

Catherine waved a diamond-encrusted hand. "Actually, we cut our trip short this time. The weather in London was just so chilly." Her eyes dropped to Stephanie's breasts, then lower. "You can't imagine how surprised Jack and I were to hear that Tal had married. And so suddenly."

"Sometimes these things *are* sudden," Stephanie murmured, praying Catherine wouldn't mention her pregnancy. She was in no mood to learn how Alison's grandparents felt about their only grandchild having a sibling.

"And difficult for children. I hope you will take care with Alison. She's so special. Jack and I worry. She's very fragile."

"Fragile?"

"Yes. She's never really accepted the loss of her mother. No child ever does, you know."

No, I wouldn't know, Stephanie thought. With only the haziest memories of her mother, how could she? Wondering how soon she could politely get away, she sent Tal another look.

He left Jack's side and moved closer. "How about a drink, honey?" With his hand at her waist, he began to nudge her away from the older couple. But Catherine wasn't quite ready to let go. She spoke to Tal.

"Now that we're home again, I hope Alison can spend some time with us during the holidays, Talbot. We thought possibly some skiing in Colorado during the days between Christmas and New Year's. If you haven't already made other plans, that is."

"That's most of her holiday, Catherine." Tal's smile was tight. "Call me and we'll discuss it."

The woman assumed a bewildered expression. "Alison seemed thrilled when we mentioned it," she said.

"When did you talk to Alison?"

"Why, today. Probably an hour ago, just before we left to come here."

He bent his head and Stephanie guessed that he was counting to ten. "Things are a little different now, Catherine," he said finally. "Since it's no longer just Alison and me, our plans for the holidays are up in the air. Stephanie's sixteen-year-old niece lives with us."

"Yes, she mentioned . . . Keely . . . isn't it?" With a glacial smile, the woman turned to Stephanie. "With all due respect to you and your. . . niece, we usually try to treat Alison to a skiing vacation each Christmas. I'm sure you understand . . ."

"I do understand, but I'm afraid that will be up to Tal, Mrs. Sterling."

"We'll discuss it later," Tal said, his tone ending the discussion.

Catherine's mouth pinched into a small knot. Stephanie moved closer to Tal.

Suddenly, Benedict Galloway materialized from nowhere. "Jack and Catherine Sterling. I thought it was you." He offered his hand to Jack, then kissed Catherine's cheek. "I see the two of you are back from . . . London, wasn't it?"

"Among other places," Jack said. "How are you, Ben?"

"Oh, holding up." He glanced at Tal. "Your son-in-law here keeps me on my toes."

"Oh?" Jack frowned.

"That infernal clinic, you know."

At mention of the clinic, Stephanie felt a chill go around the group. Did the Sterlings share Galloway's contempt for it?

"I don't think Jack and Catherine are interested, Ben." The very evenness in Tal's voice was a warning to Galloway.

"We're interested in seeing that vile place closed," Catherine said. Stephanie sighed inwardly.

"What about the clinic?" Jack asked, giving Tal a sharp look.

The Sterlings' attention was firmly captured as Galloway had obviously intended. His satisfaction was almost tangible. "We're going to be sued, Jack."

Sterling's frown darkened. "I might have known. The hospital's involvement in that place is a constant irritant."

"Our liability in this is simply incalculable," Galloway said soulfully. "This time, they've exposed us to the nasty possibility of a lawsuit."

Stephanie was tempted to bean him with her evening bag, the pompous prig. He hadn't managed to discredit Tal and the clinic with the board, so he obviously thought to do the dirty work through the back door, so to speak, by working the brass one by one. The Sterlings were a powerful start.

"Every lawsuit is a nasty possibility," Tal said irritably. "In my view, there is nothing particularly threatening about this one. I'll stand by every decision made that night under oath."

"Would somebody give me some details here," Jack demanded impatiently. "What happened? Who else was involved?"

"Me," Stephanie said quietly. "I was on duty that night, too." She looked at Galloway. "I understood this was referred to our attorneys. Wouldn't Mr. Sterling get a better perspective if he waited until he got back to work?"

Benedict's look was not pleasant. There were many ways an administrator in a hospital could make the life of a physician miserable.

Jack Sterling held up a hand. "Forget waiting until Monday morning. Tell me now."

"Oh, for Pete's sake!" Tal looked away with angry eyes.

"Irving Connaught's son showed up there—God knows how he got there or why he went to the clinic—and remained untreated until he went into cardiac arrest."

"Good God!" Sterling's shocked gaze went to Tal.

Galloway sighed. "I don't have to tell you, of all people, how I feel about that clinic, Jack. But I can only do so much. The board seems reluctant to pull the plug with so much attention nowadays on health-care reform. Perhaps you can talk some sense into Talbot."

Tal took Stephanie's hand and started to pull her away, but she touched his arm. "Wait, Tal. I think Mr. Sterling may have the wrong impression."

She looked at the lawyer. "There's more to the story than Benedict's revealing. The problem was, whoever dropped Anthony Connaught off at the clinic failed to let anyone on the staff know. As I said, I was the physician on duty, but I was occupied with a child who'd been shot. When Anthony was discovered, the child I was treating was extremely critical. Luckily, at that moment Tal dropped in. He did everything that was appropriate. It was an unfortunate incident that could have had a tragic end."

"Connaught was critical, too," Galloway said.

She stared at him. "What are you suggesting, Benedict? Should I have abandoned the little boy? If Tal hadn't appeared, Anthony would have died. Tal saved his life."

She felt Tal watching her. She was very close to offending three people whose enmity could cause her considerable harm, not only in a professional sense, but personally, as well. Not fifteen minutes ago, she'd been in a state of panic over having to be here at all. Tal must be wondering if her outspokenness could be blamed on her pregnancy.

"I loathe that clinic," Catherine said to Tal with a delicate shudder. "I don't know how you can bear to even look at the place."

"I couldn't agree more," Jack said.

"We've been through this time and again," Tal said with impatience. "I started the clinic and I'm not abandoning it. Make peace with that or not. It's up to you. The patients who come there need the clinic. Too many people depend on it. If you don't approve of it from a humanitarian viewpoint, then I suggest you think of it as good public relations for the hospital. Generally, people approve of a clinic for the disadvantaged. And the stockholders don't need to worry. Thanks to Stephanie's efforts, there is matching federal money to beef up the state's contribution."

"There are other federal projects that will show a profit for Woman's Hospital," Galloway said stiffly.

"Fine. Get them," Tal snapped, ready to walk off. "But as long as I'm chief of surgery, we're not abandoning the clinic."

Had Benedict even heard the anger in Tal's words? Stephanie wondered. The evening was turning out to be quite a revelation. She hadn't realized the full extent of Galloway's bitterness until tonight. The man was driven by his obsession to punish Tal for the loss of his son. Jack and Catherine Sterling had lost a daughter. Did they blame Tal for Diana's death? Was that the reason they'd been so cold? Or was it because of her? Did they disapprove of his decision to remarry? Did they consider her an unsuitable stepmother for Alison?

What a mess. With Tal ready to walk away, she probably should let it go, but concern for her teen parenting program gave her courage. Both projects—the clinic and her counseling group—were vulnerable to political axing, and these three people wielded a lot of power.

Although Tal was urging her to leave, she made one last appeal to the Sterlings. "I understand that the clinic represents unhappy, bitter memories for you. Alison's mother lost her life there." She glanced at Galloway. "And Benedict's son, as well. Nothing could be worse than two lives lost. It's senseless and tragic..."

Catherine Sterling had been coolly distant before. Now her expression froze. Uh-oh. Mentioning Diana and Ben, Jr., was obviously out of bounds. Oh, well, in for a penny, in for a pound. The little boy she'd treated for a gunshot wound was someone's child, too. She groped for the right words. "Nothing could be worse...except dozens and dozens more lives lost. We don't have any way to guess the numbers. But believe me, for the people who rely on it, that clinic is a lifesaver."

"Hospitals provide the same services," Galloway said irritably.

"At many times the cost," Stephanie argued.

Galloway clearly had not expected her to argue. "The project should be allowed to die a natural death! Without Talbot championing it, that's exactly what would happen." He was coldly furious. "I hoped you would persuade him to be reasonable."

"Is that a threat, Ben?" Tal asked softly.

"These are precarious times for physicians," Galloway said, his expression as hard as his heart. "I'm simply cautioning your wife that an overactive social conscience can sometimes work against someone, career-wise."

"I'm afraid I agree one hundred percent with my husband on the matter of the clinic," Stephanie said quietly. Her heart gave a little bump when Tal laced his fingers through hers and pulled her a little closer.

Galloway looked at Jack Sterling. "You see what I mean?"

A waiter appeared with a tray of canapés, a timely interruption, although no one took anything. "Aren't there other projects the hospital could pursue?" Catherine asked plaintively.

"Such as teen parenting for a bunch of children having babies out of wedlock?" Galloway asked snidely. "Yes, indeed, we have that, too."

Stephanie couldn't afford to let the administrator jeopardize this, of all things. "It's only a pilot program," she said hastily. "And so far it has been funded by state and federal grants. But it has more than proved its worth. Seven babies delivered safely." She smiled. "Maybe the mothers have even learned a little about parenting."

Galloway's smile was sarcastic. "Have they learned to prevent future pregnancies?"

"The answer is yes, they've learned about contraceptives. Will they use birth control when it's necessary? We'll just have to wait and see."

"Drugs, illegitimacy, violence, abuse..." There was distaste on Catherine's face.

Stephanie spoke quietly. "It's a cycle we're trying to break."

"I don't understand why anyone would want to get involved that way," Catherine said. "Those children are so... different from us. Where are their values? Where is their sense of... propriety? Their futures are so bleak."

"If we can change just one bleak future to something better, isn't it worth it?"

Catherine shrugged, clearly losing interest. "It's hopeless."

TAL PULLED into the driveway, activating the remote that opened the garage, then drove inside. Beside him, Stephanie sat studying her hands. Her wedding ring gleamed in the glow of the security light. She moved her hand slightly, still not quite used to seeing it on her finger. In the quiet when Tal killed the engine, neither moved for a moment. Then he looked at her.

"Tired?" he asked.

"A little."

"Was it as bad as you thought?"

"The reception? Except for the Sterlings and Benedict, not really." Being with Tal had made all the difference, but she didn't know how to say that to him without explaining all the reasons for her insecurities in the first place.

He reached for the handle on his door. "Let's go inside."

Stephanie got out before he could come around. He reached for her hand as they walked. "Beautiful night," he said, looking up at the sky. "Must be a million stars out."

"Hmm."

"I guess of all the seasons, I like autumn best," he said, strolling across the lawn. "What about you?"

"What?"

He stopped, tipped up her chin and looked directly into her eyes. "What is it, Steph?"

She returned his gaze, studying his features in the moonlight. There was strength in him, yes, but such gentleness sometimes. He was looking at her now with a blend of both. "It's nothing. Pregnant women get moody."

"I think it's more than that," he said, dismissing her attempt to use pregnancy as an excuse. "I know how much you care about the teens. What Catherine said was insensitive and arrogant. Her world is so far removed from theirs that she can't possibly understand."

"I realize that," she said, gazing at a distant star. She wouldn't admit it to Catherine Sterling, but she often wondered if what she said to the girls ever really sank in. Did she influence them to make any changes in their lives or were they simply too entrenched in negative behavior to hope for anything better?

Tal pulled her closer, wrapping his arms around her, and rested his chin on top of her head. "If you're worried that Ben and my in-laws might influence the board to end your parenting program, don't. They're stockholders, too. As long as state and federal funds are tied to your counseling program and the clinic, they're not going to pull the plug."

She leaned her head against his chest, liking the firm, steady sound of his heartbeat. It seemed natural to anchor her arms around his middle. "That's so cynical."

"Uh-huh. They're a cynical lot." He was swaying a little in the dark, one hand sweeping up and down her back. It felt good, comforting. She had become accustomed to Tal's pampering, that was the only word for it. She wondered how she'd got along without him. Her other life, before Tal and her pregnancy, before Keely and Alison, seemed mundane and monotonous now.

She stirred against Tal's chest, turning her face into his crisp white shirt. He smelled nice, clean and male.

"You were super tonight," he said, his voice coming in a deep rumble from his chest. "You made me proud."

"When?" She looked up at him.

"When you were setting them straight about the Connaught incident. Your eyes were shooting fire and your chin had that set look it sometimes gets when you wade into the mix with the girls."

"The girls?" Was he talking about the pregnant teens? How could he know what she said and did during those sessions?

"Yeah, Alison and Keely."

"Oh." She felt a little bump of joy. She liked it when he referred to her and the girls as though they were a regular family. He did that sometimes, said things that made them *seem* like a regular family.

After a while, he spoke in a thoughtful voice. "I couldn't have depended on Diana for that kind of support."

Her hand stilled. "Why not?"

"First of all, she was barely aware of my career, except as a means to an end. The end being her life-style. And even if she had known the details about the Connaught incident, she certainly wouldn't have defended my actions to Benedict Galloway."

"Was she afraid of Benedict?"

"No, she was simply uninterested."

"She must have had some purpose in life," Stephanie said, unable to imagine life the way Diana Robichaux apparently lived it.

"Just tennis and bridge and maintaining a showplace instead of a home. Oh, and, of course, cocaine."

"Tal..." She touched his cheek, then stretched a little to kiss him. He returned her kiss, his mouth warm and musky. When he finished, he spoke against her temple.

"I can't imagine Diana expressing one iota of interest in a program for pregnant teens, let alone actually getting personally involved enough to know them, to be concerned about them."

How sad for Diana Robichaux, Stephanie thought. Tal might have adored her once, but living with her and her addiction had changed that. She remembered how rarely he'd smiled that night in Boston. He was smiling at her now. Slowly, lazily, genuinely. Desire and need rose in her, catching in her throat.

With a ragged sound, Tal pulled her close, pushing his pelvis against her softness. He was hard, *so hard*. She gasped, melting against him. "Does that feel good?" he asked, his voice hoarse.

"Oh, yes."

Arms tight around her, he brushed his lips against the soft skin beneath her ear, then kissed his way to the sensitive shell, nipping it. With a helpless sound, Stephanie tipped her head back to give him access to her throat. Above her, the stars seemed to whirl away into dazzling space.

"You're tired," he reminded her, breathing heavy now.

"No."

"No?"

"Not anymore."

His hand found her breast. "I want to love you."

"Yes." More than anything, she wanted to be loved by Tal.

Oh, yes.

CHAPTER TEN

*Pregnancy is a stupendous life process.
Do you tend to neglect other things in
your life as you focus on the miracle
taking place within your body? Perhaps
you have other children. Make them a
part of the process. Prepare them for
the presence of a new person in the
household. Life goes on!*

—Ask Dr. Meredith

December 18, 1995/20 weeks

"WHAT'S THIS, Mimi?"

"It's chicken divan, Miss Keely." The housekeeper reached for a basket of dinner rolls on the serving cart and placed it on the table in front of Tal.

Keely sighed. "There you go again, Mimi. I'm Keely, just plain Keely. What if I called you Miss Mimi?"

The woman smiled. "Well, I've been called worse, I suppose."

Stephanie and Tal exchanged an amused look. This was a familiar routine between Mimi and Keely. From day one, when Keely realized that Tal employed a staff to run his household, she had set out to convince them all that she was no snob. Sometimes the gardener, a shy Vietnamese, fled to the potting shed to escape her egalitarian fervor.

With her fork, Keely poked at the broccoli that lay beneath her portion of chicken breast. "No offense, Mimi, but do we ever get southern fried chicken around here?"

Mimi whipped the glass lid off a dish of fluffy white rice and set it alongside the platter of chicken and broccoli. "If you would like it, certainly. Were you thinking of having a picnic?"

Alison snickered.

"A picnic? No, why?"

"That's the only time fried chicken is *right*," Alison said, delicately slicing through a broccoli spear.

"Right?" Keely rested both hands beside her plate, her knife and fork at attention. "You mean, all those times I ate fried chicken in my other life except when I was on a picnic, it was *improper?*"

"Girls . . ." Recognizing the signs, Stephanie spoke quietly.

"That's stupid," Keely said flatly.

"*You're* stupid," Alison retorted.

"That's enough," Tal said firmly. "Both of you."

Daggers drawn, the two teenagers waged a silent battle, then Keely shrugged and flashed a smile around the table. "Sorry, folks. It's too close to Christmas to fight."

Tal broke apart a hot roll. "Hallelujah."

Stephanie and Keely laughed. Alison made a little huffing sound.

"Not that this *chicken divan* isn't good, Mimi," Keely said, cutting into the succulent breast. "The truth is, it's very tasty."

"Thank you, Miss . . . uh, Keely."

Keely munched for a moment, then reached for water. "Speaking of Christmas, when do we go out and buy a tree?"

"We don't buy a tree," Alison said. "We have an artificial one in the attic."

"Oh, wow, no." Distressed, she looked at Tal. "Is that right? This big, gorgeous house, and you have a *plastic* tree?"

He smiled. "I'm afraid so."

"Tell me that as artificial trees go, it's really special," she said hopefully.

"Well..."

"It's real tall, right?"

"Well..."

"What's the big deal?" Alison said, giving Keely an impatient look. "A tree's a tree. Mimi sets it up every year and my dad and I have never found anything to complain about."

"*Mimi* sets up your Christmas tree?" Keely asked, truly aghast.

"Sure." Alison shrugged.

Keely looked at Tal. "She's putting me on, huh, Dr. T?"

Tal exchanged a quick look with Stephanie. "Well, actually, that is how we usually do it." He added dryly, "I take it you have other ideas."

Keely waved her hand. "This beautiful house, those tall ceilings, lots of glass to let the whole world see how beautiful and Christmassy we are, in spite of the fact that we're...uh, *you're* rich...well, sure. I guess I'd do it differently."

A small smile played around Stephanie's mouth as she sipped coffee. "Me, too."

Tal looked at her. "What's this? My lady wants to add her two cents."

Eyes bright, she set her cup down. "Let's get a live tree. A really fabulous one that smells like piney woods and is so tall it takes a ladder to decorate."

Tal leaned back, studying her intently. "I think I hear a Christmas junkie in that speech."

"I do love Christmas."

"Me, too," said Keely. "Do you have lots of decorations?"

Tal looked at his daughter. Alison, for once, had no ready reply. "I guess so. I mean, we have the usual stuff."

"This is terrible." Keely slumped back in her chair. "I thought you guys would have fabulous decorations, family heirlooms, and, you know, stuff like that."

"I have a nice collection of things," Stephanie said, glancing at Tal. "You know how it is, you pick up something here and there when you travel, little mementos of trips, incidents, people."

Tal shook his head. "I confess I don't do that."

"You can start," Keely advised. "This is the first day of the rest of your life."

Alison rolled her eyes. "Oh, please."

Keely, for once, ignored her. "So, when can we make the big trip to the forest?"

Tal chuckled. "You mean that one on Canal Street downtown?"

"That's it."

"How about tonight?"

"Yes!"

"Then what are we waiting for?" He shoved his chair back and stood up. "We're out of here."

THE TRIP was a rousing success. Even Alison seemed to get into the spirit of the thing. The two girls took relatively few potshots at each other and had only one major confrontation. Tal finally stepped in to settle which tree to buy. Alison's choice was a tall, elegantly skinny one and Keely preferred a massive blue spruce that would have looked fine in the lobby of the Fairmont. Stephanie inwardly cheered when he chose the one she'd secretly favored.

"Congratulations," she told him later, laughing softly. "You made the choice and we're all still speaking."

They were in the attic where she had stored the cartons containing her Christmas ornaments. Stretching up on her toes, she reached for a box, but Tal's hands suddenly enclosed her waist.

"Let me get that," he said, moving her aside. Instead of releasing her, he slipped his arms around her and buried his face in her tawny hair. Instantly, there was a rush of heat and pleasure. His hands moved leisurely over her waist and up, cupping her breasts, heavy and ripe with pregnancy. "Mmm, you feel nice." He kissed her neck. "You taste nice."

She shifted a little, fitting her hips against his pelvis. He groaned, pushing against her. At the same time voices came from the stairwell. "Oh, hell."

"You started it," she murmured, resting her head back against him. Now his hands were cradling their baby. At five months, there was definitely something there. She was round and firm, carrying the child right out front like a ripe cantaloupe.

"Hey," he whispered, rubbing the little mound. "It's your daddy, slugger."

"Slugger?"

"You said it was a boy. Slugger's a good nickname."

"Oh, yeah?" Smiling, she placed her arms over his and wiggled wickedly.

He groaned again.

They broke apart reluctantly just as the two girls reached the top of the stairs.

"Come on, y'all!"

"What's the matter? Can't you find the decorations?"

"No problem," Tal said, busying himself with lifting a big box, then conveniently carrying it low in front. Thanks to the dim lighting in the old attic, Stephanie's blush went unnoticed.

DOWNSTAIRS, Christmas carols that Keely had selected played softly from concealed speakers. Mimi had made punch and set it up on a sterling-silver pot on a hot tray. The spicy smell mingled with the pungent odor of the tree itself to create a festive mood. The truce between Keely and Alison was holding. As they tore into the cartons of decorations, Stephanie looked up and found Tal watching her. He was holding a mug of the punch spiked with a splash of bourbon. Holding her gaze, he lifted it in a silent toast. Her heart did a flip.

"Oooo-oo-oo, look at these." Keely held up a pair of crystal angels. "And these." Two silver snowflakes. Next came Santa and Mrs. Claus.

Alison unwrapped two tiny mice with holly around their necks. "Everything's in pairs."

"Not everything," Stephanie said quietly, pulling a ceramic bell out of its packing. It was red with a candy-striped bow. She ran her finger over the date, hand-lettered in green ink. "Nineteen seventy-two," she murmured, remembering.

That was the year she and Tessa had been placed with a foster family on a farm outside of Memphis. Along with eight other children, they had slept bunk-house-style in a detached building. Up at six, chores, then school, home by three-thirty to baby-sit the little ones, work kitchen duty, clean house, do laundry, cultivate the vegetable garden. It had been a joyless eighteen months. She'd hated it, but not as much as Tessa had. At Christmastime, they'd saved enough by sharing lunch at school to buy the bell. A single bell. It had been on the bargain table because it was damaged. That time, when Tessa ran away, Stephanie had gone with her.

"Pairs?" Tal walked over and inspected the ornaments spread out on the floor, then looked at the bell which Stephanie held. "Nineteen seventy-two. You were what, twelve?"

"Yes." Stephanie found a place for the bell to hang on the tree.

Keely appeared beside her and gave the bell a tiny push with her finger. The small ping had a hollow sound. "It's cracked," she said.

"I know. We mended it . . . in the days before Super Glue."

"We," Keely repeated, looking at the pairs of ornaments with sudden understanding. "Everything's in twos because of you and my mother being twins, am I right?"

"Uh-huh."

"Do any of these belong to my mother?"

"The ones dating back seventeen years, yes. Half of those belong to Tessa."

"Why did she leave them with you? Why didn't she ever come back and get her half? Why didn't she think of me? Her kid? If she didn't care about them, I would have."

Oh, Lord. "She had her reasons, Keely, I'm sure. She wasn't thinking about Christmas. She wasn't thinking about anything except getting away. Finding a new life."

"Huh. Some new life."

"She was unhappy," Stephanie said, desperate to defend Tessa to her daughter. "She tried to make the best of it here with Camille. We both did, but it just didn't work out for Tessa."

"*You* stuck it out. *You* managed to work it out."

"It was different for me." *I didn't wake up with a devil on my back every day.*

"How?"

Stephanie looked helplessly at Tal. He was listening as intently as Keely. Even Alison looked spellbound. How shocked they would all be to learn the whole truth about her and Tessa.

"People make choices, Keely," she began hesitantly. "Sometimes wisely, sometimes not so wisely. Tessa did what she felt she had to do at the time. You have to know a person's fears and pain to understand why one person chooses one way and another chooses a different road."

"She sure made a rotten choice," Keely said bitterly. "And I had to travel that road with her."

"I'm sorry. I know you've had it hard."

"Damn right I have."

"Maybe she didn't exactly have a choice," Alison said.

Everyone stared in surprise. Alison offering sympathy to Keely?

"I mean, maybe she had a really good reason."

Keely went to the window. Outside, tiny white lights had been strung on the limbs of a huge oak tree. She spoke without turning. "How could she not have a choice? People always have a choice."

"Maybe she was going to have a baby and ran away so she wouldn't have to tell anybody," Alison said.

Stephanie gave her a startled look. Beside her, Tal held his breath.

"Well, it wasn't me," Keely said, "because the dates don't match. Of course, I could have a sibling I don't know about." She added coldly, "My mother's capable of anything. Having a kid and giving it away, she probably wouldn't hesitate."

"No." Stephanie was emphatic. "You're wrong, Keely. Tessa wouldn't do that."

"Oh, no? I could tell you some stuff that happened before I finally hit the road that would curl your hair, but you probably wouldn't believe it because you're so different from her. Even though you look alike, beneath the skin where it counts, you and my mother are night and day. I would never even believe you're related if your faces weren't the same."

"Oh, Keely..."

She shrugged, looking as if she had said too much. "Forget it. I don't expect you to explain it. It's hopeless, I know. It's just that I've spent so many million hours trying to figure her out." She sighed. "Still...you two being twins and all, I thought maybe you might have a clue."

Oh, God. What to say? To reveal Tessa's secret, she would have to tell the whole sordid story. Stephanie looked at Tal. There was something intent in his dark eyes as he watched her, waiting.

"We had some pretty difficult times while we were growing up," she said, touching the face of a cheery cherub dangling on a limb. "Before Camille took us in. We never knew my father—he was killed in an accident when we were four years old. My mother was driving. I don't think she ever got over it. Anyway, after that she drank a lot. We were shuttled from one foster home to another for a while. She died when we were nine."

At that particular point in time Stephanie and Tessa had been living with their mother. They woke up one morning to find her unconscious on the couch. The phone was disconnected for nonpayment and Stephanie had run frantically next door to ask a neighbor for help. It was too late.

On the day of the funeral, it rained. Stephanie would never forget it. So, at age nine, they were suddenly permanent foster children.

Stephanie gazed into the tiny lights on the tree. She blinked as Tal touched her shoulder, offering her a cup of the mulled punch. "Here, it's warm and sweet." His dark eyes were unreadable, but she sensed his sympathy. Or was it pity? She didn't want his pity.

"We did okay for a while," she said after sipping the punch. "We stayed with a couple of families that were . . . okay." She shrugged, not able to find a better word. "We stayed the longest on a farm. We swore then we wouldn't grow up and marry farmers." She laughed softly and then her smile faded. "Our caseworker finally placed us with a couple in Memphis when we were fourteen. We really hated it there and finally we just ran away."

"Wow," Alison said softly.

There was more. So much more. But Stephanie didn't want to think about it tonight. Not when the Christmas tree was twinkling and everyone was mellow with Christmas spirit. Maybe another time. Maybe when she felt more certain that she and Tal would stay married.

Keely sat on the floor, legs tucked. She looked at Stephanie. "Can you believe my mom never told me any of this?"

"Maybe, like me, she just wanted to forget it."

"But aren't you supposed to tell the people you love stuff about yourself?" Keely asked. "You aren't supposed to keep secrets, you aren't supposed to bury the past like it never happened."

"Good thinking, Keely," Tal said quietly. But he was looking at Stephanie.

Keely stood up and brushed off the seat of her jeans. "I still don't know why she ran away that last time. Miss Camille is really neat. Seems to me you guys had finally gotten lucky."

"Do you think it could be that she was pregnant?" Alison asked, hanging on to her theory. "It was almost seventeen years ago. Back in those days, people were pretty hard on unwed mothers."

"There are lots of reasons teenagers run away besides pregnancy," Stephanie said, nervous over the direction of Alison's thoughts.

"Yeah, but didn't you and my dad get married because of that?"

"Because of the baby?" she asked weakly.

"Sure."

"What makes you think that, Alison?" Tal asked.

She gave them an exasperated look. "Well, I can add, for heaven's sake. You got married in August and the baby's due in April. That's eight months. It takes nine. Sex education, remember?"

Stephanie's gaze flew to Tal. Great. Wonderful. For once, her expertise with teenagers deserted her. Tal would have to handle this one.

Seeing their expressions, Alison shrugged. "You don't need to look so awful, Daddy. These things happen, I suppose, but you really should have used birth control."

"We used birth control," Tal said in an even tone.

Alison didn't blink. "Well, whatever. At least you did the right thing."

"And that's it?" Tal asked, looking like a man who has approached an abyss and somehow managed to step over it.

"Well, you're just not the type to get a woman pregnant and walk away from your responsibilities."

"No," he said faintly.

"And neither is Stephanie," she said, glancing at her.

Tal moved close to Stephanie and put an arm around her. "You're right about that, Ali." He smiled at his daughter. "I think you're growing up."

She grinned at him just as the telephone rang.

"Oh, no!" Both teens exclaimed at once.

Mimi appeared, carrying a portable phone. "It's for you, Dr. Robichaux."

He took it, spoke briefly, then cut the connection. "Sorry, guys." His gaze lingered on Stephanie. "It's an emergency."

"It's always an emergency," Alison griped.

He was already slipping into a jacket, checking his keys. "I don't have any idea when I'll be back. Probably not anytime soon."

"Go ahead," Stephanie said. "The girls and I will finish up here."

"Thanks." He kissed her on the mouth, hard. "We need to talk," he whispered. At the arched doorway, he stopped and looked back. Then he winked at them all. "Hey, nice tree."

WITH TAL MISSING, decorating the tree didn't seem as much fun. At least to Stephanie. But the girls were as eager as ever. Every time they pulled out another of Stephanie's ornaments, they wanted to know the story behind it. She told only the good ones, the funny ones. No more dismal stuff. A little bit of her and Tessa's childhood went a long way. The tree was done around midnight and Tal had not returned.

They were clearing away the empty boxes, when the telephone rang again. Keely answered.

"It's Jolene," she said, passing it to Stephanie. "Sounds like she's scared."

"Hello, Jolene."

Nearly hysterical, Jolene began talking. Between the girl's sobs and panic, Stephanie managed to piece together that Jolene was in labor. As she was only seven months along, Stephanie hoped it was false labor.

"I'm at the clinic, but I'm not goin' in without you," Jolene declared. Fear made her voice shaky.

"Meet me at the hospital, Jolene." If there were complications, Stephanie wanted the full arsenal of Women's obstetrical unit.

"I don't want to go to the hospital. My mama had her last two babies at the clinic and so did my auntie. I'm havin' my baby here, too."

"Jolene—"

"Are you coming or not, Dr. Steph?"

Stephanie sighed. "I'm coming. Go inside, do you hear me?"

"No! They'll start their whole rigmarole and I won't have no say in nothing. I'm waitin' for you, okay?"

IT WAS RAINING by the time Tal left the hospital to drive home. His patient had suffered massive injuries in an accident on the interstate after a trucker fell asleep at the wheel and hit him broadside. Fortunately, the victim was young and healthy and, in spite of the odds, would probably recover completely.

Tal was conscious only of crushing fatigue as he approached his house, then he spotted the Christmas tree through the windows, and smiled. Lights, many more than had ever been on any tree in that house, glittered and glistened through the rain-spattered panes. He felt a lessening of his fatigue and a tiny sense of anticipation. He couldn't wake Steph. Hell, it was past three. Still, the thought of crawling into their big bed and pulling her close was instant pleasure. She'd be warm and soft and fragrant. She'd murmur sleepily and settle into him as if they'd slept together forever. Using the remote, he drove into the garage. Shoving the car door open with a muttered oath, he stood up before the aching bulge in his groin got any worse.

The house was still and quiet. Peaceful. He dropped his keys softly in a tray on a small table and shrugged out of his jacket, then extended his arms high in a tired

stretch. After loosening his tie and undoing the buttons on his shirt, he rolled his shoulders a couple of
times to ease some of the strain. At the arched entrance to the living room, he glanced at the tree and
some of his fatigue lifted. It was beautiful, thanks to
his ladies. Alison and Keely and Stephanie. Stephanie. As he climbed the stairs, he thought about his wife's childhood. Until tonight, she had revealed few
details. Understandable maybe, now that he'd been
given a glimpse. He ached with sympathy for her, but
he worried that her reluctance to share her past meant
that she didn't trust him completely. Maybe she felt he
wasn't committed to their marriage or worse, maybe
she wasn't committed to the marriage or to him. No
matter how good the sex was, he wanted more from
Stephanie.

He hesitated at the door to their bedroom. Diana
had not been capable of deep, abiding love, but he
knew Stephanie was. And that was what he wanted
from her—deep, abiding love. He wanted her heart.

He gently pushed open the bedroom door, his gaze
going directly to the bed. She wasn't there, but a soft
sound came from across the room. She was sitting in
the dark in front of the window, her head resting
against the winged back of the chair.

He was beside her in half a dozen steps. "Steph!
What's wrong? Is it the baby?"

He reached toward the lamp, but she put a hand on
his arm and stopped him. "Don't. I'm all right, really. The baby's fine, too. I just had a little trouble
sleeping."

He settled beside her on his haunches. "Did you go
at it too hard today? Did the girls fight after I left?

Damn it, I thought for once they seemed almost friendly."

"I didn't overdo and the girls were great. The tree's beautiful." There was a husky sound to her voice. "Did you see it?"

"Yeah, it's gorgeous. It puts every tree we've ever had in this house to shame." He found her hand and laced his fingers through hers. They were cold. "You realize you've started a tradition, don't you? You Christmas freaks are really something."

"Really something." It was a broken whisper. She turned her face from him, but not before he'd seen her lips tightly pressed together. And trembling, anyway.

"Steph, honey, tell me what's wrong." His tone was sharp with concern. It was a cloudy night, with virtually no light filtering through the window. He touched her cheek, wanting to see her face and realized it was wet with tears.

With a muffled sound, he rose and pulled her up with him, keeping her close. Her whole body was trembling. Instead of the silk lingerie she usually wore, she had on a soft, white cotton thing, like an old-fashioned dress with a ruffle on the hem that went almost all the way to the floor. He'd never seen it.

He took her face in his hands. "What—"

"She died, Tal."

"Died? Who?"

"Jolene's b-baby."

"Jolene? She's one of your teens?"

"Y-yes." She sniffed, wiping at her tears with a half-shredded tissue.

"The little skinny one with the smart mouth."

"S-sh-she didn't have a smart m-mouth today."
Tears overflowed and she began to cry softly. "Her
heart is b-broken."

"Oh, sweetheart, I'm so sorry." Tal brought her
close and wrapped his arms around her, cradling her
as gently as if she were an infant herself.

She began to cry harder, deep, wrenching sobs that
tore at his heart. Her shoulders shook, her fingers
clutched at his shirt, her tears gushed in a wild tor-
rent. He stroked her back and she leaned into him,
utterly vulnerable in her grief.

"Shh, baby, you're going to make yourself sick."
He crooned the words, knowing she couldn't control
the anguish any more than she could have controlled
the event that brought it on. "C'mon, let's go over to
the bed."

He urged her along and they sat down together. He
ducked a little to see her face. "Some light, okay?"
She nodded mutely and he reached over, snapped it
on, and in the soft glow he looked into her eyes. Sad,
sad eyes.

"You want to talk?"

She shook her head as fresh tears welled up.

"Don't, sweetheart." He scooted back against the
pillows and pulled her close. Pressing her head against
his heart, he ached to say something to make it easier.
But he knew nothing ever made death easy. Especially the death of a newborn.

He rubbed her back, infinitely glad that she wasn't
weeping so desperately anymore. He bent and brushed
a kiss on her temple. She drew in a long, uneven breath
and slipped her hand into his open shirt. Tal's heart
bumped. He felt heat pooling in his middle, felt the
instantaneous swell of his manhood. She moved her

head, pressed her lips to his chest, sifted through the dark curling hair with her fingers, found his flat nipples. Kissed him.

Ah, Stephanie, Stephanie. What are you doing?

"I want to make love," she whispered, as if she'd heard his question.

He caught her face between his hands so that he could look at her. See into those sad eyes what she needed. "Are you sure?"

"Yes."

No force on earth could stop him from lowering his head to kiss her pain away. He meant to be gentle, to go slowly. She was wounded. He didn't want to take advantage of her.

But Stephanie wasn't behaving like a woman wounded. She was like a woman starved. She opened to him, welcoming the heated hunger in his kiss. With her mouth sealed to his, she pushed his shirt off his shoulders, wresting a small grunt from him as she pulled it free at his waist. She paused, sat back on her knees and, holding his gaze, drew her nightgown slowly over her head. Caught in her fire, he watched her fling it aside, then reach to unbuckle his belt. He felt a fierce surge of desire. And delight. If this was escape for her, then so be it.

Impatience made him push her hands aside and tear his belt open. He lifted to pull off his pants and briefs, looking at her, telling her with his eyes how much he wanted her. His breath caught at the beauty of her breasts, the ripe weight of them. His gaze lowered to the rounded swell of her belly. His child. The thought was so arousing that it stunned him.

He had always been the aggressor in their lovemaking, but with her like this, he only wanted to lie back and experience whatever she had in mind.

And then she straddled him.

"DON'T SAY A WORD."

Tal turned his head lazily and looked at her. She was gazing at the ceiling, her hair a tawny tangle on the pillow, the sheet pulled up primly beneath her arms. To his disappointment, her beautiful breasts were covered. "Not even one?"

"Well..."

"Wow."

She almost smiled.

He shifted suddenly, raised himself onto one elbow and pulled a strand of hair away from her cheek. Something about the sweet curve of her jaw touched him. "Stephanie, Stephanie, Stephanie." He shook his head. "You want to tell me what was going on just now?"

"Are you complaining?"

"Are you crazy? You are one incredibly sexy lady. I must have been wearing blinders for the past few years not to have snatched you up long ago. Or I was dead from the neck up. Or..." his glance grazed the window, then came back to her "...was it none of that? Did you purposely keep a low profile? You didn't want to be noticed, did you?"

"Not by you, no."

It hurt to hear her say it. She turned on her side then, propped on one elbow the same as Tal so that they were face-to-face. "What I mean is that I never allowed myself to think of you in that way."

"Why not?"

"Not because I didn't fancy you," she said with a chagrined smile. "But fantasies like that are dangerous."

"Dangerous?"

"Yes. I like to keep my feet solidly on the ground. You set yourself up for pain and suffering if you believe dreams can come true. Reality is just too harsh."

The sheet had slipped a little, baring the curve of one breast. He touched a dusky areola and smiled at the small catch of Stephanie's breath. He looked into her eyes. "Pretty."

"I don't know how you do that," she said. It was almost a wail.

"Do what?"

"Just a touch or a look and I get . . . breathless."

"The same thing happens to me," he said, slowly stroking her breast. "From you, all it takes is a touch or a look and I get hard."

"Really?"

He drew back to see if she was serious. "Really, Stephanie." He took her hand and proved it.

She blushed and he laughed softly, not resisting when she placed her hand on his waist. They looked at each other for a few moments, thinking private thoughts. When Tal spoke, his smile was gone. "Do you want our marriage to be permanent, Stephanie?"

He could tell from her expression, she hadn't expected his question. "What is it? Shouldn't I have asked that?"

"No. No. It's...you just surprised me." She stared at the ring on her third finger. "Of course I want our marriage to last."

"Do you think it will?"

"I don't know," she said so softly he barely heard the words.

"Why?"

One pale shoulder lifted. "So many reasons."

"Alison? Keely? The baby? Our careers? Our different backgrounds—as you so often point out—to name a few."

"Yes."

"I don't think any of those reasons will be what does us in, sweetheart."

She searched his face, letting her gaze roam all over it. "What, then?"

"It'll be because you don't believe in fantasy."

She frowned, wrinkling a patch of freckles on her nose, and he forced himself not to haul her into his arms and kiss away that frown. She was so beautiful even without makeup, natural and fresh-looking. He couldn't believe his luck. If only he could make her believe in their marriage. Believe in him.

He slipped his fingers through her hair just below her ear, cupping her face and drawing it close to his. "Listen, just because you were unlucky in your childhood and with that jerk you were first married to doesn't mean that you're destined to be unlucky forever. You found Camille, didn't you? You have a career many women envy." He smiled crookedly. "You're married to a helluva nice guy now. Forget how you're challenged daily by two teenage daughters."

"I'll be happy to."

He grinned. "So fantasize all you want. I sure as hell plan to. I want this marriage to last and I believe in it. In you. We've got everything it takes to make it work."

She studied him candidly. "What makes you think Donald was a jerk?"

He made a face. "Was that his name, Donald?"

"Uh-huh."

"Any man who let you get away is a jerk."

She laughed softly. "Thanks."

He sobered. "Want to tell me why it went sour?"

"He hated my choice of profession, can you believe that?"

Tal looked confused. "You were an intern when you married, weren't you?"

"Yes, and he thought it would be neat having a wife who was a physician. He'd already finished law school. I think he imagined we'd set up a practice doing medical liability and get rich. He didn't count on the time and energy it would take for me to get through residency. He didn't do dishes and he didn't cook," she added dryly. "But he found somebody else who did and brought her right into our house. One day I opened our bedroom door and there they were. It's so different being married to you."

"No wonder you hate picking up after me."

"Well, I may be a tad compulsive when it comes to neatness."

He touched her nose. "It's your way of having some control over your life. You need to keep your world tidy and straight. Your childhood offered enough chaos and uncertainty to last a lifetime."

She smiled into his eyes. "Thanks for understanding."

He didn't want thanks. He just wanted her to keep talking, to tell him as much as she would about herself. "Do you realize that I've learned more about you tonight than in all the rest of the time we've known each other?"

She dropped her eyes. "It's not personal. I hope you believe that."

He didn't think it was, but now he knew about her first marriage, he wondered if she would ever really trust him. "Have I made you happy, Stephanie?"

"Yes, of course."

He nodded with satisfaction. "Good. There's more where that came from."

Stephanie gazed somewhere beyond his shoulder. "Maybe that's it, Tal. It's scary when things are too good. When you feel too happy, the gods become jealous."

"Or the gods reward deserving people," he said quietly.

"Not always," she said, the sad look back in her eyes.

"You're thinking about Jolene?"

Her eyes filled again.

"Don't cry again, sweetheart."

She shook her head mutely, while he struggled to find something to say to ease her pain. But he knew exactly how she felt. Fortunately, it didn't happen too often, but sometimes you worked over a critical patient, probed into blood and tissue and muscle, battled the clock ticking away precious seconds, only to watch death snatch the life away.

"The baby was just too tiny, too sick," Stephanie said, wiping away a tear. "And Jolene was so brave." Her hand moved idly across his skin. "She wanted that baby, you know. The father was some street tough who couldn't have cared less, but she decided right away that she didn't need him. Didn't need anyone except her baby." She looked at Tal. "What will she do now? I'm afraid she'll just give up like her mother has. She's smart, Tal. And funny and quick and...and a *good* person. A wonderful human being. Why did it have to happen to Jolene?"

He pulled her close, settling back with her head on his chest, next to his heart. "You know better than to ask that one, Steph. Bad things happen to good people."

She was silent. It was one of the mysteries for which there was no answer.

CHAPTER ELEVEN

*Pregnancy takes a full nine months out
of your life. Other events are bound
to occur, some good, some bad, which
may challenge your ability to cope.
Try to keep your stress level low
during pregnancy. At trying times,
your mate's moral support can make all
the difference.*

—*Ask Dr. Meredith*

February 13, 1996/28 weeks

THE NURSES' STATION on two-west was the usual bustle of activity. While the patient load in other areas usually dropped after the holidays, it was business as usual in the maternity ward. Babies had their own personal calendars.

Stephanie stopped at the counter. As she pulled her pen from her lab-coat pocket to make a note on a patient's chart, she spoke to Pete Haywood, who gave her a distracted wave without breaking rhythm as he dropped medication into tiny paper cups. Laughter came from the visitors' lounge. Seinfeld reruns, she thought. A couple strolled by the station, hands linked, faces happy. Across the way, a new grandfather proudly showed a picture of his two-hour-old grandson to a relative who'd missed the birth. The ward overflowed with cheer and flower arrangements.

With her pen poised over the chart, Stephanie smiled. The mound that was her own child was pressed against the counter. He gave a firm kick in protest. She chuckled and Pete looked up. At seven months, she considered herself huge, no matter how Tal chose to phrase it. She was not "blooming" and "earthy" and "fruitful", she was huge. But she was happier than she'd ever been.

That thought instantly stirred old ghosts. In spite of Tal, she felt a little wary to be so happy. She stopped, looked outside where bright February sun made the fierce pink of azaleas appear even more startling. It was almost spring in New Orleans. Eight more weeks to go. A sonogram taken after Christmas had confirmed her belief that the baby was a boy. Tal had chalked one up for her, but he couldn't hide his joy and pride.

She shifted from one foot to the other and put down her pen to rub her right thigh. It had been the strangest thing. A few hours ago, she'd been standing with her stethoscope against a patient's heart when a blinding pain had made her gasp. Her thigh and neck had been aching ever since. Suddenly, Tessa came to mind. She used to—

"Dr. Sheldon?"

She turned to acknowledge her name and saw a uniformed officer. She read the patch on his shoulder; "Louisiana Highway Patrol."

"Dr. Stephanie Sheldon?" he repeated, looking at her intently.

She smiled politely. "That's right."

He glanced around the busy station. "Could we go someplace private, do you think?"

Her heart began beating heavily. She didn't move. "What is it, Officer?"

Making a quick survey, he found the coffee room off the nurses' station and gave a little jerk of his head in that direction. "If you'd just step over here, I'd appreciate it, ma'am."

He extended his arm, not touching her, and she moved numbly into the coffee room. He followed and closed the door behind him.

"Please," she whispered. "What is it? Is it my husband? Is he all right?"

"It's not your husband, ma'am, but I do believe it's your sister. Would you happen to have a sister by the name of Tessa Hamilton?"

She squeezed her hand into a fist. "Tessa?"

"Yes, ma'am. She noted on her ID that you were to be notified as next of kin."

"Oh, my God." She reached behind her, clung to the edge of the counter.

"Ah, ma'am—" He looked around for a chair, then jerked the door open. "I need a chair in here!" he yelled.

Pete rushed inside. "What's wrong? Dr. Sheldon!"

"She needs to sit down," the officer said.

"No, I...I'm okay." She touched her mouth. "What...what happened?"

"There was an accident on the interstate," the officer said, flipping open his notebook. "At the six-ten split where traffic merges heading to Metairie, this lady was westbound when an eighteen-wheeler forced her against the guardrail. She—"

"Please . . ." She pressed her hand hard against her lips. "How bad is it?"

"Yeah, get to the point, Officer!" Pete shoved a chair toward Stephanie, who sank into it gratefully.

"The vehicle looked worse than it actually was," the officer said, referring to his notes.

"How bad was it, Officer?" Pete demanded evenly.

"Well, Ms. Hamilton has a broken collarbone, I know that. Could tell it from other accidents I've covered. She's banged up pretty good, and she broke her leg."

With a weak sound, Stephanie rubbed her thigh.

"I'm no doctor," the patrolman continued, "so I can't speculate on internal stuff, but the EMTs said nothing was life-threatening, barring complications, naturally. They brought her to the emergency room here. Somebody recognized Dr. Sheldon's name."

"My sister is downstairs right now?" Stephanie demanded.

"Yes, ma'am. Sure is. I mean, she's definitely your sister." He shook his head. "You two are bookends, is what you are."

Stephanie stood up. Pete tried to stop her. "Dr. Sheldon, I can't leave the station, you know that. If you'll wait a second, I'll page Dr. Robichaux and he can—"

"Tell him to meet me there," she said, shoving the chart into his hands, and before he could object, she was gone.

"STEPHANIE."

With a small cry, she rushed into Tal's arms. He held her tight, feeling her fear and bewilderment.

"I was in surgery, sweetheart. I just heard."

"It's okay, I knew . . . I remembered later that you had an early surgery. And I haven't been able to see Tessa. They took her straight to O.R."

He took her hand and walked with her over to a sofa and sat down with her. "How bad are her injuries, honey?"

Stephanie swallowed, drew in a cleansing breath to try to get herself together. She wasn't acting like a physician, she was acting like a hysterical wimp. But with Tal beside her, she found she was able to think again. Rationally.

"I think she's going to be all right. She has a damaged spleen, that's what the surgery is about. Sheila Carson is doing it."

"She's good."

"Uh-huh. She also has some bruised ribs and her leg is broken. Her right leg." Unconsciously, she massaged her own thigh as she spoke. Reaching over, Tal covered her hand and she winced.

"What's wrong?"

"Oh, nothing. Tessa's break must have been there."

"And so your thigh aches?" He looked taken aback. "I thought that was a twin-myth thing."

She shrugged. "Not really. It used to happen all the time with Tessa and me, but after she left and time passed . . . it just went away. Sort of. Once in a while, I still got little flashes, but I suppressed them because they were too painful. I didn't know where she was, or if she was even alive."

She turned her hand and clasped his. "Then after I married you, and Keely came, I stopped resisting them. I think I was trying to communicate with Tessa. To tell her to come back. Tell her that we needed her."

Her voice broke. "But not like this. I didn't want her broken and bleeding."

Tal slipped an arm around her and pulled her close. "She's going to be all right, honey. From the sound of her injuries, she'll recover." He tipped her face up and gave her a quick kiss on the nose. "Who knows? Sounds like you might have summoned her up with those mysterious flashes."

She searched his dark eyes, thinking he was teasing her. And he was, in a way. And yet, there was something more—sympathy, a sincere effort to reassure her, affection. In that instant, lost in his gaze, Stephanie realized how important this man had become to her. She honestly couldn't imagine living without Tal now. It was a scary thought. Her old demons were having a field day. Was it only this morning that she'd been at the nurses' station daydreaming about the husband that she'd fallen in love with, communing with their unborn son, savoring a life that was pretty special?

Her thoughts were interrupted when the doors opened and Sheila Carson appeared. A colleague of Tal's, Sheila was a redhead in her midforties and one of Women's Hospital's finest surgeons. Stephanie scrambled off the seat. "Sheila, how is she?"

"She's fine." Sheila pulled the cap from her wiry curls and shook her head. "She's healthy, a fighter." A smile appeared. "She mentioned you."

Stephanie drew a quick breath. "She's awake?"

Sheila shrugged. "Not really. You know what happens with anesthesia. Some folks talk. Your twin is one of them." She gave Stephanie a keen look. "It's remarkable, really. The two of you are incredibly alike. Two peas in a pod."

"Yes." She felt Tal's arm come around her waist and drew in a cleansing breath. "How about her spleen?"

The physician launched into a technical analysis of Tessa's injuries, finally convincing both that the danger was past. If there were no complications, Tessa would be out of recovery and into a hospital room within two hours, she told them.

"I want to see her now," Stephanie stated.

"Of course," Sheila said.

Tal walked with Stephanie to the double doors of the recovery room and stopped. "Do you want me to come with you?"

This was a moment she'd wondered would ever happen, a reunion with Tessa. Should it be shared? Even by Tal who sometimes seemed to understand Stephanie better than she did herself? But could anyone understand the mystifying link between twins? The unspoken communication, the shared joy and hurt, the discoveries and disappointments?

She lifted on her toes and gave him a soft kiss. "Thank you, but no, not this time."

TEARS WELLED instantly in her eyes as Stephanie looked at the woman lying on the bed. Tessa, her mirror image. She was pale, neck and one cheek slightly bruised, but otherwise unmarked by her ordeal. Her right leg was encased in a thick cast and elevated. Thankfully, she was sleeping peacefully, but it would be different when she awoke. A broken leg was painful, but when coupled with surgery, it was doubly traumatic. On a pole hung plastic bottles supplying medication through the IV in Tessa's left hand.

Her right hand lay across her waist. Stephanie touched it and felt an instant connection.

"Tessa," she whispered brokenly.

There was the faintest movement of Tessa's eyelids.

Stephanie took the hand, as familiar as her own, and squeezed gently. "It's me, Tee." The childhood nickname came naturally.

Tessa stirred and the beeping of the machine monitoring her heartbeat accelerated. Fear. Vulnerability. Panic. Stephanie felt everything as if the electrodes were connected to her body, too.

"Don't worry," she reassured her. "You're safe now, Tee. I'm here."

Don't leave me.

"I won't leave you."

The recovery nurse appeared beside Stephanie. "She's coming along beautifully, Dr. Sheldon." She glanced at the big clock on the wall. "Another thirty minutes and she'll be on her way to her room. You can meet us there."

"I can't leave her," Stephanie murmured, holding on to Tessa's hand.

The nurse turned, prepared to do battle. A quick visit in recovery was one thing, an indefinite stay—regardless of rank—was against the rules.

"Please," Stephanie whispered, reading the woman's mind.

"Well..."

Suddenly, Tessa spoke weakly. "Steph...is it... really... you?"

Stephanie laughed softly, cradling Tessa's hand against her cheek. "Yeah, it's really me, Tee." She managed a watery smile. "Welcome back. I've missed you."

"What..." Tessa licked dry lips "...h-happened?"

"You were in an accident."

Tessa made a small sound, remembering. "Um...big...truck."

"You were lucky. You're going to be okay."

"Huh." Derisive and blunt. Vintage Tessa.

"Cross my heart," Stephanie said with a smile in her voice. "It's nothing we can't fix."

"So...so sorry."

Stephanie squeezed Tessa's limp fingers. "There's nothing to be sorry about, Tee. The truck driver was at fault."

"No..."

Stephanie realized she wasn't talking about the accident.

"Years..." Tessa couldn't open her eyes, but her fingers fluttered. "So many years."

"We'll make them up," Stephanie promised huskily.

Seconds ticked by silently. Stephanie was sure Tessa had drifted back into a drug-induced sleep, when she felt the hand in hers stir again. "Keely..."

Keely? Did Tessa know Keely was here? "Keely is with me, Tessa."

Tessa managed to nod. "I...know. Good...thing."

"She's beautiful, Tee."

"Tell...I love...her."

"I'll tell her."

There were no more words. With a tight throat, Stephanie watched a tear slip from the corner of Tessa's eye and roll slowly down her bruised cheek.

"Rest now, Tee." She bent and kissed Tessa, then moved aside as the nurse appeared. Tessa's heartbeat, monitored by the machine, evened out in sleep.

TESSA WAS WHEELED out of recovery around 6:00 p.m. As the orderlies and the charge nurse on the floor were making her comfortable, Stephanie and Tal talked outside.

"It's the most incredible thing, Tal," she said, unconsciously rubbing the small of her back. "Tessa is the administrator of a halfway house for troubled teenage girls."

"No kidding?"

"Yeah, in Florida. How's that for a coincidence?"

He moved her hand and began a gentle massage of her back. "You mean, 'Twins separated at birth choose identical careers?' Why are you surprised? That kind of thing has been documented many times in studies about twins."

"I suppose." Stephanie closed her eyes as Tal touched a tense muscle. "Mmm, that feels good... I don't have many details. I found out when the Juvenile officer from the New Orleans Police Department stopped by to check on Tessa after learning about her accident from the highway patrol. Tessa was driving to New Orleans to pick up two runaways who were in custody here. She's been working with Juvenile authorities in Pensacola for over two years, Tal. Two years!" She sighed. "I don't know what to make of it. Her own daughter a runaway, a waif of the state, and she's taking care of other people's children."

"It's puzzling, but there may be a perfectly logical reason, honey. Don't judge yet."

Relaxed a little by the magic of his hands, she nodded. "You're probably right."

"How about grabbing a bite in the cafeteria while they're getting Tessa settled?" he suggested.

"I'm not sure I should leave her just yet, Tal." She glanced in the room where Tessa lay quietly as the nurse took her vitals. "If she needs me, I should be nearby."

"That's why I suggested the cafeteria instead of going home. I knew you wouldn't want to leave the hospital."

"Well . . ."

"She's fine, Stephanie. You've been hovering over her since the moment she was admitted over six hours ago. You need to sit down yourself, relax; eat something. Remember the baby."

She put her hand to her forehead. "I know. It's just . . ."

"It's just that after all these years, suddenly Tessa is back. All the more reason to step back and get a grip on the situation."

She almost smiled. "Am I losing my grip?"

His arm around her tightened. "No, and you won't." He rested a hand on her waist just as the baby thumped hard against her side. "Yo, what was that?"

She chuckled. "Your son. He had his feet up and you disturbed him."

He moved his hand directly over her belly. "Little rascal," he said, his tone dropping. He smiled into Stephanie's eyes. "So, what do you say, Mama? Break time?"

The nurse came out of the room. "Oh, hi, Dr. Robichaux. Dr. Sheldon, your sister is resting well. The femur fracture was a clean one, luckily. It'll ache a bit, no doubt. She's also having a little pain with the incision, but she refused the narcotic that was authorized. I noted it on her chart. Her temperature and blood pressure are normal." She passed the chart over.

"If you want to grab a bite, now's a good time. I promise we won't neglect the patient."

Stephanie met Tal's eyes and laughed. "Okay, okay, let's go."

THE LOUNGE was deserted. Tal set a tray on the coffee table while Stephanie eased down onto a leather sofa. Before she could prevent it, a groan escaped.

"Here, drink this." Tal handed her something pink and healthy-looking.

"What is it?"

"A shake with banana, yogurt, strawberries and papaya."

She took it, wrinkling her nose. "My kingdom for a gin and tonic."

He chuckled, lifting his own glass, which held something dark and alcoholic with tons of ice. "Eight weeks and counting."

She drank a little of the concoction and rested the glass on her tummy. "I'm still trying to take it in, Tal."

"Tessa?"

"Yes. After all these years."

He nodded. "It's a shock, all right."

"It's the strangest thing." Stephanie traced the design on her glass. "She knew Keely was here with me. It's one thing to cut me out of her life, but her own daughter... I just don't understand it, especially now that I know about her job."

"What did she say?"

"Nothing, really. She hasn't explained anything yet."

"She's still very groggy, Steph. And in pain. It's probably beyond her to deal with anything else right now."

"I know that, of course," Stephanie murmured, leaning her head back and closing her eyes.

There was a moment of silence. From the hall came the sounds of the hospital, the constant ding of the telephone system, voices as people passed by. Beside her, ice cubes clinked softly in Tal's glass.

"I knew you had a twin," he said suddenly, "but still it's odd to see someone who looks exactly like you, and yet isn't you."

"Odd in what way?"

"It's hard to explain. Tessa is a carbon copy of you, but I didn't feel any special connection with her. She's a complete stranger in spite of being your mirror image. The differences in you go deeper than your physical resemblance." He sat hunched forward, cradling his drink in both hands, elbows on his knees. "That surprised me."

"Why?"

He looked at her, making no attempt to hide anything. "Because I'm intensely aware of you, of everything about you. The way you walk, the way you talk, the look you get when you're happy or sad or aroused." He smiled when she quickly looked away. "Even the way you look when you're embarrassed."

"I'm not embarrassed."

"Oh, no?"

"I'm ... well, I'm ... I guess I'm embarrassed."

"You're adorable, is what you are."

She looked warily at the door. Anybody could come in and find them ... what? Talking? Having a drink together?

No. Anybody could come in and catch me being seduced by my husband.

As the thought formed, the door burst open. It was Keely, out of breath and agitated. "Is it true?" she demanded. "Is my mother here? Did she have an accident on the interstate?"

"Keely, she's okay." Before Stephanie could stand up, Tal put a hand on her knee.

"No, don't get up." Then he looked at Keely. "Your mother is here. There was an accident. She had some surgery and came though it without any problems. She's being settled in a room right now. We'll take you there if you'll wait for Steph to finish her drink. She's been on her feet since your mother was admitted."

"Why didn't you call me?" Keely cried, talking to both of them.

"We thought we should wait until she was out of recovery," Tal replied. "You wouldn't have been allowed in, anyway."

"She could have died!"

"No, Keely. There was never any danger of that," Tal said.

Keely swallowed convulsively, looking from Stephanie to Tal and then back again. She seemed rooted to the floor, her eyes bright and anxious. She was nothing like the brash, tough-talking teenager whose precociousness entertained them nightly at the dinner table. She was the homeless waif who had appeared in Stephanie's class looking for a substitute mom. Wordlessly, Stephanie opened her arms, and with a choked cry, Keely flew to her, burying her face in her aunt's embrace.

Stephanie held her close while the young girl sobbed. She stroked her bright hair, murmuring comforting words until the storm of weeping eased.

"I—I n-never thought I'd s-see her again," Keely said. With her head resting on Stephanie's breast, she gazed bleakly through the window. "I thought sh-she was *dead!*"

"I know, love," Stephanie said, her own thoughts in nearly as much turmoil as Keely's. But she had known Tessa was somewhere out there. She had felt it.

"Have you talked to her yet?" Keely asked.

"Only briefly and she was still groggy from the anesthetic." She tucked a strand of hair behind Keely's ear. "She said she loved you."

Keely sniffed, took a swipe at her nose. "Did she say why she . . . why she . . . just . . ."

"She hasn't explained anything, Keely."

The girl sat up then, wiping her eyes with both hands. Her young mouth was set, her chin firm. "Because she can't. There isn't any explanation for what she did."

Tal and Stephanie looked at each other, both silent. What was there to say to that?

"YOU LOOK GOOD, Steph." Tessa plumped her pillow and settled on her side. It was the first time they'd had a chance to really talk.

Stephanie laughed. "I'm big as a hippopotamus, my ankles are swollen, I need help sitting down and getting up again, I cannot find a comfortable sleeping position, no matter how I try, and you say I look good?"

"You look happy."

Stephanie's smile softened. "Now that you're here, Tee, I'm very happy."

"I meant marriage and motherhood. Tal Robichaux is a lucky guy. He almost deserves you."

Stephanie stared, tilting her head. "You sound as if you know Tal."

"I know *of* him."

"How, Tee? How could you know anything about Tal?"

"I checked him out soon after the two of you were married."

Stephanie leaned forward, hands on her thighs. "You *checked him out?* How did you do that? And how did you know I was married? It was sudden. Everyone was taken by surprise."

"I called Camille. She told me all about him."

"Camille? Camille told you about— You've been in touch with Camille? Camille knew all along where you were?" Stephanie got to her feet, a struggle, considering her bulk. "Are you telling me that Camille has known your whereabouts all these years? She let me wonder and worry and fret, when with a word, she could have—"

"No! No. She only knew when Keely went to live with you."

Stephanie stared speechlessly for a long moment. "I think you need to start from the beginning, Tessa," she said quietly. "Keely is filled with doubt and anger and questions that I'm finding difficult to answer. Now you drop the bombshell that Camille has known your whereabouts for months. It's three days since your accident. Let's have it, the whole story." She folded her hands in her lap and waited.

"You've got that look, you know," Tessa said, shaking her head.

"What look?"

"The one you used to give me when I was contemplating something bad and you were determined to save me from myself."

"But I never could, could I?"

"Save me from myself? No, Steph. You were only human, after all."

Memories crowded in on Stephanie. The misery of their childhood, the drudgery of the farm, the horrors of the house in town, the scandal that broke over their heads, the panic and fear that sent them fleeing from Memphis into the night. The bus boarded before dawn after collecting every penny they could scrape together for the fares, winding up in Jackson, Mississippi. From that point, hitching to New Orleans on a cold, rainy day in January. Then Camille. Ah, thank God for Camille.

A brief knock sounded on the door and a nurse came into the room bearing medication. "Tessa Hamilton, right?"

"That's me." Tessa eyed the contents of the tiny paper cup suspiciously, then pressed a button elevating the top of the bed. "What's that?"

"One is an antibiotic and the other is for pain." The nurse smiled, handing it over, then filled the plastic drinking cup from the decanter on the bedside table. She looked puzzled when Tessa took only the antibiotic. "You don't want the pain medication?"

"No, no narcotics."

"Well, if you're sure." She chuckled. "However, it's a rare patient who refuses the painkillers, isn't that right, Dr. Sheldon? Most of the time, we have our hands full trying to keep them from taking too much of the stuff." She made a notation on Tessa's chart and slipped it back in the rack mounted on the wall. "See you later."

Stephanie waited until the nurse was gone. "I know that leg has to be throbbing, Tee. Your incision, too. You're also running a low-grade temperature. The pain medication would relax you, help you rest. That's what your body needs right now to get you on your feet again."

Tessa gave a short, humorless laugh. "That's the last thing *my* body needs."

"Nothing's wrong with taking medication to relieve pain, Tessa. Even the bravest man would groan over a ruptured spleen, a broken collarbone and a fractured femur."

"I would rather suffer the tortures of hell than to take a single narcotic ever again, Steph."

Stephanie sat down and settled back, hands folded on her swollen middle. "Do you want to explain that?"

Tessa turned her face toward the window and spoke softly. "I was a terrible mother, Steph. I got pregnant about a year after leaving you and Camille. The father—" she made a derisive sound "—was the guy you hated who had been trying to sell us drugs in high school, remember?"

"Ray Somebody? Big senior with biceps?"

Tessa nodded. "Thanks to steroids. Yeah, Ray Hytower. He disappeared even before Keely was born. Which I know now was a good thing. All that responsibility, you know."

"Oh, Tessa."

"So, there I was, eighteen and unwed, uneducated, scared and penniless. I vowed to be a good mother, which shows what a naive twit I was. I got a job at the hospital where Keely was born, in the administrator's office. A year later, I married a guy who sold pharmaceuticals, Richard Hamilton. Big mistake. He was into cocaine, but when he was clean, he was actually decent. He adopted Keely. But eventually, the drugs took over and I had to get out."

"Were you using then?"

"A little. But after the divorce, the pain, more failure, a child . . . yeah, if there was a point where I truly lost it, then I would have to say that was it. Keely was seven."

"She says she went into foster care for the first time when she was seven."

"That's right. I checked out the couple." She glanced at Stephanie and shrugged. "I wanted to be sure she was in good hands. Then I went into rehab."

"Good for you."

Tessa laughed humorlessly. "The program didn't take, not that first time."

"What then?"

"After that first attempt at rehab, I got Keely back and began a merry-go-round of rehab, then a job, then a relapse and more rehab." She gave Stephanie a clear-eyed look. "I didn't sleep around, Steph. I did a lot of things I'm not proud of, but not that. Besides, men and relationships...you can imagine the trouble I had with that."

"You had reason, Tessa. You had been . . ."

"Raped. Say the word, Steph."

"It sounds so . . . I can't say it, even now."

Oddly, it was Tessa who reached for Stephanie's hand. "You need to say it, Steph. You need to face what happened to us. I don't think you ever did."

"I don't want to think about it, Tessa. It's a part of the past that I want to forget. I was lucky. It was you who—" She swallowed, closed her eyes. "Do we have to talk about this?"

"Not yet, huh?" Tessa squeezed her hand. "It's okay. I've gotten beyond it. God knows, I had enough therapy to wash out a thousand bad pasts."

"In rehab, you mean?"

"Yeah. I kept trying to clean up my act, Steph. But good intentions just aren't enough sometimes. I kept falling back into my need for drugs. And the real victim was my daughter. I really hit bottom when Keely was taken from me. Then, when she ran away—just disappeared off the face of the earth—I thought I would die. She was thirteen. I went into the program that time with a changed attitude, I can tell you. Nothing like losing your child to make you straighten up and fly right. I've been clean and sober ever since."

Stephanie was confused. "But you said you knew Keely was here, with me. Why didn't you come? This has devastated her, Tessa."

Tessa turned to the window again. "You probably won't understand this, but from the day I left, you've never been far from my thoughts. I was in New Orleans several times over the years just to see how you were getting along. Sometimes I think keeping that link with you saved my sanity."

All that time, worrying and wondering. Stephanie was shaking her head.

"I knew when you went to med school and when you married that bonehead Donald McNeil."

"You must have been talking to Tal," Stephanie muttered.

"What?"

"I assume you cheered when I filed for the divorce."

"No. I knew firsthand how painful it felt to fail, especially at marriage. Knowing you, I knew it would be particularly hard."

"That doesn't explain why you cut yourself off from Keely." Stephanie repeated.

"When she turned up in your teen-pregnancy class—"

"You know about that?"

"Yes. I was terrified that she was pregnant. It would have been a repeat of the dysfunction and wrong choices that had ruined our mother's life and my own. But Keely's different, she's strong. Like you." There was pride and love in Tessa's smile and bright tears in her eyes. "Somehow...s-somehow, she had managed to track you down, the good twin, the best half of a matched pair, the twin who should have been her mother."

"Tessa!" Stephanie's eyes widened in shock.

Tessa drew a deep breath. "It's true. Having Keely here with you is a thousand times better than the life I could offer her. Look at your career, where you live, your family life... Why, Keely has a sister now."

"Alison?" Stephanie asked weakly. Sisters? Those two seldom exchanged a civil word.

"It was meant to be, Steph."

Stephanie was shaking her head. "I can't believe you're saying all this, Tee. I can't believe you *believe* it. Keely is your daughter, not mine. You have a job just as important as mine, maybe even more. You've overcome astonishing adversity. As a role model, nothing is as strong as that. If I hadn't seen you refuse that pain pill, I'd say drugs were making you crazy."

Tessa lay back, folding her hands on top of the sheet. "Just think about it. You'll see I'm right."

Stephanie was almost amused. It was so like Tessa to come up with a cockamamy idea like this, worry it through in her head to some goofy conclusion and settle back satisfied that everybody else would see it her way, too.

From the look on her twin's face, she knew better than to try to convince Tessa how wrongheaded she was this time. That argument could wait.

Just then, there was a brief knock on the door, left standing ajar by the nurse. Tal came into the room.

His gaze went directly to Stephanie. Something about his look made her heart flutter. His smile was . . . cool, that was the only word. He kissed her, a quick peck on the mouth, then greeted Tessa. "Hey, how's it going, Tessa?"

"Hi, Tal. I'm okay."

He was in his lab coat, opened to reveal the blue oxford button-down and a tie that Keely had given him for Christmas. He looked good, fiercely masculine. Her eyes narrowed. Fierce, definitely. What was wrong?

"You two have a nice visit?" His tone was clipped as they made their way across the parking lot. They'd spent only a few more minutes with Tessa, and then, because Stephanie sensed Tal's impatience, they had left, promising to bring Keely later.

"We were just catching up," she said, waiting for him to unlock the car. "You'll never believe what she said."

He looked directly at her with eyes that were flashing dark fire. "Try me."

She slipped into the seat uncertainly, buckling up while searching her mind for reasons that Tal was angry. It had been a long time since she'd seen this side of him. Chewing her lip, she watched him stride around the car and then get inside. He didn't start the engine, but sat in his seat and looked straight ahead. At nothing.

"What's wrong, Tal?"

"What could be wrong?" His voice was curiously flat. "You were going to tell me your sister's secrets. Come on, I'm waiting. I know damn good and well I'll never hear yours, so I guess Tessa's are the next best thing."

"What on earth are you talking about?"

He did look at her then. "The rape, Stephanie. I was standing at the door when the two of you were talking. I knocked, but you were so caught up in the past that you didn't hear me. Why? What did you think would happen if you told me? *What the hell kind of marriage do we have if you can't tell me something like that!*" He emphasized every other word by banging his fist on the steering wheel.

Her heart dropped. God, here it was. What she'd feared would happen some day. Oh, it was so ugly. So sordid. She covered her baby protectively with her hands, as if to shield him from the truth.

"How many other secrets are you keeping, Stephanie?"

"I want to go home now," she said quietly.

He didn't move. She watched him struggle with frustration and a purely male need to bend her will to his. More seconds ticked by while he gazed beyond her into the twilight, then with a smothered oath he reached for the ignition, brutally racing the engine when it caught.

"Home it is," he said, sarcasm tainting the word. When he pulled out of the car park, gravel spurted wildly beneath the tires.

Stephanie remained silent.

CHAPTER TWELVE

*It shouldn't come as a surprise that
your mate is subject to some of the
emotional upheaval that you are
experiencing. Men are generally not as
forthcoming about their feelings as
women. Look for signs that your mate
may be feeling needy. Real
communication flows in a relationship
built on love and trust.*

—Ask Dr. Meredith

February 13, 1996/28 weeks

"I DON'T WANT to go and see her. I've thought about
it and made up my mind."

"She's your mother, Keely. She loves you."

"Huh! Some mother. Some love."

Stephanie closed her eyes, too easily understanding. "You don't want to go tonight, or you don't want
to go at all...ever?"

"Not tonight, for sure. Maybe never."

Stephanie studied the stony little profile. "I can
understand that, Keely. I'm feeling pretty stunned by
all this myself, but the alternative is worse. I don't
want Tessa to walk away for another seventeen years."

The baby shifted suddenly, giving her a hefty kick. With a grunt, Stephanie sat down on the edge of Keely's bed. It had been a terrible day. Fatigue lay like a lead weight on her shoulders. Downstairs, Tal was holed up in the den, barely speaking to her. Alison was in her bedroom pouting, bewildered by the tension pervading the whole house. Even the baby was cantankerous.

Unlike the others, Keely at least had good reasons for her attitude. Having had no contact with her mother for three years, she had been harboring the secret fear that Tessa was dead. Worse yet was discovering that Tessa knew where her daughter was once Keely got to Stephanie in New Orleans. The girl's emotions had been in upheaval since her mother's sudden appearance. An adult would have difficulty dealing with this; for an adolescent, it was nothing short of traumatic.

Keely turned with a bewildered expression. "Why did she act like she did, Steph? Did she think a kid didn't need a mother? That's dumb, no matter how old the kid is." She looked upward, clearly holding back tears, then said fiercely, "You know what? The real miracle is that I didn't run away sooner!"

Stephanie took her hand. "I understand how you feel, Keely. And you know what? I think those questions should be answered by your mother, not me. Tessa is the only person who can answer them."

"I don't want to see her *or* talk to her," she repeated.

"I'm afraid you'll have to, sooner or later."

Keely looked defiant. "Why? She hasn't shown any interest in me. Or you, either. You should be as mad as I am."

"Maybe I am a little bit," Stephanie admitted. "I think it's okay for us both to be ticked off. Honest feelings are okay." She touched the mutinous little chin. "As for her forgetting about us, I know you're wrong about that. But, again, you need to ask *her* about these things."

"Huh. We'll probably get there and she'll have disappeared again."

Stephanie stood up. "I don't think so, sweetie. With that broken leg, your mom will be anchored for a while."

"I guess that could be a real problem for her, couldn't it?" Keely got off the bed and reached for her Nikes.

Stephanie waited, hoping the girl would say more. When she didn't, Stephanie prompted her, "Got any ideas?"

Before looking at Stephanie, Keely's gaze swept over the room that she had occupied since September. Between them were thoughts of the vastness of the Robichaux house. Four bedrooms were unoccupied. "Not really."

"C'mon, Keely. You must have a couple of ideas."

"You mean . . . maybe she could stay here?"

"I'd like that. At least for a while . . . until she's on her feet again. Of course, I'd have to ask Tal."

Keely shrugged. "It's your house. You can invite anybody you please, I guess."

Stephanie watched as Keely pulled on her Nikes and began lacing them. Her long hair fell forward, hiding her face. Despite what Tessa had said about not being a fit mother, Stephanie knew her sister hoped to start over with her daughter, but at the moment there was no forgiveness in Keely's attitude. Stephanie sighed, hoping she was doing the right thing.

Closing the door quietly, she left.

STEPHANIE COULDN'T ask him anything if he wasn't speaking to her. She didn't count "Pass the salt" and "Have you seen the book I was reading?" She stole a look at him propped against two pillows in bed beside her. With his reading glasses on, his attention fixed on his book, he was as unapproachable as a stranger.

She sighed, and a small muscle ticked beside his mouth. His gorgeous mouth. She watched him turn a page. Nice hands, too. Appropriately so. He was a surgeon. Her gaze dropped lower, skimming his flat stomach to the point where the sheet was bunched. He no longer wore the sweatpants. He no longer wore anything in bed. Not that it meant anything tonight. Maybe never again.

Why can't I tell him about it?

"Something on your mind?" he asked, startling her.

"Um . . . ah, Keely."

"What about Keely?" He was as cool as the icy drink beside him.

"She almost refused to visit Tessa tonight."

"Hmm. This has been tough for her."

"Yes."

"That's it?"

"Well…actually, I never finished telling you about Tessa."

He set his book aside, a little too deliberately. "That's right, you didn't."

Stephanie touched her forehead briefly. "She's got this crazy idea that she'll just let Keely stay here with me…with us…for good. That she's not a fit mother for her own daughter.''

"What do you think?"

"Well, it's ridiculous! She's Keely's mother, not me."

"I can understand her dilemma."

"There's no dilemma. She's a good person, kind and sensitive, unselfish. She's turned her life around under circumstances that have destroyed other people."

He removed his glasses. "There's no need to defend your sister to me, Stephanie. I like her. She's honest. She's straightforward. She's exactly who she claims to be." He let that sink in before putting his glasses back on. "I think she sees Keely settled here with you and me and Alison. It's simple, really. We appear to be a loving family."

Stephanie's heart stumbled.

He picked up his book. "Looks can be deceiving."

She swallowed, then spoke quietly. "I intend to make it clear to Tessa that Keely will naturally live with her."

He paged through the book until he found his place. "Incidentally, she is welcome to recuperate here. For as long as it takes. We'll get extra help if necessary."

Stephanie felt utter dismay. Even though Tal was saying exactly what she wanted to hear, his tone was ice-cold. Somewhere deep in her chest, the pain was crushing. She wanted to reach over, grab his book and fling it against the wall, tear those stupid glasses off his face and…and what? Feel him hold her close again? Have him reassure her that the brick wall of her silence wasn't something that would destroy their relationship?

"You'd better get some rest," he said, his eyes on the book once more, not her.

Beneath her breasts, the baby gave her a swift kick. Her hands went to her stomach. She felt fat and unattractive. She felt like the hippopotamus she'd complained about to Tessa. It had been a joke then. Not now. She studied her hands. Because she was retaining fluid, her wedding ring was tight.

She lay back and closed her eyes. The last thing she wanted was for him to see her cry.

March 6, 1996/31 weeks.

FOUR POUNDS GAINED. *Blood pressure up. Fluid retention.*

Stephanie left Evelyn Duplantis's office with the bad news hanging like a millstone around her neck. She shouldn't have eaten that scrumptious crabmeat au gratin that Travis sent over last night. She should have stuck to the salad Mimi had made for her. Instead, she'd eaten both.

When the elevator pinged, she stepped inside and chose Tessa's floor instead of the second, where a stack of patients' charts and at least two hours of dictation awaited her. She felt a need for another woman's sympathy, one who'd experienced pregnancy. Especially if that woman happened to be Tessa. It was an old habit to seek out her twin when she felt bad.

Staring at her feet—what she could see of them— she admitted what was really wrong. It was ridiculous to assume that Tal had left the house at dawn this morning just to avoid looking at her, hippopotamus that she was. He'd had an early surgery.

But he hadn't kissed her. Over two weeks since the chilly little exchange in their bedroom and he hadn't kissed her.

She pushed Tessa's door open after a brief knock and stopped in surprise. Her sister had company.

"Travis?" She looked blankly from Tessa to her brother-in-law. "I didn't know you two even knew each other."

"Hey, pretty lady." Travis rose lazily and kissed her on the cheek. "We didn't until fifteen minutes ago."

"Well..." She shrugged, almost speechless. "I guess I don't need to bother with introductions, then, do I?"

"Nah, I took care of that," he said. Leaning against Tessa's bed with his legs crossed at the ankles, he looked entirely at ease. "The truth is, sugar, I had to check and see if Tal was exaggerating. There couldn't possibly be two like you." He gave Tessa a sexy wink. "But here she is."

Despite herself, Stephanie smiled. "Look out for this guy, Tessa. I hear things."

"I'm protected by a fifty-pound cast," Tessa said dryly.

Travis grinned, wagging a finger at her. "But it won't be there forever."

To Stephanie's amazement, Tessa blushed.

Apparently satisfied with that reaction, Travis turned his attention to Stephanie, running a swift eye over her. "So, how's the Robichaux heir? You're blooming, sugar. Bet my big brother is counting the days."

Until he's free again, maybe, but they didn't have to know that. Yet. Stephanie spanned her gigantic stomach with both hands. "I'm *awful!*"

"Hey, you're beautiful, honeybun." He tilted her chin up. "Pregnant is beautiful! Haven't you heard?" He motioned her to the settee and helped her sit. When she looked up, Tessa was studying her, narrow-eyed. "What's wrong? You look like somebody ran over your puppy."

"My back aches, I've gained four pounds, my blood pressure is off the stick, I can't eat any more salt or fat, a good night's sleep is impossible, and...oh, hell..." She leaned back gloomily. "I guess I just wish it were all over."

Tessa smiled softly. "It will be very soon."

"Another month...at least!"

"Well, it does take nine."

"Enough about me. What's the good news from your doctor?"

"You just missed Sheila," Travis said.

Tessa knocked twice on the hard cast. "She's releasing me this morning. I left a message with your service."

"I haven't checked my messages. But no problem. Mimi's standing by as a home-duty nurse. We're all set up for you."

"I don't know what to say." Tessa put a hand against her cheek. "Inviting me into your home... Are you sure it's no imposition?"

"What? In that rambling residence Tal calls home?" Travis said, pushing away from the bed. "He could have twenty houseguests without noticing."

"I was asking the woman who's married to him, Robichaux," Tessa said evenly.

Travis put out an eloquent hand, clearly expecting Stephanie to back him up. And of course she did.

"My house is your house, Tee. And it was Tal's idea."

"See?" Travis's grin flashed again. "I know Tal's schedule is crammed. Do you need help getting Tessa to the house?"

"Thanks, Travis, but we'll manage. Keely promised to come if Tal can't get away."

"Isn't she in school?" he asked.

"She'll be here, anyway. She sometimes meets with the teen class, so I called the school, clearing it for today." She glanced at her watch. "That's in twenty minutes."

"Do you think she'll drop by and see me?" Hope and doubt mingled in Tessa's voice.

Maybe. Maybe not. Time hadn't done much to smooth relations between mother and daughter. Only Stephanie's promise that Keely could drive had made her agree to be on hand to transfer Tessa from the hospital to the house.

Tessa sighed. "Probably not, huh?"

Stephanie squeezed her hand. "She'll come around, Tee."

"Sure."

"Gotta go," she said. "Remember, be ready to leave as soon as I finish the teen group session, okay?" She kissed her sister and Travis, and left them to enjoy each other.

In an otherwise gray day, at least that was one bright spot.

ALTHOUGH SHE WAS running a little late, Stephanie took a moment to put her feet up in her office and drink a cup of tea—herbal—before meeting with the group. She did a few stretching exercises to relieve a nagging little ache in her lower back. The patient charts were still there, but she didn't have time for dictation. Maybe after the session with the girls. To tell the truth, she didn't feel like doing much of anything.

When the phone rang, she was tempted to let her voice mail pick it up, but it could be Tessa. Or Keely. Even Alison. Not Tal. With a sigh, she answered, hoping in spite of everything that it was Tal.

It was Margaret Steele, Benedict Galloway's secretary, requesting a "minute of her time" later in the day.

"That's about all I can spare, Margaret," she said, wondering what bone the administrator had to pick with her this time. "I've got my group in about five minutes, then I'm checking my sister out of the hospital and driving her home. And I have a stack of patient charts awaiting dictation. Are you sure it must be today?"

She was and it must be. Reluctantly, Stephanie agreed and replaced the receiver. Only then did she think to check her messages. Her heart lurched at the sound of Tal's voice. And then sank at the message. He was heading into an emergency surgery and would be tied up for most of the afternoon.

So much for their driving Tessa home together. Keely was drafted, whether she liked it or not.

"THIS PLACE is beautiful, Steph." Balanced on her crutches, Tessa surveyed Tal's house and grounds from the driveway with an expression of awe.

"I think so, too. Watch your step on these bricks. They're uneven in places."

"Because they're old," Keely put in. "They were laid over a hundred years ago."

Tessa smiled. "My goodness, is there a ghost, too?"

Keely shrugged, clearly still not ready to warm up to her mother. "Alison says there is, but she's full of baloney most of the time."

Stephanie reached to unlatch the wrought-iron gate leading into the back courtyard. "It's a long walk to the front door. Let's go inside here."

"A real French courtyard," Tessa exclaimed, looking around with pleasure. "It's gorgeous."

Stephanie smiled. Azaleas and wisteria were in full bloom. Wafting around them was the pungent scent of sweet olive. "I knew you'd like it. Do you want to sit outside for a few minutes? Since you've been cooped up in the hospital for nearly three weeks, you can enjoy some fresh air for a while. We have coffee or iced tea, lemonade—you name it."

"Sounds wonderful." She propped her crutches against a glass patio-table and sat down.

Keely edged toward the steps at the back door. "I'll tell Mimi we're here. Do you want coffee, or what?"

Stephanie frowned at her curt tone, but was hesitant about correcting her. Now that Tessa and Keely were reunited, she didn't relish her role as disciplinarian.

"Coffee, I think," Tessa replied quietly. "Thanks, honey."

When the door closed behind her, Tessa sighed. "Will she ever forgive me, Steph?"

"Yes. Give her time."

"It's going to be uphill all the way, I'm afraid. I hope the discord doesn't disrupt your household. So close to the birth of your baby, you shouldn't have to cope with me and my problems, too."

"We'll manage, Tee. It's good to have you in my life again." They both heard the screen door. Tessa looked worried as Keely approached with their drinks.

"Let's hope you don't change your mind."

The teenager plunked a mug down in front of her mother. A chipped mug, Stephanie realized with dismay. She wondered where Keely had unearthed it in Mimi's impeccable kitchen. "Here's your coffee. And mineral water for Steph." She set a glass in front of Stephanie with less rancor, then looked at Tessa. "Mimi has your room ready."

"There's no rush, Keely," Stephanie told her. "Give us a minute to drink this."

"Well, I've got some stuff I want to do." She stood with hips cocked, fingers drumming impatiently. "I don't have to hang around here and wait on her, do I?"

"Keely!" Stephanie frowned, setting her glass aside. "That's enough rudeness. Now, apologize to your mother."

"Why should I apologize?"

Tessa finally spoke. "Because it's good manners."

"What would you know about manners?"

"Keely!" Stephanie said. What was happening here?

"I read a book," Tessa said.

"When?" Keely's mouth curled with scorn. "Not in the first thirteen years of my life."

"Three years have passed since then, Keely."

"Big deal. You're claiming you've changed? Hah! Wait'll dinner when you get a chance at the wine bottle. We'll see how you've changed."

"I haven't touched alcohol or drugs since the day you disappeared." Tessa's hands were trembling.

"Could I see that in an affidavit?"

"Stop it! Both of you." Stephanie managed to haul herself upright, bracing her aching lower back with one hand. "What is going on here? Keely, you will show some respect for your mother or I—"

"Why should I?" the girl demanded in an unsteady voice. "Just because she gave birth to me? It takes more than that to be a mother. Isn't that what you tell the teen group? When you have kids, you're supposed to nurture them, care for them, *stay* with them through thick and thin. Or you're supposed to give them up to some adoptive family who will value them." She turned accusingly on her mother. "And that's not a foster family! It's not some county- or state-run agency."

Looking pale and stricken, Tessa seemed unable to reply.

Keely turned to Stephanie. "She shows up here after all this time and expects everybody to open their arms and welcome her back," Keely said in a disgusted tone. "Well, you can if you want to. She's your twin. Maybe that's a stronger bond than a kid can claim."

Tessa put out a hand. "Keely—"

"The truth is," Keely said, firming up her voice, "I've been calling the shots for myself long enough that I think I've earned the right to make my own decisions. You know we had an understanding about that when I came to live with you, Steph." She was unflinching as she looked at her mother. "This may sound hard, but I don't have to show you any respect just because you gave birth to me. I don't have to treat you special."

It was a harsh indictment. One look and Stephanie could see that Tessa was devastated. Keely had tapped right into Tessa's guilt and remorse. She would be more convinced than ever that her decision to leave Keely here with Stephanie was right. And if Keely knew that, the situation would be a thousand times worse.

"Could I say something?" she asked, bracing herself on the back of the chair.

Keely shrugged.

Tessa looked away.

"It breaks my heart to hear two people I love so much tearing each other apart." With the ache in her back, she was forced to sit down. "Look, a mother/daughter relationship is complicated, even in the best of families. Tessa and I certainly didn't have much of a role model in our mother. I suppose some of the dysfunction in our lives comes from that. But people grow up. And sometimes, if you're very lucky, you get a second chance. That's what has happened here with the two of you. The way I see it, you're being offered a time and place to rebuild your relationship. To mend fences. Don't throw it away, for heaven's sake."

The silence was as heavy as the humidity. Neither Keely nor Tessa looked convinced. Stephanie sighed, wondering if she was breaking a confidence by what she was about to do. "Alison, for instance, was not so lucky," she said.

Alison's name snagged Keely's attention.

"Tal's daughter can never have a second chance with her mother," Stephanie explained. "There will be no reunion for Diana and Alison, at least in this life. Diana's craving for cocaine led to her death."

Keely's eyes widened. "Wow, I didn't know that."

"Nobody does. I'm telling you this for a reason, Keely."

Keely's gaze encompassed the house and court-yard, the sweep of lawn and expensive landscaping. "She had everything, a nice husband, a kid, this big house. She must have been crazy."

"She was ill."

Keely's chin set stubbornly. "At least she stayed with her family. She didn't just walk away."

"No, but she might have if she'd lived long enough. If her addiction had pushed her far enough. As it was, her need for a fix drove her into a dangerous neighborhood one night and she was shot."

"Jeez."

"No second chances there," Stephanie said.

"I guess."

Stephanie leaned forward, holding Keely's gaze intently. "Your mother has somehow found the strength to overcome her addiction, Keely. The years apart from you and me can never be reclaimed, but she has turned her experiences to good use. She counsels teenagers. She turns lives around. She deserves a fair hearing from you."

"I gotta go."

Stephanie half rose to stop her, but Tessa put out a hand. "Let her go, Steph." They watched her rush for the back door, then fumble a little before managing to yank it open.

"I guess I botched it," Stephanie murmured.

"No, *I* botched it." Tessa's eyes were bleak. "And it may take more than a second chance to fix it."

CHAPTER THIRTEEN

*The final weeks of pregnancy may seem
endless. Twinges of false labor may
trigger anxiety. Fatigue may sap your
ability to cope. Worries about weight
gain, your overall health, the
possibility of something going wrong
may plague your waking hours.
Inability to sleep may make nights seem
endless. Cheer up! Only a few weeks
to go.*

—Ask Dr. Meredith

March 6, 1996/31 weeks

STEPHANIE WAS DRIVING back to the hospital for the
appointment with Benedict Galloway when she felt a
strong, knotting contraction. Her hand went instinctively to her stomach and she sat absolutely still. *False
labor.* It couldn't be the real thing. She still had almost six weeks to go. She had seen Evelyn Duplantis
just that morning. Surely there would have been some
indication and Evelyn would have spotted it.

She drove the route to the hospital on automatic pilot, tensed for another contraction, but nothing happened. She got out of her car cautiously and breathed
a thankful sigh when everything seemed normal.

There was still the nagging back pain that had plagued her all day, but even that seemed to have eased a bit. The meeting with Benedict Galloway was the last thing on her schedule. Afterward, she was heading home—patient charts be damned—home to the sanctuary of her bedroom and a quiet evening with her feet up. Her family would just have to let her have some time to reflect and regroup.

She had plenty to reflect on.

She headed down the hall, straightening her lab coat—now impossible to button—as she walked. Waddled was more like it, she thought. Tal had suggested that she begin maternity leave now, but she had resisted, thinking she would have too much time on her hands. The last weeks would surely pass faster if she kept busy. But if Tessa was going to be around for a while, maybe she would consider taking the time, after all. She could still meet with her teens; she had planned to do that all along, even after the baby came.

At Galloway's office, she brushed her fingers through her hair and drew a deep breath—as deep as was possible with the baby crowding her lungs—and went inside.

Because the door to his inner sanctum was open, she could see Galloway behind his desk. His expression was...odd. Frowning, Stephanie walked past his secretary with an absent nod and entered the office.

"Hello, Benedict."

"Dr. Sheldon." He gestured for her to sit, but did not rise or smile.

Her relationship with the administrator had never been warm, but professionally there had been respect and cordiality between them. She guessed that this meeting would not reveal either.

"Yes, by all means have a seat, Steph."

Startled, she realized that Tal was here, too. Behind her, at a side window. He was simply standing there, hands shoved deep in his pockets. She tried reading his expression, but it was guarded. Still, something about him worried her. With a sense of foreboding, she slipped into a chair. Tal took the seat beside her.

"Our friend's been doing a little sleuthing, Steph."

Sleuthing? She looked blankly at Galloway, who ignored Tal.

"It's all here, Dr. Sheldon." He slid a large brown envelope across his desk.

The last time she and Tal had been summoned by Galloway, his concerns had been scrawled on a yellow pad which he'd pushed across to her exactly as he was shoving the manila envelope at her now. As bewildered now as she had been then, she reached for it, but was stopped by Tal.

"No, not this way, Ben." He put his hand on the envelope, fingers spread wide.

"What's going on? What is it?" she asked, frowning.

"I'd hoped I wouldn't have to resort to something like this," Galloway said stiffly, "but you've forced my hand. To my eternal bafflement, a majority of this hospital's board members seem determined to support the two of you in your pet projects. I've never made a secret of the fact that I don't approve of Women's Hospital sponsoring a clinic that attracts mostly riffraff. We have Charity Hospital for that."

"Get on with it, Ben," Tal snapped. "We know the size of your heart."

The older man huffed with indignation. "I prefer to keep personal attacks out of this discussion, Talbot."

"What the hell is that if it isn't personal?" Tal demanded, pointing at the envelope.

"What is going on?" Stephanie cried. "What's in the damned envelope?"

"Your secrets, Dr. Sheldon. Your husband may blanch at the truth, but I have no reason to tiptoe around your sensibilities. With this material, I can prove that you've misrepresented yourself for years at this hospital and, I suspect, in your personal life. If you force me to reveal all I've learned about you, then you risk destroying your professional reputation. Frankly, I don't think you'll be able to salvage much of a career." He did not look disappointed at the prospect.

"What secrets?" she asked, her face pale.

"Steph, he's been digging around in your past. He sent a private investigator to Memphis." Tal reached for her hand, but she moved, clenching both in her lap. "He discovered the reason you and Tessa ran away."

"We were children. Only fifteen."

"But old enough to sell your bodies," Galloway said, sneering.

"We didn't! That wasn't true! It was all a lie."

"There was no scandal at the farm where you and your twin sister lived?" Galloway asked.

"Yes, but—"

"I don't think these headlines lie." Galloway pulled a folder from his desk drawer and spread the contents on the top of his desk.

Sex and Sin—Juveniles in Custody—Teen Prostitution Ring Thrives in Rural Setting—Twins Are Star Attraction.

In one glance, Stephanie took in everything. After all, she'd seen it all before. The scandal had dominated the front page of the newspaper in Memphis for a week, while she and Tessa had huddled together in a dingy holding cell in juvenile court waiting for their future to be decided by nameless bureaucrats in a system that had neglected them. It had been horrible. Outside, reporters had clamored, demanding interviews with the "Twin Lolitas." Their questions had been insensitive, insulting, intimidating. Their articles, packed with lies and insinuations, had hurt unbearably.

"It was never like that," Stephanie murmured, cupping her stomach. Protecting her baby from the slime. She did not—could not—look at Tal.

"About the child, Keely," Galloway said. "Your so-called niece."

So-called? Stephanie watched Galloway gather the copied clippings and slip them back into the folder. As if they were snakes, she thought. He was stuffing them back into the hole they'd come from, but as with snakes, the horror did not pass even when they were out of sight. "What about Keely?" she whispered.

"She isn't your niece, is she, Stephanie? She's your child. Born as a consequence of your stay at the foster farm. She's as illegitimate as those that you nurture through that ridiculous teen-pregnancy class of yours. You wouldn't want the whole world to know that, would you?"

"Just a damn minute, Galloway! That's slander and you don't have one iota of evidence to support it." Tal started up out of his chair, but Stephanie stopped him with a hand on his arm.

"No, wait, Tal." She felt his shock. With all her secrets, did he think she was going to say that Keely was her child, after all? But Tal could wait. Inside her, the turmoil of years swirled hotly. Galloway, with his pale, accusing eyes, could have been the judge in Memphis, or the fat sheriff, or the caseworker, or any of a dozen people who had somehow let her and Tessa down when they had needed kindness and care more than food and shelter.

"I'm going to tell you something, Benedict," she said. Now that she had nowhere else to hide, she found she wasn't afraid of the truth. "Not because I owe you any explanation for what you think you have discovered about me, but because it suddenly feels good to know I'm not a victim any longer. My sister and I were placed by social services in the care of a monster. This man systematically seduced most of the teenage girls assigned there and then coerced them into prostitution. For children starved of love and attention, jewelry and clothes and special favors can be powerful inducements. Tessa and I refused to be manipulated, but we were tarred with the same brush when the scandal broke."

She stood up, getting to her feet with surprising grace. "I can't see much difference between what that monster did to Tessa and me and what you're threatening here today, Benedict. But this time, I'm not a scared, orphaned girl. I've earned everything I have. Keely is not my child, although that's none of your damn business. What you're threatening is blackmail, Benedict, and I'm not buying."

"I support my wife a hundred percent, Ben." Tal picked up the brown envelope and dumped it in Galloway's trash basket. "You've crossed the line with your obsession to destroy the clinic and now this ugly effort to discredit Stephanie, but two can play this game. I never wanted you to know this, Ben, but you've forced my hand. It wasn't a stray bullet that killed your son. It was cocaine. Ben, Jr., was an addict.''

Shock came and went on Galloway's face. His hand holding an expensive fountain pen started to shake. ''That's preposterous!'' He stood up abruptly. ''It's a filthy lie.''

''How I wish it were,'' Tal said quietly. ''Diana and Ben, Jr., were not at the clinic that night for the reasons everyone assumed. They were in the neighborhood to buy cocaine. After the deal, they didn't leave. Instead, they stayed to take a hit right on the street. That's when they were caught in a drive-by shooting.''

Galloway sat down heavily. ''I don't believe it.''

''Diana died instantly from her wounds, but that is not what killed your son. Maybe the drugs were contaminated, I don't know, but Ben, Jr., suffered cardiac arrest. Exactly like Anthony Connaught a few months ago.''

''It's not true.''

''Believe it, Ben. Your son died in my arms. The irony is, if he'd been inside the clinic, I might have been able to save him.''

The pen clattered as Galloway dropped it. He raked a shaking hand over his face. In ten minutes, he'd aged ten years.

''I'm sorry, Ben. I honestly never wanted you to know.''

Stephanie gave Tal an anxious look as Galloway swiveled his chair around and stared out the window.

She started to speak, but the administrator put his hand up abruptly. He would not welcome sympathy.

They turned to go, but Tal stopped at the door. "Burn both those packages, Ben."

"Get out," he said, but the hostility was missing. He simply sounded defeated.

IT TOOK enormous effort, but Tal somehow managed to keep from bombarding Stephanie with the questions churning in his mind. At least until they left the hospital. He couldn't allow himself to think about how Galloway had behaved before Stephanie appeared. First, he'd informed Tal that the Connaught lawsuit had been withdrawn. He'd been grudging with the news, almost as if the politician's decision not to sue the hospital disappointed him. And then he'd gotten down to the real reason for wanting to see Tal. His face had been sly and mocking as he'd produced the investigator's report and watched avidly as Tal read it. He had gloated over Tal's stunned reaction to Stephanie's secrets. And then, when he'd presented the newspaper clippings, he'd almost crowed with triumph. Tal had thrust everything back into the envelope and, unable to sit waiting for his wife to walk into the trap, had paced the office, seething, until she appeared.

What had been revealed about Stephanie was only the tip of the iceberg, he realized. He didn't know her at all. Just when he thought he was beginning to, something else, some little trickle of information from her past cropped up. If he hadn't stumbled on a private conversation between Tessa and Stephanie, he would never have known about the rape. *Rape,* for God's sake! Didn't she know how a man felt when the

woman he loved had been violated? Ever since he'd
found out, he'd been a wild man. He'd fantasized
about killing the culprit. The violence of his thoughts
had shocked him. He hadn't trusted himself to ask for
details, so he'd closed himself off from her. Now this.
He swore savagely, silently. How many more secrets
did she have? And when would she tell him? If she was
truly committed to their marriage and to him,
wouldn't she trust him enough to tell him everything?

He knew his hand at her waist was unsteady as they
stepped from the garage elevator to the floor where
both their cars were parked. He knew she was devastated by the encounter with Galloway. She'd want to
go home and hide. That was the way Stephanie coped.
She made to veer off toward her car, but he caught her
by the arm, intending to guide her to his Jaguar. He
wasn't about to let her out of his sight right now.

She pulled free, turning on him fiercely. "Stop! I'm
tired of being...manhandled and manipulated
and...bullied and—"

"Hey..." He backed off, both hands up. "I'm not
the enemy, Steph. I'm your husband. Although
sometimes I think you manage to forget that."

She wrapped her arms around herself. In spite of her
flare-up, she looked fragile. And extremely pregnant.
"What is that supposed to mean?" she asked.

"Can we get into my car? You look ready to drop
right here."

"I'm okay. I can drive."

"Indulge me. I'll get someone to take your car
home."

"So we can talk?" She gave him a defiant look. "I
know what you want, Tal. You've got some...some
dumb idea that if you know everything about me, it

will somehow be a good thing. Good for our relationship. Our marriage. Our future. The way things are going, I'm wondering if there's going to be any of the above."

He stopped, pulled back and looked at her. "Explain that, if you can."

"You want me to believe in fantasies when you don't know the first thing about real life." She waved a hand behind her, somewhere in the direction of Galloway's office. "What you heard in there is real life, Tal. I've spent twenty-one years trying to forget it."

"Our marriage is not a fantasy, Stephanie, not to me. It's real. I know we got married quickly, but I took my vows seriously. I wanted this marriage to work but I wonder if you can say the same thing? Except when we're in bed. At least there I know you're with me a hundred percent." He ignored the blush that colored her cheeks. "But we're intimate only in a physical sense, Steph. How do you think that makes me feel? Think about it—I find out you have a twin sister only when Keely shows up. I learn about the pain of your childhood only when Tessa shows up. I discover the worst this afternoon when Galloway dumps that garbage out on his desk and watches me read it."

He had his hands propped on his hips. They fell away then, as he looked around, frustration and anger momentarily drying up his tirade. He blew out a long breath. "I feel used, Steph. I want to know, is it always going to be like this?"

"You feel used." She said it softly. Too softly. "You feel used," she repeated. Narrow-eyed, she gazed out over the sea of cars in the garage, then swung back to look at him. Her gray-green eyes were blazing. "*You* feel *used!* Well, do forgive me, Tal, but who the hell do you think you are? You wish I had bared my soul before now. Why should I? How could I? We both know you only married me because I was pregnant. And what's this about physical intimacy? As opposed to what? Emotional intimacy? You told me yourself, up front, that you had nothing to give in an emotional sense. Diana had killed everything, you said. Okay, I accepted that. But for you to come back complaining when you yourself set the tone for our marriage is just too much."

"Stephanie—"

"Don't touch me, Tal." Her gaze dared him. "As you've guessed, those headlines in there are only the tip of the iceberg. The whole truth is a lot uglier. Tessa and I picked up the pieces of our lives as best we could and got on with it. Do you think *you* could have managed better?"

"I—"

"Maybe you've seen your mother drunk for three days in a row."

He said nothing.

"Maybe you've wondered what you're going to eat when there is nothing, zip, nothing in the cupboard."

"Stephanie—"

"No? How about school? When you entered the gated schoolyard at posh Sacred Heart, did your sweater have holes in it? Were your shoes a little tight because they were bought secondhand?" She shook her head. "I don't think so. Your childhood was trouble-free and loving and secure. I give you credit for your efforts to do good things now, Tal, but you can never really understand what it was like. You can't know how it would have affected you years later, either."

"No, I can't," he said without missing a beat.

She was put off for a second. "Well, then . . ."

"Can we get something else cleared up here?"

"What?"

"We did get married because of an unplanned pregnancy. And when I told you I felt I had nothing to give, it was before we made love that first time in Boston. By the next morning, I felt different. Maybe it was a mistake not saying something then, but—tell the truth Steph—if I'd said then that you made me feel alive again, that I was stunned because you'd been right under my nose for three years and I hadn't grabbed you for myself, that I was elated at the thought of courting you when we got back to New Orleans, would you have believed me?"

"Probably not."

He could see only the top of her tawny head as she stared at her hands. Her vulnerability touched him. But there was so much more he liked about her—her courage, her sweetness, her intelligence, her eyes, her hands, her spunky chin. But not the way she stonewalled. Because she had become so dear to him, he needed to have her open up and share her past—all of it, the good and the bad.

"We need to talk, Stephanie," he said, ramming his key in the lock on the Jaguar, and jerking open the door. "But not here."

She hesitated, looking at him intently, but after a moment, she climbed in. He knew he hadn't won the battle yet, but getting her to go with him, knowing what he expected, was the first victory.

"I know a little bar that's quiet," he said, looking at her before starting the car. She was tired. He felt momentarily guilty about keeping her out but—damn it!—she owed him some answers. He reached for the ignition. "That'll give us more privacy than we could get at home."

"Fine." She leaned back against the headrest as he drove out of the parking garage and closed her eyes. He wasn't sure what that meant, but at least she was giving him this chance. By the time he pulled up in front of the bar, he was tense with the depth of his need to have more than answers. He wanted her to trust him.

He wanted her to love him.

The bar was quiet. Music came from a lone guitarist playing something melancholy. Standing in the doorway with Stephanie, Tal found himself thinking about that night in Boston. Two lonely people had come together in a fateful moment. Something special had happened that night. He was determined to build on it.

They found a table in a corner and Tal ordered mineral water for her and a scotch for himself. When it came, he lifted his drink. "To trust," he said, looking into her eyes.

"To trust," she echoed softly.

Was that a hint of a smile in her eyes? If it killed him, he would not screw up as he'd done before, he vowed. He would hear her out and be understanding. Sensitive. And if he felt like hitting someone, he'd silently count to ten.

He wanted to coax her, prompt her, but he dared not. Failing that, he wanted to touch her. It was all he could do to sit, both hands curled around his glass, and wait. When she started to talk, something gave inside him. Like tension wire snapping.

"It's so sordid, Tal." She fiddled with her napkin, folding and refolding it. "When we left Memphis, I thought it was over. We had gotten away. Camille was wonderful. For months after we first came to her house, I used to hold my breath whenever the phone rang. Or when someone came to the door unexpectedly. But gradually, when nothing happened, I came to believe I could have a normal life. Like an ordinary person." She laughed bitterly. "I should have known better."

"You do have a normal life," Tal said, "but you're hardly ordinary."

She looked toward the musician. "There was a scandal at that farm in Tennessee, just as the headlines proclaimed. No matter how conscientious caseworkers are, some kids tend to drop through the cracks of our system. The couple—their name was Curtiss, Buck and Lila Curtiss—had a fabulous little enterprise going. They ran a teen-prostitution ring out of the farmhouse. To the Social Services people, the setup seemed innocent enough, even ideal—a dozen or so teenage girls in a rural family setting. A mom and pop built in. A tranquil, healthy environment. What could be wrong with that?" Tal saw that she was hardly aware of him. She was back in the country. Except that it wasn't pretty and pastoral. It certainly wasn't healthy.

"Buck seduced the girls." She grimaced. "He was a big, good-looking man, a charming liar. He used smiles and promises as much as trinkets and other things. Anything to get them to do what he wanted—to quote-unquote, 'be nice to his friends.'"

Tal swore. "How did he get away with it?"

Her gaze returned to his. "I'm sure he greased the right palms." He glanced away, unwilling for Stephanie to see in his eyes the violent urge to kill Curtiss. It was an old story, one that was not uncommon. The media exposed bastards like Buck Curtiss with enough frequency that people weren't shocked for long. But Tal had never been touched personally by one of the victims. He had never been married to one.

"Who blew the whistle?" he asked in a curt tone.

"Tessa, of course. In a roundabout way." She paused, studying her hands briefly. "I tried to stay out of his way, but Tessa was always the defiant one." Her voice lowered so that he could barely hear her. "I think that's why he chose her first."

"Chose her?"

"Buck knew he was never going to bring us around. You know that old saying, United we stand? It was like that with Tessa and me. The two of us had an advantage the other girls didn't have. They were individuals, we were twins. We were strong in our togetherness." She looked at him. "That only made us more of a challenge to him."

"The spineless bastard," Tal said, trying to control his rage.

She gave a dry laugh. "Yes."

"Couldn't anybody help?"

"It happened in the barn." She put her fingers on her mouth.

"The barn."

"Buck knew Tessa loved to ride. She was allowed to sometimes, but only if she cleaned out the stalls every day. Still, she liked that better than housework. One afternoon, I saw Buck go into the barn when I thought

Tessa was inside by herself. He had been working on us, trying every way he knew to bring us into his scheme. Twins, identical ones, at that, would get special attention, he promised."

"Scumbag."

But Stephanie didn't hear him. She was back in the barn. "It was late. I remember that it was raining. I can still smell the damp hay. And the animals, wet and steamy."

Tal listened with a knot in his stomach as Stephanie recalled the details. Even after seventeen years, her memory seemed remarkably clear.

"I knew she'd be in trouble by herself, but I thought he wouldn't dare do anything if he had to deal with both of us. So I went inside, too."

It was all Tal could do to sit still. His scotch was gone and he didn't remember drinking it. Inside him, violence was building . . . frightening in its intensity.

"He was waiting for me just inside the door. I nearly jumped out of my skin. He grabbed me from behind, pulling my arms behind me, hurting me as he wrapped some kind of rope around my wrists."

Tal wondered if she realized she was rubbing the soft underside of one wrist.

"I wanted to get away. I screamed, I begged, I kicked and struggled, I tried to bite him, until finally he hit me so hard that I was stunned into silence."

Tal didn't want to hear any more. He wished he hadn't pushed this, hadn't hounded her for details. Maybe she'd been right not to tell him these things. But deep inside, he knew better.

"Then he tossed me like a sack of animal feed. It knocked the breath out of me. I lay there, thinking everything in me was broken . . . wondering . . . won-

dering . . . when was he going to . . . do it.'' Her eyes
narrowed as if even now she was still wondering.

"But he didn't rape me," she said, her unfocused
gaze somewhere in Tennessee on a long-ago rainy afternoon. "He really wanted Tessa and she came rushing into the barn just then. She'd sneaked a fast gallop
and was drenched in the rain. She stopped short when
she saw Buck. Then she saw me. I wanted her to run.
I tried to tell her to run, but she didn't. She came toward me, she *flew* toward me." A small, dry sob escaped. "And Buck grabbed her."

Stephanie bent her head low, massaged her forehead, brought up her other hand and rubbed both
temples. Tal could imagine how many times she'd tried
to erase this memory.

She looked up then, gazed helplessly into his eyes.
"Buck raped her, Tal. He threw her down on that
filthy, muddy floor and ripped her jeans off her like
the animal he was and he raped her. And he did it all
right in front of me."

Nearby, the guitarist was pouring out his soul in an
unrecognizable song, but Tal could see that Stephanie
was hearing only rain drumming on a barn's tin roof,
cringing as lightning cracked with frightening power,
screaming as her sister was brutally violated before her
eyes.

Tal touched her hand, wanting to pick her up and
cradle her in his lap as if he could protect her. "You
were next?" he asked with soft sympathy.

She looked at him. "No," she said.

"You got away?" he asked, surprised.

"Got away? I escaped the actual act, if that's what
you mean. But I was raped as surely as Tessa. Watch-

ing it was the most hideous moment of my life. My innocence was shattered along with hers. Afterward, I lost my reputation with the scandal that followed just as Tessa did and neither one of us was ever the same. But no, I was never sexually violated."

Her hands lay beneath his, limp and still. He guessed she'd relived the rape as many times as Tessa herself must have. More, perhaps. Knowing Stephanie, she still felt the guilt of having escaped while Tessa hadn't.

"What happened afterward?" he asked, stroking the knuckles on both her hands with his thumbs.

"Fate," she replied dully. "There was an intercom system in the barn—you know, for security, fires, whatever. Anyway, it was inadvertently on and a caseworker just happened to make an unscheduled visit that afternoon. They do that sometimes. She was in the kitchen with Lila and heard the ruckus. By the time they got to the barn, it was too late to save Tessa."

"And you," he added softly.

She shrugged. "Tessa and I were both taken straight to the hospital. We told everything, but the rape was hushed up. Buck was charged with several counts of criminal activity, but not rape. Tessa didn't care; she was satisfied to see him jailed and to reveal what had been going on at the farm."

The guitarist finished abruptly. In the silence, the spots on the performer were turned off and the lights in the bar grew dim. Around them, people were engaged in casual conversation, relaxing after a day's work. After what he had just heard, it seemed almost bizarre to Tal that ordinary people were doing ordinary things.

"So now you know," Stephanie said.

"Could we get out of here?" he asked.

She looked at him without responding for a second, then reached for her purse. "Sure."

They drove home in silence. Tal had hesitated pulling away from the bar, tempted to check into a hotel because there were so many people waiting at their house and there was so much he wanted to say to his wife. But he knew she would never go for it on Tessa's first night in their home. So he took the turn that would take them home, then drove along St. Charles Avenue, oblivious to everything but the emotion crowding his chest. At the house, he popped the gate and then the garage door, and finally glided to a stop inside the garage. With his wrist draped on the steering wheel, he wondered how he could get her past the crowd and into the privacy of their bedroom with minimum delay.

"I knew it would shock you."

He realized she had misunderstood his silence. "I'm shocked, sweetheart, who wouldn't be? But mostly I'm humbled by the way you've turned your life around, by everything you've accomplished when so many other people would have simply quit." He reached over and touched her cheek. "The reason we're sitting here is because I have a lot I want to say to you and no place private to say it."

She studied him in silence, obviously not sure what he meant. "I thought you'd be totally repulsed by what happened."

With that look on her face, that hesitancy in her voice, she was irresistible to Tal. "How could I blame you for something you had no control over? How could anyone blame you or Tessa?"

She suddenly pushed her door open and managed to get out of the car. By the time he was around at her side, she was heading not in the direction of the house, but deeper into the courtyard. He started to speak, but she put a finger to her lips, looking toward the back door. "I know a place," she whispered. Taking his hand, she pulled him deeper into his own backyard.

It was a swing near the back of the lawn beneath an old magnolia. Tal wondered why he hadn't thought of it, too, as he sat down beside her.

She turned to him then. "What was it you wanted to say?" Her mouth quirked in a smile. "And you'd better hurry, because even in March the mosquitoes are as big as bats out here."

"But at least we've got privacy." Feeling the first sting, he slapped at the side of his neck. "Well, almost."

"Do you think we'll laugh about this in years to come?" she asked, brushing her hand between them to wave the pesky insects away.

He caught her hand before it settled on her stomach. "That's what I'm counting on, sweetheart."

"What?" she asked, puzzled.

"That there will be years to come. For us. Together."

There wasn't much illumination in the deepest corner of Tal's backyard, but there was enough for him to see that Stephanie was startled. Her eyes were wide as she stared at him.

"What exactly are you saying, Tal?"

"That I want us to stay married, sweetheart. And not because you're pregnant, but because I love you."

She dropped her gaze suddenly. Since he was holding her hand, he felt the tremor that went through her.

Was it fear or uncertainty or joy? Because he didn't know, it scared him. He knew then how much he wanted her, how much he needed her. "Stephanie? Maybe it's not a good time..."

"No, it's...I'm just...don't...didn't..." She touched the corner of her eye. He could see the gleam of tears. "I don't know what to say."

He grinned crookedly. "Not, I love you, too, huh?"

She rummaged around in a pocket of her voluminous smock and found a tissue, then wiped away a tear. "Of course I love you. How could I not love you? I love you so much that when Benedict Galloway started telling you all that...well, all I could think about was that I didn't want you to find out that way, and—"

He put a finger on her lips. "How did you want me to find out?"

"I don't know. I should have been the one to tell you. Maybe after I presented you with an heir."

He tucked a finger beneath her chin. "Bribing me with our baby?"

She laughed with chagrin. "Sounds awful, doesn't it?"

He pulled her into his arms, longing to banish her ghosts along with her tears. "Yeah, but I'll take you any way I can get you. Haven't I already proved that?"

"Even pregnant and big as a—"

"Uh-uh, don't say it." He gave her a little shake. "No negative remarks allowed. The mother of my child is beautiful."

They swung gently back and forth for a few minutes. With one arm around her, she was as close as her advanced pregnancy allowed. "So, you were going to tell me about yourself eventually?" Tal said, idly stroking the side of her neck. "Even though you think it's a dumb practice."

She sat up a little and looked at him. "I didn't mean that. I was just mad." Taking his hand, she held it to her cheek. "You seemed so angry lately. I wanted to tell you everything, but I was afraid to risk it."

"I *was* angry," he admitted, rubbing a thumb back and forth on her lips. "It meant you didn't trust me, Steph. And if you didn't trust me, how could you love me?" He leaned forward and kissed her. It began gently. Then, because the taste of her excited him, he took the kiss deeper. She opened to him, as always. Heat and lust concentrated instantly in his loins. She was the most desirable woman he'd ever known.

He knew she had to be exhausted, but his body had a will of its own. Hers, too, it seemed. Stephanie pressed closer, crushing her breasts against his chest. Wrapping her arms around his waist. Making those sweet little moans.

Cupping her chin, he angled his head to keep her mouth just where he wanted it, while with his other hand, he shifted her so that he could wedge himself against the heat of her. This couldn't go anywhere, he knew that. He groaned with the intensity of desire clouding his brain. Just a few more minutes, he told himself, then he'd take her inside. With luck, maybe they could find some time alone together in their bedroom.

He felt the vicious sting on his neck.

"Ow!" He cursed, slapping at his neck.

Stephanie looked up and they made eye contact. She began to laugh. At the same instant, Tal did, too. It was frustrating and funny and it felt good. They laughed until they were weak, then Tal stood up and caught Stephanie's hand to help her out of the swing. Still wrapped in the glow of love and laughter, they headed for the house.

CHAPTER FOURTEEN

*Nerves may tend to fray in the final
weeks before delivery. Family dynamics
are affected by the prospect of a new
baby in the house. These expressions
of stress are nerve-racking, but
essentially harmless. A considerate
mate can help by smoothing troubled
waters.*

—Ask Dr. Meredith

March 6, 1996/31 weeks

KEELY KICKED at a pair of athletic shoes that lay in the
middle of her bedroom, enjoying the solid *thwack!* as
they slammed into the armoire. Under her breath she
whispered all the swearwords she was no longer allowed to utter since she'd started living with Stephanie and Tal. She was tempted to holler them, but she
didn't want her mother to hear her. She didn't want
her mother to think she talked like that anymore. Now
that she lived in a beautiful house and had beautiful
things—including security and a decent family—she
wanted her mother to think she'd changed. A lot.

She felt awful. Just frigging awful. She had been
thinking about it for the three weeks since her mother
showed up. She had been scared out of her gourd

when she thought her mother might die from her injuries in the accident, but almost the instant she realized Tessa was going to be okay, her feelings had changed.

She was so confused.

She plopped down on her bed and stared dejectedly at the rotating ceiling fan. Everything had been going just fine in her life until her mother decided to reappear. So what if she had made a miraculous transformation? Keely still remembered when she was only eight or nine trying to sober Tessa up so she could go to work.

She turned her head slowly on the bed and gazed at the costly artifacts so taken for granted by the people who lived here. Not Steph, though. No, she had a few secrets in her past just like Tessa and Keely, but these other people—Tal and Alison—they'd never understand. They'd never know what it was like having your stomach in a knot when the welfare people came around, or listening to every tiny sound when it was time for your mother to come home and it was midnight and then one o'clock in the morning and then two and she still didn't show.

How could Ali understand stuff like that?

Her door flew open suddenly and Alison herself appeared. "What do you think you're doing?" Her hands were fisted on her hips. "Would you just answer me that? Huh? Your mother's in her room, and it's her first day in the house, and you're closed up in here looking like a gloomy gus. What's going on?"

Keely got off the bed, but she took her time doing it. "Welcome home," she said sarcastically. "How's Grandmama and Grandpapa?"

"I had a nice visit," Alison said coolly. "And when I got home, I found your mother sitting by herself looking like she'd rather be back at the hospital. Now, what's *wrong?*"

Keely walked to her CDs and started sifting through the collection. "Mind your own business, princess."

Alison sat down on Keely's bed. "It won't work. You're not gonna make me mad calling me names."

"Shut up, Ali. I'm not up for it tonight."

Alison studied her in silence. "You've been acting funny ever since Tessa came back. Aren't you happy about it?"

"Not particularly." She could see that she'd shocked the little princess. She found the CD she was looking for and put it on. Suddenly, hard rock blasted from the speakers, guaranteed to end any attempts at intruding on her privacy, she thought with satisfaction.

Alison walked over and punched the Off button. With a yelp and a few choice words, Keely had it back on. For a minute or two, it was a heated standoff, with the passionate intensity only two adolescents can generate. Then Keely gave a disgusted huff and turned off the music. "Okay, are you satisfied?"

"So, are you happy your mom's here, or not?" Alison said, taking a seat again on the bed.

"Why should I be? She's been gone so long, I don't even know her anymore."

"Are you gonna go live with her when she goes back to Florida?"

Keely stalked over to the window. "You'd like that, wouldn't you?"

Alison shrugged. "I don't know. I'll have to think about it. Heck, what difference does it make, one more person? When it was just my dad and me, it was kind of quiet around here." She tapped her lips thoughtfully with one finger. "There's the baby to consider, too. If you take off, I'll be stuck as the only baby-sitter."

Keely turned around. "You are *so* selfish!"

Alison grinned. "Yeah, I guess so."

Keely rolled her eyes.

"Now, let's figure this out," Alison said in a tone remarkably like her father's. "Don't you love your mother anymore?"

"I don't know."

"Really?" Alison was wide-eyed.

"Yes. Really. I don't know."

"Hmm, maybe I can understand that, too. She does look like she's been around the block a few times."

Keely was up off the bed in a flash. "You little brat! That's a snotty thing to say. My mother's been through hell and back and she's survived. That takes guts and character! What would you know about that?"

"Nothing, I suppose," Alison said, seemingly unfazed. "I haven't had to go through hell and back . . . unless you count my own mother dying in a drive-by shooting."

"Yeah, talk about going around the block a few times."

Alison frowned. "What do you mean?"

"Your mother wasn't such an angel, *princess*," Keely said, wanting to hurt somebody as she was hurting.

"You didn't even know my mother!"

"No, you've got it wrong, Alison. *You* didn't know your mother."

Alison scrambled off the bed. "You're talking stupid, Keely. I'm getting out of here. I don't know why I tried to talk some sense into you, anyway." She started for the door.

"What's the matter? Too chicken to hear the truth?"

Alison stopped. "What truth?"

"Your mama was a junkie, Alison. She was in that seedy neighborhood buying coke and along came some street thugs and she got it. *Bang!* All she wrote."

Even before she'd finished, Alison had clamped her hands over her ears. "No! You're lying! That is not what happened. My mother would never do that! She was a wonderful person. She was good. She was nothing like your mother. She was a *nice* person!"

"What is going on here?" Pale from exertion, Tessa pushed the door open. Propped on her crutches, her eyes went first to her own daughter, then to Alison, who was nearly hysterical. Her fists were pressed against her mouth, her tearful dark eyes fixed on Keely. Alison seemed frozen for a long moment, then she whirled away, nearly bowling Tessa over, and ran wildly from the room.

STEPHANIE AND TAL strolled across the courtyard, arms looped around each other's waists. "My hair's a mess," she said, catching a look at herself in the glass on the back door.

"You look delicious," Tal said, reaching around her with his key. "That damn swing is no place to make love. As soon as we decently can, we're heading upstairs and locking our door. I'm not on call tonight and neither are you. Nothing short of a hurricane can ruin the plan."

Stephanie spotted movement in the kitchen. "Uh-oh, I think something's wrong."

Tessa threw open the door before Tal could fit his key in the lock. "Oh, thank God, you're back!"

"Where have you been?" Keely wailed, right behind her mother. "We've been trying for hours! The hospital said you'd been gone forever. We tried your car phones, both of them." She was nearly in tears. "You never do this!"

"We've been right here," Stephanie said, slipping off her sweater. "Sitting on the swing in the backyard."

"What's wrong?" Tal demanded.

"It's Alison!" Keely cried. "And it's all my fault."

"Alison?" Tal paused in the act of removing his jacket. "I thought she was with the Sterlings."

Tears were standing in Keely's eyes. "She came home from there, but now she's gone. Oh, you're going to hate me!"

"Hush, Keely." Tessa took Keely's arm and led her to a kitchen chair. "Sit down and let me explain. We don't want to upset Stephanie."

"I'm going to be extremely upset if somebody doesn't tell me what's going on," Stephanie said.

"What *about* Alison?" Tal repeated.

"She's run away!" Keely announced.

"Run away?" Tal looked at Tessa. "What is this all about, Tessa?"

Stephanie realized that Tessa looked pale. "Tessa, you need to sit down. You've just gotten out of the hospital. I know that leg must be painful. And your incision—"

"We can all sit down as soon as somebody tells me where Alison is," Tal snapped.

Tessa closed her eyes, sinking onto a stool that Stephanie shoved toward her. "Keely's right, I'm afraid. It appears that she has run away, Tal. I'm so sorry. I heard them screaming at each other, and when I—"

"Who?" Stephanie asked. "Keely and Alison?"

"Yes. Like two banshees."

"There's nothing new in that," Tal said dryly, pulling Stephanie over to a chair and firmly urging her into it. "What makes you think she's run away?"

Tessa bent, rubbing her forehead with a shaky hand. "Oh, it's what they argued about, Steph. Alison was devastated. By the time I'd wormed it out of Keely, Alison was nowhere to be found. At least, not in the house. We've called the Sterlings. We've called her friends. Keely seems to think—"

"I don't think, Mom! I *know!* We oughtta be looking instead of talking." She grabbed Tal's sleeve. "Tal, you know she shouldn't be out at night alone. Nowhere in this city is safe after dark!"

"What was the argument about, Keely?" Stephanie asked.

Keely looked stricken. She sent a pleading glance at her mother, who started to speak, when Tal said impatiently, "Spit it out, Keely! How unspeakable can a squabble between two teenagers be, for God's sake!"

"I told her about her mother." The words were so faint that at first they didn't fully register to Stephanie. Twisting her hands in front her her, Keely's gaze flicked from Stephanie to Tal, uncertain what to expect.

"What about her mother?" Tal looked baffled.

Keely licked her lips. "You know...about when she was... when she died."

Stephanie closed her eyes. "Oh, no."

"I'm sorry, I'm sorry, I'm so sorry," Keely moaned, looking on the verge of tears again.

Tal was looking at Stephanie. "What is she sorry about?" His face had grown hard with suspicion. After the tender moments in the swing, it hurt to her heart.

Keely saw his expression. "I was mad," she said, rushing to repair the damage. "We were arguing. She...she said something about my mom." Tessa looked startled, but Keely didn't notice. "I wanted to hurt her back. But I was sorry the minute I said it. I don't know how I could have done something so bad, Stephanie," she said, looking imploringly at her aunt. "It was awful! Her face...the look...I've ruined her memory of her mother *forever*." Covering her face, she sank into the chair beside Tessa.

"How did Keely know about Diana?" Tal asked Stephanie coldly.

Knowing the futility of trying to explain, Stephanie tried, anyway. "I told her. I'm...sorry. It...we...Tessa and Keely and I were discussing their...ah...problems. It seemed to me they might look at each other differently if...they knew..." She waved a hand as weariness washed over her. "I'm sorry. I know you told me in confidence."

"You and I can talk later," he said, moving directly to the telephone. "Right now, we need to concentrate on finding my daughter."

"Who...who are you calling?" Stephanie asked, watching him pick up the receiver.

"I'm calling the cops." He dialed. "It's a long shot whether they can help. I'll go out and look for her myself, of course."

"I want to go with you," Stephanie said, getting to her feet. She felt a twinge, low and deep, but she ignored it. It was no time to wimp out over false labor. "This is all my fault. You can't drive and search very well at the same time. It'll be easier with two of us."

"Don't be ridiculous, Stephanie!" he said sharply. "You've had a long day already. Go upstairs, get some rest."

"I can't rest!" she exclaimed, looking at him in disbelief. "Not with Alison lost. She's hurt and bewildered and no doubt scared—"

"It's too late to think of that," he snapped. Sweeping up his jacket, he started for the door.

"Tal! Dr. T... let me come with you!" Keely pleaded. "It's *my* fault. Besides, I want to help. Alison..." She gulped back a sob. "I feel like Alison is my sister. I know we fight a lot, but it doesn't mean anything. It's normal, isn't it?"

"Stay with your mother and Stephanie," he ordered, yanking the door open. "I'll be back when I find her."

"Will you at least call us," Stephanie asked, walking toward him. "Everyone will be worried."

He stopped with his hand on the door, his dark eyes unreadable. Only a minute before, he'd been holding her, loving her, laughing with her. Now he seemed as remote as he had once been before their marriage. "I'll call," he promised, then added, "If you hear from her, or she shows up or calls, get me on my car phone, okay?"

"Of course." As she turned away, she was suddenly struck by a strong, sharp contraction. She sucked in a quick breath and stood still, unable to move until it passed. She was vaguely aware of the door closing behind Tal, but she concentrated on making her way slowly toward the hall where there was a powder room.

"Stephanie?" There was concern in Tessa's voice, but she ignored it. Her need to get to a bathroom was urgent.

"I'm just going in here," she said. As she pushed open the door, she battled another urgent need: to cry. Just when things were beginning to come together for her and Tal, she had to go and mess up everything. It wasn't Keely's fault for telling Alison about her mother. She was just a child. Stephanie should never have betrayed a confidence—no matter what her reason was—especially one with such dire consequences.

As she stood leaning against the door, the sting of tears threatening, a soft knock sounded. "Stephanie, it's me . . . Tessa."

As if she didn't recognize the voice, Stephanie thought with a spent smile. "I'll just be a minute, Tee."

"Are you okay?"

"Uh . . ." She sniffed, wiped both eyes with her fingers, then straightened to move to the toilet. That was when she felt the warm gush between her legs.

"Omigod."

A sharp knock. "What is it, Steph?"

"Tee, oh, Tee . . ."

"Please let me in, Steph."

Stephanie put out a trembling hand and flipped the lock. Tessa stood at the door balanced on her crutches. She took one look, and instantly yelled over her shoulder, "Keely, go outside and stop Tal! Tell him it's Stephanie. Hurry!"

"What's wrong?" Keely appeared, trying to crowd into the small space.

"Go!" Tessa ordered sharply. "Didn't you hear me? Stop Tal before he leaves!"

Keely's gaze skimmed over Stephanie, stopping at the dark stain on her maternity pants. Her mouth fell open, then she whirled when her mother gave her an urgent push. "For heaven's sake, Keely! He'll be gone."

Stephanie made her way shakily toward the sink. Leaning on it, she made an attempt to pull off her pants, but another contraction struck. Grasping hold of the counter with both hands, she breathed in deeply, riding it out. Panic came then, dark and overwhelming. It was too early—almost five weeks too early.

Tal, come back. I need you.

"Here, let me give you a hand." Tessa's crutches were too new to her to be managed with grace. She shoved them aside, where they fell with a clatter against the ceramic sink. "Just what we need," she muttered, leaning against the sink herself. "The crippled leading the stricken." She helped Stephanie pull off the soaked pants, then handed her a towel to wrap around herself. They left her smock on.

The moment they heard Tal and Keely hurrying toward them, Tessa hobbled out on only one crutch. "I'll call your doctor."

"What's wrong, Stephanie?" Tal asked, stopping short at the bathroom door. "Keely thinks you're in labor. She—" He glanced down. "Oh, Lord."

Two steps and he had his arms around her. She sagged against him, feeling her panic subside. "It's not blood," she told him. "My water broke."

He started to speak, then broke it off. Instead, without turning, he shouted, "Tessa! Call Steph's doctor. Her name's by the phone. Evelyn Duplantis."

"I'm right here," Tessa said, hovering at the door. "I've already called. I got her answering service."

"Damn it! This is an emergency."

"I made that clear, Tal."

"She'll call within ten minutes, Tal," Stephanie said weakly. Another major contraction had just struck, nearly sending her to her knees. Sensing it, Tal held her, rubbing her back until the pain subsided. Spent, she could only cling.

He drew back, looking at her. "This isn't false labor, is it?"

"No. This is it."

"Okay." His voice became energized. "The hell with Evelyn. We can't wait for her. I'm driving you to the hospital."

"You can't do that, Tal," she reminded him. "You have to go find Alison."

"Alison." For one heartbeat, he looked as if he had forgotten his daughter. "Oh, God."

She clung to his shirtfront. "It's too early," she whispered, her own fear returning.

A measure of calm seemed to come to him then. Sliding his arms around her, he turned his face into her hair. "It isn't too early if our baby says it isn't, sweetheart." The lump in his throat made his tone gravelly.

"Five weeks, Tal. Something's wrong."

"Look at me." He turned her around and took her face in his hands. "You've done everything right, you're healthy, the last sonogram was normal. Sometimes babies don't follow the rules."

"I'm scared, anyway."

He pulled her close, both of them conscious of the mound that was their child between them. Tal braced her with his big hand warm and solid at her back. "I thought tonight when we were on the swing that the little rascal was unusually calm," he said, chuckling softly in her ear. "He's ready, babe. We both know that when the water breaks, the show's on the road."

"Yes."

"I called 911," Tessa said, shuffling to the door of the powder room.

"They'll think some crank lives at this address," Stephanie said with a weak attempt at humor.

"Come on." Tal urged her toward the door, then swung her up into his arms, ignoring her startled protest, and carried her to the living room, where the paramedics could get to her with a minimum of fuss. Keely scrambled ahead of him to stack pillows to try to make her comfortable. Tessa drew up the rear, moving very slowly.

"I know you're exhausted, Tee," Stephanie said as Tal eased her onto the sofa. "Keely, help your mother to her room upstairs. She needs to rest. Her incision could reopen. Tal, you can't wait for the paramedics. You have to find Alison."

"I'm not leaving until I see you to the hospital," he said flatly.

"I'll rest when you've had your baby," Tessa stated with equal stubbornness.

"Let me go and look for Alison," Keely suggested brightly. "I have my license. I'll be okay."

None of the three adults dignified her suggestion with a reply. The telephone rang and Keely surged toward it. "Maybe it's Alison!"

"It's probably Evelyn," Stephanie said. Eyes closed, she was resting up for the next killer pain. The only good thing she could find in this was that her contractions were irregular. Once they settled into a measured pace, things would begin to happen. Hopefully, she would be at Women's Hospital by then.

But she might be there alone.

She felt Tal clasp her hand and opened her eyes to look at him. He looked worried. The strain on his face was unmistakable. "I don't want to leave you," he said, bringing her hand up to kiss.

"You have to go," she insisted. "I'll be okay, really."

Keely went to the door to let the paramedics in. Tal stood, refusing to release her hand even when the two EMTs were at Stephanie's side.

"Hey, Dr. Robichaux, I thought this was your house." EMT Eric Gonzales was a regular at the clinic. "And Dr. Sheldon. Well, look at you." He slapped a blood-pressure cuff on her arm. "Having that baby right here at home, hmm?"

"Not if I can help it," she said weakly.

"Hey, no problem. We're six minutes from Women's." He signaled to his cohort and they prepared to transfer her to the stretcher. "You can let go now, Doc," Eric said, glancing at their clasped hands. "You can ride in the ambulance with us or you can follow. Your choice."

Tal met her eyes, frustration and misery clouding his.

"Alison is your first priority right now," she told him, finding the strength somehow to sound firm and calm. "The baby and I will be fine. Now, go."

"I'm sorry," he said, giving her a kiss. Releasing her hand, he got slowly to his feet.

"I'll be okay. *We'll* be okay." She patted her tummy and closed her eyes as they swung her up to go. She didn't tell them that she felt a crushing contraction closing in. "The heir and I will wait for you."

Please, God.

IN THE END, Keely's driving skills had come in handy that night. Tessa could not drive with her cast and she had refused to stay home and wait. With Tal searching for Alison, Keely's chance came and she grabbed it.

In spite of impassioned argument, she had been banished from the room where Stephanie lay in labor. Her mother was in there, which made sense, Keely reluctantly conceded. Next to Tal himself, there was probably nobody Stephanie would rather have with her during labor than her twin. Those two had a very special relationship, even after all the years apart. Two minutes around them and anybody could see that.

She had probably destroyed any sisterly relationship with Alison, she thought, gazing morosely at the television. She had done a few harebrained things before, even a few things that were, well, illegal...strictly speaking. But she'd never felt the sense of shame she felt over what she'd said to Alison. What she'd done to Alison.

If only she could fix it.

Now here they were in the hospital. Stephanie was having Tal's baby, and he was somewhere on those dark, mean streets looking for his daughter. His innocent, thirteen-year-old daughter. She may as well be a toddler for all she knew about the stuff going on out there.

With her hands hanging dejectedly between her knees, Keely tried to think what to do. She was blind to the television, blind to two would-be fathers, the only other occupants in the room. Suddenly, an idea came to her. Springing up from the chair, she left the waiting room. Outside in the hall, there were four public telephones in an alcove. Digging deep in her jeans, she found a quarter to make the call, then dialed a number.

"Hey, Jolene, this is Keely."

"What's up, m'frien'?"

Keely stared down at her shoes, oblivious to the traffic in the hall. "Jolene, I got problems. I was just sitting here in the hospital thinking and it came to me suddenly. If anybody could help, it'd be you."

"Why you in the hospital?"

This was the ticklish part. Everybody who knew her understood that Jolene had nearly lost it when her baby died. It was difficult bringing up the subject of babies to her, but this was a difficult situation, Alison being lost and all. "Well . . . you know Stephanie's pretty far along in her pregnancy."

"She's not due for five weeks."

Damn. She was keeping track.

"The truth, Jolene? She's in labor right now."

"Is everything goin' okay?" Jolene asked in a voice that wasn't anything like her usual one at all.

"Well, you know they don't tell kids anything, but I think if it was bad, my mom would probably let me know."

"Your mom's there?"

"Yeah, she's about to fall over because she only got out of the hospital herself today, but she's stubborn and I guess she's tough, too. She insisted on staying right by Steph's side."

"That must run in the fam'ly, that stubbornness."

Keely laughed ruefully. "Yeah, it must." She paused, then picked it up again. "Jolene, we got big trouble tonight and I'm the cause of it all."

"What trouble?"

"I went and told Alison some things about her mother that upset her and she's run away. She's somewhere out on the streets tonight, and Dr. T's looking for her when he should be here in the hospital with Stephanie while she has their baby!"

There was silence while Keely visualized Jolene taking in the bad news, processing it, but not judging. Jolene wasn't into judging other people.

"This ain't good news," Jolene said. "The little princess could meet some subjects who don't respect her."

"Why do you think we're all crazy worried!"

"Uh-huh. I'm thinking maybe me and some people I know might put out an APB, try to locate her."

Keely sagged against the wall. "Would you do that, Jolene?"

"What are frien's for, Keely-girl?"

"Thanks, Jolene." She gave her the number to call if she found out anything, and hung up. After a minute, she headed back to the waiting room. Plopping down in front of the television again, she said to no one in particular, "And *that's* the reason I don't go to Sacred Heart Academy."

She ignored the startled looks she got from the two almost-fathers.

WITH A SENSE OF FOREBODING, Tal cruised the edge of the French Quarter. As usual, the place was teeming with tourists, and he was forced to drive excruciatingly slow. There was no sign of the slight, dark-haired teenager.

Trying not to succumb to panic, he drove to the end of St. Peter and turned onto Esplanade, praying he would not find Alison here. He had already checked with the clinic, which was nearby. How could he expect his daughter to seek refuge there? Her mother had been slain in that neighborhood.

But where else to look? He'd tried everywhere.

Picking up his car phone, he punched the automatic dial for the hospital. Beneath his panicked concern for Alison was his tormented need to be with Stephanie. Everything in him cried out to be at her side.

"Two-west," came the clear voice of an anonymous nurse.

"This is Talbot Robichaux. How is my wife?"

"She's progressing nicely, Dr. Robichaux. As we reported to you ten minutes ago—" she emphasized the words "—she's dilated to seven centimeters. Do you want me to call Dr. Duplantis to the phone?"

"No...no, thanks. I'll keep in touch." He started to press the disconnect button, then added, "You'll call me if...when the baby...if my wife is wheeled into delivery, right?"

"Of course." The nurse's voice gentled. "No luck finding your daughter, Dr. Robichaux?"

"No. Nothing." He pushed the disconnect button and resumed his search.

He stopped at a traffic light and rubbed a hand over his face. His eyes felt gritty and it was hard to swal-

low around the tightness in his throat. He couldn't recall a night as terrifying as this, ever. He desperately
wanted to find Alison and at the same time he wanted
to gather Stephanie in his arms, take the pain of her
labor on himself, be with her to share the moment
when the child of their love came into the world. Yes,
it was love. He adored her, he treasured their marriage and the prospect of a relationship that would
grow and be enriched with the years. And with other
children.

*Hold on, Steph. Wait for me, my little son. Wait for
Daddy.*

He looked out of the window, feeling bereft. He
stared at objects, but saw nothing.

Ali, where are you?

He snatched up the telephone almost before the ring
was completed. "Hello."

"Hey, Dr. T, this is Jolene."

"Jolene?" Behind him a car honked impatiently.
He ignored it. "Jolene of Stephanie's teen group?"

"Yeah, that's me. What is this? You know some
more Jolenes?"

"No..." Distracted, he pulled to the side of the
street beneath a No Parking sign. "Is this about Alison?" he asked, not daring to hope.

"Yeah. We found her."

CHAPTER FIFTEEN

*Labor and delivery is a time when pain,
joy and excitement are mingled. You
will want your mate close by. Allow
nothing to prevent the two of you
sharing the miracle.*

—*Ask Dr. Meredith*

March 6, 1995/31 weeks

STEPHANIE COULDN'T decide whether the huge clock on the wall in the labor room was a blessing or a curse. It reflected accurately the minutes between her contractions, while ticking away the hours of Tal's absence. She drew in a deep, exhausted breath, but before she felt its cleansing effects, another punishing contraction started to build. Her pains were coming with increased, well-paced frequency now. This one was no wimp, either. Seeking relief—any kind of relief—she tapped into methods she'd been teaching pregnant women for a decade.

"Go with it, don't fight it, flow into it, let it take you..."

She realized the words were Tessa's, not her own. She gave her twin a tired smile. "Are you sure you want to read my mind at a time like this?" she managed to say. Closing her eyes, she licked her dry lips.

"You're doing great. Holding at seven centimeters, Steph."

"How's the fetal heartbeat?"

"Perfect." Tessa gave her a tiny piece of ice.

"My blood pressure?"

"Couldn't be better. Stop being a doctor and let Evelyn worry about that stuff."

Because the contractions were sporadic, Evelyn had wanted to administer a drug to intensify and regulate the course of her labor, but Stephanie had refused. She was hoping to hold out until Tal could be with her.

"Tal," she whispered, holding on to Tessa's hand. "He's never going to forgive me." She groaned as she was assaulted by another wave of pain. Seven minutes... pant... pant... pant.

"He'll forgive you anything when he sees his newborn son," Tessa said, her gaze fixed on the overhead mirror. "Way to go, Steph. That one was a doozy."

This was not the way she had envisioned the birth of their child. In her imagination, Tal had been there, holding her hand, counting with her, coaching her breathing techniques.

Another pain struck. They were getting closer together and harder to bear. She rode it out, calling upon every shred of control to keep from crying out at the peak. Six minutes... pant... pant.

"Scream if you want, Steph," Tessa advised. "This is no time for bravery."

"Alison..." She licked her dry lips again. "What about Alison?"

"Don't worry about Alison!" Tessa cried, reaching for the ice cup. "Here, suck on this. Alison is fine, wherever she is. I know it!"

"Right, sweetheart. Alison is fine."

At first, Stephanie thought Tal's voice was a figment of her imagination. Or wishful thinking. Or an answer to her prayers. Her eyes flew open as his hand clasped hers.

In green hospital scrubs, he was the most beautiful sight she'd ever seen. He bent and kissed her, hard, on the mouth. "Hey, pretty lady, let's get this show on the road."

She burst into tears.

"Sweetheart, don't cry. Save your energy, you're going to need it." He took the ice cup from Tessa, who was literally fainting on her feet with fatigue. With a weak wave, she shuffled to a chair and collapsed into it.

Stephanie wanted to know about Alison, but another fierce pain began and all thought was crowded from her brain in the primitive urge to bear down.

"Don't push yet, love," Tal coached. "Breathe short, pant...remember?"

"I have to!" she cried, losing control. It was as if her body had simply bided time until Tal arrived. Now he was here, there was no holding back. With a grueling wail, she gathered strength and pushed with all her might.

Suddenly, she was in the delivery room. Vaguely in the background, she heard Evelyn cautioning against pushing, but Tal's was the only voice that mattered. She was oblivious to the team bustling around her, startled into action after several hours of sluggish labor.

"Not yet, not yet," Tal chanted. Turning her face with his hand, he forced her gaze to his. "Look at me, Steph. Don't push. Evelyn's rushing trying to do her thing, but you're jumping the gun. Don't push, baby. Breathe instead, pant...pant...pant...remember?"

"I...hate...this...Tal," she moaned, panting with every word. He was going to think her such a twit after it was over.

"You're brave and wonderful," he told her, glimpsing the baby's crown in the overhead mirror. "You'll be a fantastic mother. You're *already* a fantastic mother."

"I'm sorry about Alison."

"Hush." He gave her a quick kiss. "Right now, just think of our baby," he told her, caressing her cheek with his thumb. He urged her attention to the mirror. "Look, we can see him now. Black hair. He's going to be hale and hearty, beautiful—"

"Yes," she panted, "like his daddy. Oh!" She closed her eyes. "Here it is again...please, I have to push."

"Okay, push now," Evelyn ordered, as if on cue.

That was all it took. In the mirror, Tal watched as Stephanie gathered herself once more. With a final mighty effort that wrenched a primeval cry from her, the baby slithered out, a wet, warm, tiny miracle.

As she lifted him, Evelyn was smiling behind her mask. She gave them a quick look. "Hey, you two...say hello to your baby boy!"

KEELY CAME AWAY from the door of the waiting room and dropped down in a chair beside Tessa and Camille. The turmoil of the past few hours had forged a new connection between mother and daughter. The hostility was missing, replaced with a shared concern for Stephanie and sincere relief over Alison, who, together with Jolene had been picked up by Tal and driven to the hospital.

"How much longer do you think, Mom?"

"Soon, I'm sure," Tessa replied, glancing at her watch. "I wasn't ousted until the last minute. It can't be much longer."

"Do you think the baby will be all right?" Alison asked, looking worried.

Tessa gave her a reassuring smile. "I do, Alison. His fetal heartbeat was strong on the monitor, and Evelyn Duplantis is the best. She didn't seem concerned over anything except that Steph wouldn't let her administer a drug to speed up her labor."

"She wanted to wait for Daddy." Alison looked guilt-stricken.

"And she did," Keely said. "Everything's cool, Ali."

"Yeah, everything's cool." Jolene spoke from the door where she was trying to get a reading on what was happening down the hall behind the secured entrance to the delivery room. She was smiling, looking better than she had in a long time. Finding Alison had obviously helped. The kid had been hunched in a rear seat on the St. Charles streetcar when Jolene spotted her, too scared to leave the relative safety of the streetcar to try to get home. Jolene had called Tal and they'd all made it to the hospital in ten minutes flat. Jolene had lectured Alison sternly the whole way. Alison told Keely no trip had ever seemed so long.

"Just remember the words of your stepmother, kid. Behavior has consequences," Jolene said now, apparently unwilling to pass this chance to impress upon Alison some of her own newly acquired wisdom. "You might want to keep that in mind next time you're tempted to split. And before you go brushin' off free wisdom, little princess, there are some of us thinks that lady walks on water.''

"I'll never do it again," Alison replied. It was an indication of her state of mind that she didn't react to the hated title. "I guess nobody will ever forgive me for almost making Daddy miss the baby's birth," she said, hanging her head in shame.

Keely stood up suddenly and went to sit beside her. "If we're talking guilt here, then I should be first in line. I'm the one who set this whole situation in motion, Ali. I owe you an apology. I was totally out of line. I had no business ever mentioning your mother like that.''

"It's okay," Alison said. "I had a lot of time to think while I was riding the streetcar. I'm not a little kid anymore. I'm old enough to know the truth, especially about my mother. Even if it hurts.''

Jolene spoke from across the room. "Well, lookahere," she said with an approving grin. "I think the little princess has found some wisdom tonight.''

Keely gave her an exasperated look. "Quit calling her that, Jolene!''

"Hey, you got it." Jolene addressed the group. "Hear that, y'all? The little princess is dead. Long live Alison!''

"Knock it off, Jolene," Keely ordered without heat.

Jolene shot her a friendly bird.

For the tenth time, Keely went to the door and scowled in the direction of the delivery room. A couple of gowned nurses came out, but passed without speaking. Keely crossed to her mother and flopped down beside her. "This is a time when I should be doing yoga," she said, her chin on her chest.

"To relax?" Tessa asked.

"Yeah."

"I believe in the relaxation techniques of yoga, too," Tessa said, turning slightly to look at her daughter. "In fact, I teach a class at Harbor Haven. It's a big favorite."

"Really?"

Tessa smiled. "Really."

Resting on her spine, Keely studied her linked hands. "What exactly is Harbor Haven?"

"It's a halfway house for girls whose crimes are usually misdemeanors. It's a controlled environment. School, work and play are supervised. We think Harbor Haven works better than conventional punishment to help troubled teens back into the mainstream."

"I'll be honest here and say I'm pretty ticked off that you have all that time for somebody else's kids," Keely said.

There was pain on Tessa's face. Above the girl's head, her eyes met Camille's, soft with understanding. "I know, Keely. I can never make up to you for those years when I was drinking. But once I stopped, I didn't rest until I located you. You'll never know how I felt when I knew you were safe with Stephanie."

"Are you serious about leaving me with her and Tal forever?"

"Are you serious about wanting to stay with them?"

Keely straightened then, looking with candor into her mother's eyes. "To tell the truth, I don't think it's right, Mom. Stephanie's had a few problems of her own with Tal and Alison. Her marriage was sort of unexpected, you know. There was her pregnancy and then I showed up. But she faced it all. She worked hard at making everything mesh."

"Yes, she did."

"I've been thinking about what she said about second chances, you know?"

Tessa studied her daughter's face. "I've been thinking about that, too."

"Maybe you and I could give it a shot?"

For a minute, Tessa was unable to talk around the thickness in her throat. "I thought you would want to stay with Stephanie," she said, her voice strained. "I've made so many mistakes, Keely." Her voice caught.

"Nobody's perfect, Mom."

"Good for you, chère." Camille touched the girl's hand.

It was all Tessa could do not to throw her arms around her daughter and promise her blue skies and sunny days for the rest of the time they had together, but looking into the beloved blue eyes, she knew her daughter was too smart, too much a realist to believe that kind of rhetoric. But there was the beginning of understanding between them now. Maybe they could have a second chance, after all.

"I've been thinking," Camille said softly, drawing the attention of Tessa and Keely. "Has anybody thought about the teen group, now that Stephanie's leaving? She's going to be tied up with the new baby. She can't abandon her practice, but there are only so many hours in the day. Those girls need someone who understands their problems, someone who's experienced dealing with their special needs, someone they can rely on. Someone with heart."

Keely nodded. "Someone like my mom!"

Camille smiled. "Well, the thought did cross my mind that your mom would be a pretty good replacement." She looked at Tessa. "This isn't something I pulled out of the blue, Tessa. Stephanie mentioned it a few days ago."

Tessa looked both hopeful and uncertain. "Do you think I could do it?"

"I'm absolutely certain you can do it. With the experience you gained in Florida, you'd be the best and most logical choice to take Stephanie's place."

"I could never fill Stephanie's shoes."

"You can and you will." Camille caught her hands and squeezed them. "You'll be perfect for the job, Tessa. Who better than you to warn kids about the hazards of making the wrong decisions?"

Tessa glanced at Keely, who was nearly bouncing in her chair. "I never dared hope—"

"You and Keely could move in with me," Camille said. "You'd be more than welcome, you know that."

"You'll do it, won't you, Mom?" Keely asked, her heart in her eyes.

"Well..."

"She will!" Keely cried, turning to the room at large. "Did y'all hear that? My mom and I are going to be the new counselors for the pregnant teens."

"Wait a minute!" Tessa grabbed at Keely, but the girl was already up and away. She glanced at Camille, who shrugged with her usual nonchalance. "Are you sure you're able to take us both in? Keely's sure to be a handful."

Smiling softly, Camille patted her hand. "I can't wait."

"Here he comes!" Jolene cried.

There was a general exodus from the waiting room. Tal was emerging from the delivery room wearing hospital scrubs and a big grin. "It's a boy!"

"All right!"

"Is he okay?"

"How's Stephanie?"

"Does he weigh enough so he won't be put in an incubator?"

"So... what's his name?"

His eyes bright, Tal rubbed the back of his neck, looking as if he could use a drink and eight hours of sleep. "Stephanie's fine, our son is an eight on the Apgar, he weighs exactly five pounds and his name is—" he shrugged, spreading his hands sheepishly "—Talbot Jean-Claude Robichaux III."

"Allll-riiiight!" Jolene high-fived with Keely.

"Is he in an incubator?" Tessa asked.

"At the moment, but it's routine," Tal said, running a hand through his hair. He smiled at the happy faces around him. "They'll wheel him out for us all to look at in a few minutes."

"Promise?" Alison seemed as thrilled over her baby brother as anybody else in the room, but her big dark eyes were hesitant on his. Her traumatic escapade on the streetcar had left grimy tear tracks on her cheeks. Tal's heart turned over. He reached for her. "I promise, Alley-cat." Oops. He hadn't called her that in a long time. Standing there, with Alison's face buried in his shirt and her small arms tight around his waist, he wondered if a man could be any happier.

STEPHANIE STRUGGLED UP through a cottony fog of exhaustion, not quite certain where she was. Heavy-lidded, her eyes refused to open as she floated, semiconscious. Then she remembered, and suddenly she was awake.

Tal was dozing beside her bed in a chair. Propped on one elbow, he looked uncomfortable, but he seemed deeply asleep. For a long, loving moment, she watched the regular rise and fall of his breathing. His hair was a mess and he needed a shave. He was still wearing the pants and blue oxford shirt he'd put on yesterday morning. Which meant he hadn't been home.

He stirred, as though sensing her regard, and forced himself awake. He let out a groan. Stretching his stiff neck muscles, he raked both hands over his face. She knew the instant he remembered. He went still, then looked at her, and his whole face softened.

"Hi, Little Mama. How're you feeling?" He leaned forward and took her hand in his.

"I'm good." Her smile broke. "Have you seen him?"

His dark eyes gleamed. "Who?"

"Talbot Jean-Claude Robichaux III," she said, pretending exasperation. "Who do you think?"

He brought her knuckles up to his lips. "Only about thirty times since 4:05 this morning."

"Is he still as wonderful as he was when I fell asleep?"

He stood up, brushed a lock of her hair away from her cheek and kissed her sweetly. "He is, my darling. Thank you."

"Oh, Tal." He was a beloved, blurry image through her tears. She couldn't have spoken if her life depended on it. Nothing had prepared Stephanie for the sheer power of her feelings at the birth of their baby. She would never be able to thank God enough for sending Tal to her in time. Sharing their son's birth was a moment never to be forgotten. One generation joined by another, that instant in time when a man and a woman are linked forever.

For a few seconds, they simply gazed at each other, enjoying the look of the other, hands still clasped. Tal smiled suddenly. "Wait a minute." With a quick touch to her cheek, he turned and headed for the door. "I'll be right back."

He left her staring at the door with a bemused smile. She could see hospital personnel passing in the hall, a janitor mopping the floor wearing a stereo headset, and a new mother walking in the slow, careful gait familiar to all women who have given birth. She felt a sudden, overwhelming need to see her baby, to hold him. She heard Tal's voice, along with a fussy newborn cry.

"Hey, Daddy knows what you need, little man." He was crooning softly. Her breasts began to tingle. "We didn't like it in that old nursery with nobody to talk to, did we? No, sir."

And there they were. Stephanie's heart turned over as she took in the sight of Tal in a hospital gown that was too small for his shoulders, their infant son nestled high on his chest. The baby's head, black as his father's, was no larger than a small orange. His tiny bottom filled Tal's palm.

"Oh, how did you manage this?" she cried, holding out her arms to take him.

"It pays to have friends in high places." He handed him over and watched with a gentle smile as the baby immediately began rooting around, his tiny mouth like a bird's, open and seeking. Shifting slightly, Stephanie slipped her gown off her shoulder and exposed one breast. Gently, she guided him, stroking his cheek, watching indulgently as he searched for and then discovered her nipple. She gasped as he latched on, looking with startled eyes at Tal.

"Does it hurt?" he asked, concerned.

"Yes. No." She settled back, now that the first fierce tugs were past. "No, it feels . . ." She shook her head, smiling softly. "There are no words." While he sucked, she sought his tiny hand, examined it with fascination. Smiled as miniature fingers closed over one of hers.

"What a greedy little guy," Tal said, watching him tug at her breast. With one finger, he gently stroked the baby's head.

"I was so worried," Stephanie said.

"Because he was small? I think we can put that behind us. Look at the little rascal go!"

Closing her eyes, Stephanie enjoyed the unique sensation. For a premature infant, he was remarkably strong. Good genes, these Robichaux genes.

"How is Alison?" she asked, guessing that Tal was purposely avoiding that touchy subject.

"She's fine, a little embarrassed about her escapade, but thrilled over the baby."

"There's nothing for her to be embarrassed about. There was no need for her to know about Diana's addiction. *I'm* the one who's embarrassed."

"Let it go. It's water under the bridge." Tal leaned back in the chair. "I've been thinking about that, Steph. How I've hounded you about secrets in your past, and yet with Alison and with Diana's parents, haven't I been guilty of the same thing? Maybe I didn't have the right to keep the truth from them."

She looked into Tal's eyes while holding on to their son's tiny fist. "Do they know now?"

"Not quite everything. I explained why Alison was missing when I called there looking for her. I'll see them later and try to tell them in a way that won't disillusion them too much."

"It might improve your relationship with them, Tal."

"Or it might not," he said, watching her lift the baby to her chest and begin gently patting his back to bring up a burp. Drowsily content now that his small tummy was full, little Talbot was snoozing on the cushiony softness of his mother's chest.

"What'll we call him?" Tal asked, envying the baby's position. "Talbot Jean-Claude Robichaux III is a mouthful."

Stephanie smiled at him. "How about T.J.?"

"T.J. it is."

She stroked the baby's back, thinking of the odd twist of fate that had brought them to this moment in time. How odd that that night in Boston could have such far-reaching consequences. Good consequences. She studied Tal as he relaxed, lazily content, his eyes on their son. She realized she was just where she wanted to be.

"I love you," she told him.

"I love you, too," he said. He left the chair and sat on the bed, gathering Stephanie and the baby into his arms. He settled back, a happy man.

A few minutes later, the door was gently pushed open. Heads appeared, four in a row—Alison, Keely, Tessa and Camille. Already, the room was a bower of flowers. Numerous balloon bouquets stretched to the ceiling. A big teddy bear was propped in a corner. And amidst the color and profusion of good wishes, Tal and Stephanie, heads together, gazed contentedly on the face of their newborn son.

The four stopped short. In spite of the chilly March day outside, sunshine poured through the windows, bathing mother, father and child in warm, golden light. Their loved ones were motionless for a moment as if sharing in a blessing. Then, laughing, they came inside.

With a quick, loving kiss, Tal and Stephanie turned and smiled a welcome.

UNLOCK THE DOOR TO GREAT ROMANCE
AT BRIDE'S BAY RESORT

Join Harlequin's new across-the-lines series, set
in an exclusive hotel on an island off the coast of
South Carolina.

Seven of your favorite authors will bring you exciting stories
about fascinating heroes and heroines discovering love at
Bride's Bay Resort.

Look for these fabulous stories coming to a store near you
beginning in January 1996.

Harlequin American Romance #613 in January
Matchmaking Baby by Cathy Gillen Thacker

Harlequin Presents #1794 in February
Indiscretions by Robyn Donald

Harlequin Intrigue #362 in March
Love and Lies by Dawn Stewardson

Harlequin Romance #3404 in April
Make Believe Engagement by Day Leclaire

Harlequin Temptation #588 in May
Stranger in the Night by Roseanne Williams

Harlequin Superromance #695 in June
Married to a Stranger by Connie Bennett

Harlequin Historicals #324 in July
Dulcie's Gift by Ruth Langan

Visit Bride's Bay Resort each month wherever
Harlequin books are sold.

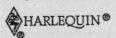

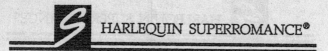

HARLEQUIN SUPERROMANCE®

MARRIED TO THE MAN
by Judith Arnold

Jane Thayer has it all. Or she will as soon as she rids herself of one little problem—an ex-husband she didn't know she was still married to. Her fiancé will never understand. So Jane does the only thing she can do. She goes to New Orleans to track down Cody Sinclair, a man she hasn't seen since their wild and reckless youth.

Cody's *still* wild and reckless. A photojournalist for a major newspaper, he's a magnet for trouble...and women. Right now he needs a lawyer—Jane. The woman who wants to be his *ex*-wife. But suddenly he's not so sure that's a good idea. Jane wants to talk about it, but Cody has other things in mind....

Reunited

First Love, Last Love

**Available in March, wherever
Harlequin Superromance novels are sold.**

REUNIT9

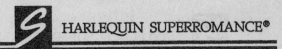

HARLEQUIN SUPERROMANCE®

From the bestselling author of
THE TAGGARTS OF TEXAS!
comes

Cupid, Colorado...

This is ranch country, cowboy country—a land of high mountains
and swift, cold rivers, of deer, elk and bear. The land is important
here—family and neighbors are, too. 'Course, you have the chance
to really get to know your neighbors in Cupid. Take the Camerons,
for instance. The first Cameron came to Cupid more than a hundred
years ago, and Camerons have owned and worked the Straight Arrow
Ranch—the largest spread in these parts—ever since.

For kids and kisses, tears and laughter, wild horses and wilder men—
come to the Straight Arrow Ranch, near Cupid, Colorado. Come meet
the Camerons.

THE CAMERONS OF COLORADO
by Ruth Jean Dale

Kids, Critters and Cupid (Superromance#678)
available in February 1996

The Cupid Conspiracy (Temptation #579)
available in March 1996

The Cupid Chronicles (Superromance #687)
available in April 1996